BUYER, BEWARE

By Diane Vallere

SAMANTHA KIDD IN

Buyer, Beware

A STYLE & ERROR MYSTERY

2

Diane Vallere

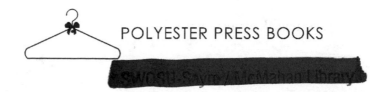

POLYESTER PRESS BOOKS

BUYER, BEWARE
Book 2 in the Samantha Kidd Mystery Series
A Polyester Press Publication

Second Edition
First published March 2013

Copyright © 2013, 2019 Diane Vallere
All rights reserved.
ISBN 13: 978-1-939197-01-6

Printed in the United States of America

To Angela Baez, who gave me my first buying job.
You're fabulous!

1

NOT A THIEF

*T*his wasn't how I'd planned to spend my Saturday night. It was one thing to be home alone waiting for the phone to ring. The man I wanted to call was in Italy, and I'd gotten used to Saturday nights by myself. Maybe that's why I was hiding in a bathroom with a naked man. He quickened my pulse, shortened my breathing, and inspired thoughts that would make a more innocent woman blush. Never mind that he was made of wood and tucked inside my handbag. Never mind that five minutes ago I'd stolen him from his place of honor in the admissions hall of the local design school.

I'm not a thief, my inner monologue cried out. *I'm not a crook, or an opportunist, or the kind of person who breaks the law.*

Well, maybe, on occasion, I *was* the kind of person who broke the law, but only in very specific situations of the life-or-death variety.

I bargained with the patron saints of thieves and fashion: *If I make it out of here safely, I promise to never wear sweatpants in public again.*

From the hallway, I heard the resonant strike of leather soles on the marble floor. I promised myself if I could make it fifteen more seconds without breathing I could have two bowls of cherry vanilla ice cream when I got home. If I got home. If I didn't get caught.

Not the best strategy for not breathing.

The footsteps faded, and I exhaled. The naked statue shifted lower in my handbag. I relaxed for a moment and rooted around, making sure my wooden companion was hidden inside the slightly worn Birkin handbag I bought on eBay back when I had a disposable income. At least if I was hauled off to jail, it would be locked up with the rest of my outfit, patiently awaiting my release. How long do you get for stealing art? Ten to twenty years? Good thing the Birkin was a classic.

The door to the bathroom creaked open. Before I could scream, climb through a vent, or adopt a really cool fighting pose, a man in a black turtleneck, black knit hat, black gloves, black cargo pants, and black Vans grabbed my wrist and pulled me toward the exit. It was Eddie Adams, my closest friend and occasional bad influence.

"Did you make the swap?" Eddie whispered.

I nodded.

"Good. The security guard is on the other side of the building. We have to go. Now!" He shoved me into the bright hallway. We raced past closed classroom doors and bulletin boards filled with colorful slips of paper that announced campus activities and tutor sessions. We burst out the exit, down the concrete stairs, to the parking lot. I dove into the back of the waiting getaway car, otherwise known as our other friend Cat's Suburban, and pulled an open sleeping bag over my body. Eddie disappeared into the night on foot. I snuggled against the backseat and remained curled in the fetal position around my Birkin while Cat drove to the edge of the lot.

The car stopped. Why did the car stop? There was no way we were out of the parking lot. It was too soon to stop.

"Can you tell me how to get back to the highway?" Cat asked in an innocent tone. I pictured her flipping her red hair over her shoulder and tipping her head to the side. A male voice described a series of exits and turns. She thanked him. A set of tires peeled out of the lot past us, the voices ceased, and off we drove, me clinging to the naked man like it was our third date.

And that describes my first premeditated robbery.

THE NIGHT WAS a success, if success can be measured by things like theft and clean getaways. We'd done it. We'd pooled our collective resources and talents and swiped a statue from the Institute of Fashion, Art, and Design, or I-FAD, as it was known in fashion circles. My careful planning had taken us from concept to execution, but success was a team effort. Eddie, visual manager for Tradava, Ribbon, Pennsylvania's oldest retailer. Cat, owner of Catnip, a discount designer boutique in the outlet center, and Dante, Cat's brother, had made it happen. Even more impressive than the success of our mission was the fact that I'd planned the whole thing less than a week ago.

Things had been quiet around my hometown of Ribbon, Pennsylvania. Life was normal, or as normal as it can be when you're in your early thirties, out of work, trying to figure out how to pay the bills. Six months ago, I'd given up my glamorous job as the senior buyer of ladies designer shoes at Bentley's New York for a chance to move into the house where I grew up. Things hadn't turned out exactly as planned thanks to a murder investigation. I lost my job, my mentor, and came darn near close to losing the house. I'd taken to obsessively reorganizing my wardrobe, first by color, next by silhouette, and finally by decade. With my savings account rapidly dwindling thanks to things like the new mortgage payment and cat food for Logan, I was a starving fashionista living off the contents of my closet.

And then the contest had been announced in the *Ribbon Times*.

Interested in a Heist?

Ribbon's hottest new store opens on July 14. Join us for the Pilferer's Ball to get a sneak preview of our unparalleled assortments at criminally low prices. Daring attendees are challenged to arrive with one of the following items in tow, "borrowed" from their current place of residency. Should you successfully lift said loot without notice, you can win a $10,000 shopping spree at HEIST. Rules and regulations listed below.

It was right up my alley.

Eddie, a high school friend I'd reconnected with during the aforementioned murder investigation, seemed the perfect person to help. Plus, safety in numbers and all that.

"The best time for the theft is in the early morning, like three or four o'clock. It'll be dark, the night guard will be tired, and there will be minimal traffic on the campus since the bars and parties shut down at two. Anyone wandering around will probably be drunk and not a credible witness," I had said to Eddie, while we hung out in my living room, discussing my plan.

When I first moved in, the house was a study in post-college hand-me-down. I'd painted an accent wall with a gallon of aqua paint from Home Depot's "Oops" rack and decorated the wall with fabric cuttings framed in black plastic document frames from the dollar store. Three rows of nine frames each filled the wall opposite the large bay window. A white afghan, crocheted by my grandmother, covered the back of the gray flannel sofa Eddie bought me from a prop sale at Tradava, the store where he currently worked (and I thought I'd be working—but that's a different story for a different time). Two black and white chairs sat opposite the sofa, set off by blue tweed fabric I'd found in the markdown bin at the local fabric store and fashioned into curtains.

"We need to not look suspicious around the campus, because people might remember us if we seem like we don't belong," I added. "I think you should pretend to be a security guard. That way the real guard won't spend too much time watching the areas where you already are."

Eddie sat sideways in one of the black and white chairs, his knees bent over the arm, his checkered Vans bouncing on the outside of the fabric. His pencil flew over a pad of drawing paper, making sketches.

"I don't think I'll make a very convincing security guard."

I ignored him. "My new neighbor is the head of the fabric curriculum at I-FAD. I'll volunteer to talk to one of her classes or something."

I was interrupted by a knock on the door.

"Hold that thought," Eddie said. He spun to a sitting position and pushed himself out of the chair.

"You invited someone to my house?" I asked, shoving incriminating plans and schematics under the sofa. I followed him to the door.

Standing on my porch were a man and a woman. I recognized the woman as Catherine Lestes, Catnip boutique owner. The last time we'd spoken, we shared a couple of not very nice words. (She'd accused me of murder, and I don't take well to that.) Next to her was a stranger attractive in a bad-boy way. His outfit could have been assembled from the greats: black leather jacket from Brando, white T-shirt from James Dean, faded denim jeans from Paul Newman. His jet-black hair and sideburns like Elvis in the 1968 comeback special. His scuffed and worn black leather boots probably protected his feet from snakes while walking through the jungle. Out of Africa, maybe. Redford. I looked back at his face. Dangerous and brooding. Not Redford.

"Are you Samantha Kidd?" he asked.

"Yes."

"I've heard a lot about you." He held out a hand. His black leather sleeve rode up, exposing flame tattoos around his wrists.

"I'm Dante. You know my sister, Cat." He tipped his head to the side.

Not sure of the protocol to welcome a formerly hostile fashionista and a strange biker dude on my doorstep, I looked at Eddie. He stepped to the side and held the door open.

"Glad you guys could make it. Come on in," he said.

Not what I'd expected. I glared at him, communicating thoughts that he appeared able to tune out.

"I get the feeling you didn't know we were coming," Dante said to me.

"Eddie invited me. We're here to help with the theft," Cat added. "I invited Dante to join us. You don't mind, do you?"

"Sure, fine, no problem." I turned to Eddie. "Can I see you in the kitchen for a moment?"

Logan, my frisky black feline, slinked into the room. I turned to Cat and Dante. "Watch out for my cat. He's very selective about the company he keeps," I said. Logan crossed the room and sniffed the toes of Dante's boots. Fickle cat.

In the kitchen, Eddie said, "Before you say no, think about it. We can't pull this thing off by ourselves."

"Cat doesn't like me."

He waved my protest away like the scent of stinky cheese. "She didn't like you when she thought you were a murderer. Things change. Let them stick around and listen what they can do. Cat has connections at I-FAD, so she can be our person on the inside. And she tells me her brother has all kinds of hidden talents."

"Like what?"

"I don't know, sneaky stuff, by the looks of him. But listen, we might need another man besides me."

The problem was, I already had another man besides Eddie: Nick Taylor. Only, I didn't.

In terms of style, Nick was Redford. And Clark Gable and Cary Grant. He was Hamptons preppy with a side of early Duran Duran. Nick was a shoe designer I'd worked with in my former (glamorous, financially successful, emotionally draining) life. When I gave up that job for a lifestyle makeover and moved from the Big Apple to the small town—Ribbon, Pennsylvania—Nick's name moved from the "colleague" column of my life to the one labeled "you've got potential." And then, like all good shoe designers, he left for Italy, where he'd been for the past month. I was pretty sure that, in addition to keeping the secret about our planned theft at the museum, keeping the secret of the hot tattooed biker who had all kinds of hidden talents might be a bit of a challenge.

"Fine," I said, though it was anything but.

We returned to the living room. Logan was curled up next to Dante on the gray flannel sofa. Cat sat on one of the black and white chairs, flipping through the Halston coffee table book I kept on my glass and chrome coffee table. Her legs were crossed, and she bounced one patent leather lime green pump against her calf.

I sat next to Dante and retrieved the plans and schematics from under the sofa. I outlined my general plan to get them caught up.

"I'll come up with assignments for both of you tonight. In the meantime—"

"Dante will make a better fake security guard than I will," Eddie said. He pulled a piece of paper from his manila folder and held it out to Dante. "Plus, that will give me more time to work on the fake."

Cat chimed in next. "I'll set up a guest professorship with the college, Samantha. I've done it before and already have the contacts. The college probably won't respond to your offer to guest lecture since you're currently unemployed." She brushed a stray lock of vibrant red hair behind her ear. "Now we just need something for you to do." She leaned forward, her elbows on her olive pants, her fingertips tapping against each other while she thought.

"I got it!" Eddie said, spinning to the front of the chair and leaning forward. "You can go undercover as a student."

We all turned toward him. Expensive moisturizers and a box of Miss Clairol could only do so much, and I think the ship had sailed on undercover student ten years ago.

"Undercover *grad* student," he clarified. "What?" He said, addressing the doubtful expressions in the room (which numbered more than just mine). "Get her into a sweatshirt and jeans and she'd look like half the students on campus." He looked at me and cocked his head to one side. "A tan, less eyeliner, no lipstick, some highlights …"

"We get the point," I said.

"To make sure I'm up to speed," Dante said, "Eddie's going to make a fake sculpture. Cat's going to get inside the college and look around. I'm going to pose as a security guard. And Samantha's going back to school."

Everyone nodded but me.

"Eddie, how long will it take you to make the replica?" Cat asked.

"Not sure. I need measurements, pictures, specs. I need to conduct recon."

Dante pulled a folder of his own from inside his motorcycle jacket and tossed it on the coffee table in front of Eddie. Cat leaned forward, and Eddie opened the folder. I watched out of the corner of my eye. Eddie fanned a series of photos across the table. They featured every conceivable angle of the statue, along with newspaper clippings describing the material, installation, security, and measurements.

"Is that what you need?" Dante asked.

Eddie's eyes went wide. "Where'd you—"

"You guys aren't the only ones who read the newspaper. Just seemed easier to be part of your team than try to steal it on my own. How long?"

"With this info? I'll review it tonight and work on materials tomorrow. I'll take a couple of days off and can have it ready by the weekend."

"Good. We all know our assignments?" Dante asked.

The heads around the table bobbed. I pushed my chair away from the table and walked into the kitchen. Dante followed. I pulled a Fred Flintstone juice glass from the cabinet and filled it with tap water, pretending I didn't know he was there.

"You don't like that we changed your plan," he said.

"Doesn't really matter. It's not my plan anymore."

"Sure it is. The players may have changed, but the game is still the same. Just because people swapped parts doesn't mean you didn't design it. Besides, it's best everyone take the role they're most comfortable in."

I turned around and faced him. "You really wanted to try to steal the statue on your own?" I asked, leaning against the counter.

"The thought occurred to me. I like a challenge."

"How do I know we can trust you?" I asked, swirling the water around in the glass. "I know nothing about you."

"You can keep me under surveillance if you'd like."

"What do you mean?"

"I've got nothing to hide. Spend the next couple of days with me."

Heat climbed my face. "I—I can't," I said, cursing my shaky voice. "I have to stay on task," I added.

He shrugged. "I have to split. If Cat wants to stick around, tell her to call me when she's ready for a ride." He took my hand in his and flipped it so it was palm-side up. He picked up a pen from the counter and wrote a series of numbers across the fleshy part. "That's my number."

"You're her brother. I think she knows the number."

He capped the pen and set it on the counter. "I know she knows the number. That's for you."

He walked to the front door, calling good-byes to Cat and Eddie, who were flipping through the Halston book. As much as I wanted to dive in and show them the outfit on page 157, I followed Dante because it was the hospitable thing to do.

"You sure you can keep them focused?" he said. "Because this won't work unless everyone stays on task."

"I'll do my best."

He reached down, tipped my chin back, and stared at me for an uncomfortable couple of seconds. "This turned out to be a pretty good night," he said. He turned and left.

TURNS OUT, EDDIE was right. Rarely do professionals move as quickly as beauticians who hear the phrase, "I need to look younger," and the professionals I'd chosen from the back of the yellow pages were no exception. My brown hair had been highlighted and layered into a tumble of curls that hadn't been allowed this kind of freedom in a decade. My blue-green eyes stood out against sun-kissed skin, the result of a week's worth of spray-on tanning and bronzer to achieve a post-spring break glow. I traded foundation for tinted moisturizer, lipstick for lip-gloss, and fought my eyeliner habit. Cat bought me an I-FAD sweatshirt, laundered and dried a dozen times to give it a lived-in look. I drew the line at matching sweatpants, pairing the sweatshirt with a kicky pleated plaid skirt.

It was uncanny to look in the mirror and see a face that only slightly resembled my own. It was even uncannier to spend the next week wandering the college campus. Surprisingly, that's all it took. One week of surveillance to figure out what we needed to know to pull off our plan. The uncanniest part of all of it was that it worked.

After the theft, our hodge-podge team regrouped at my house for a celebratory drink. It was close to two in the morning, but we were hyped up by the fact that we'd gotten away with (sanctioned) thievery. Dante popped a bottle of champagne and we toasted our success. At least, Cat, Dante and I toasted our success. Eddie was upstairs getting the shoe polish off his face.

I pulled the bundle out of my handbag and unwrapped it. A wooden Puccetti statue on permanent loan from the Philadelphia Museum of Art to I-FAD. It was one of the few known works by Milo Puccetti, a student of Brancusi. It had resided on the college campus for the past five years, and we'd managed to swipe it, all because of a contest in the newspaper.

"Who's going to be in charge of Woody until the party?" Dante asked.

"Woody?" I asked.

Dante pointed toward the Puccetti. "Woody."

Cat rolled her eyes. "You can't call him 'Woody.'"

"We can't call him Puccetti," Dante countered. "What do you suggest?"

"Allen. Get it? Woody Allen." Cat said.

"What about Steve?" I asked.

"Steve?" they answered/quetstioned in unison.

"Woody Allen—Steve Allen. Steve."

"We're naming him? Can I get in on this?" Eddie asked, towel drying the side of his bleached blond hair.

"We went from Woody to Woody Allen to Steve Allen. Where do you want to go? Tag, you're it. You pick the final name."

Eddie repeated after me. "Woody ... Woody Allen ... Steve Allen ...." He dropped the towel and shot two fists in the air. "Steve McQueen!"

I dipped two fingers into my champagne glass and dabbed the base of the statue. "I hereby dub thee McQueen."

We stared at all twenty-four inches of him. It was the figure of a well-sculpted man, and I know size doesn't matter but his twenty-four inches were impressive. Now we just had to get him to Heist and present him to the judging committee. That was the last detail on our agenda, and it would happen tomorrow night at the Pilferer's Ball, the store's opening party.

Cat yawned. "Time for me to get home and go to bed. Dante, you want a ride?"

Dante looked at me. I was still wearing my college-girl outfit, and even though the outfit included a bulky oversized sweatshirt, it felt a little like he was seeing me in my underwear.

"Yes, Dante wants a ride," I said.

Eddie was back to his usual shade of surfer-dude. He tossed the damp towel on the end of the sofa. "You guys are leaving already? The party is just getting started."

With sound effects. Because that's when we heard the sirens.

2

THE PILFERER'S BALL

I grabbed the towel from the sofa, wrapped up the statue, and pushed the bundle under the cushions. The sirens grew louder. It was obvious they were headed our direction. There was nothing to do but wait for them to come to the front door, announce themselves, and take us into custody. And, contest or not, we all knew we were guilty—guilty of theft from a public institution.

I fed my hand behind the blue tweed curtains and created an opening wide enough to look through. The cars didn't turn into my driveway. They turned into my neighbor Nora's. The sirens turned off, but the flashing lights pierced the darkness at evenly spaced intervals. We may have been tired fifteen minutes ago, but we were wide awake now.

"Should we leave?" Cat asked.

"At two o'clock in the morning, with the cops right outside the house? I don't think so," Eddie said.

Dante reached down and untied his shoes. "Those aren't police cars, they're campus security. They're parked in front of your neighbor's house, and they're going in."

Then he put his feet up on the ottoman and put his hands behind his head. "Looks like I'm staying after all."

"Eddie, can I see you in the kitchen, please?" I went to the kitchen. He knew the routine by now.

"I don't think Dante staying over is a good idea," I said.

"After tonight, I think you can trust him."

"It's not him I'm worried about," I said. I leaned forward and peeked into the living room. Logan sat in the chair with Dante. He stared right at me, and I felt myself blush. "Having Dante around is going to be a little distracting, if you know what I mean."

"What's wrong with a little distraction?"

I stepped backward, out of Dante's line of vision, and pulled Eddie with me. "I'm finally in a place where I can start a relationship with Nick. Just because he's halfway around the world right now doesn't mean I'm going to blow that chance. Cat can crash upstairs with me. You have to keep an eye on him. Can you help me with that?"

"How's Nick going to know? He didn't even call you tonight."

"Shoot." I scampered to the living room to get my handbag. Cat was asleep on the sofa, half-covered with the white afghan. Dante studied my face with an amused look on his.

"Looks like my sister took the sofa. Got anywhere else I can sleep?"

"The floor." I returned to the kitchen. When I powered on my phone, the missed message alert beeped. One message.

"Samantha? It's Nora. Your neighbor. Call me as soon as you get this. I need to talk to you about something."

"It wasn't Nick. It was Nora," I said to Eddie.

"As in next-door Nora?"

22

"As in the-professor-for-the-college-we-just-stole-a-statue-from Nora. As in campus-security-is-at-her-house Nora." We both looked at the wall between my house and hers. It would have made more sense if there'd been a window there.

"Find out what she wants," Eddie said.

"Not tonight," I said. "I'll call her in the morning."

I WOKE UP thinking about that message. What was it Nora wanted to tell me? I called and left a message. I called two more times and hung up on the third ring. Around lunchtime I crossed the yard between us and rang the doorbell, but there was no answer. Her car was gone from her driveway, so I figured she'd gone out for the day. I'd try to call her later, but I had other things to think about.

Tonight was the party at Heist, and after succeeding in our small-time perpetration, we were juiced to collect our prize money. The last part of our plan had been to arrive at the new department store with the statue bundled in my handbag. And don't think it wasn't hard to find an evening bag that accommodated a twenty-four-inch tall Puccetti statue, either.

Scrub as I had, my new fake tan wasn't budging, so I based my evening attire around my new carefree seventies-look. I pulled on an amber silk caftan with gold beading at the neckline and cuffs, gold shoulder duster earrings, and an armful of colorful bangle bracelets. The time I saved by not straightening my hair helped me still arrive on time.

Eddie waited for me in the parking lot. His black tuxedo jacket opened to a Frankie Say Relax T-shirt. He paced back and forth, looking nervous, despite the message on his Tee.

"What's wrong?" I asked.

"Did you talk to your neighbor?"

"No. I tried to call her, but she wasn't home. Why?"

"I didn't want to tell you this, but I signed the fake statue that we used for the swap." He shrugged. "I guess it was a matter of pride. If anyone came along and stole the one we left, I wanted to prove they didn't have the real one."

"It's a priceless statue. They probably have better tests of authenticity than that."

"Okay, fine. I wanted to show off how well I copied it."

"So why are you asking about Nora?"

"You said Nora was a professor at I-FAD. We stole the Puccetti from I-FAD, and they'd know it by now. I keep thinking about the campus security at her house. I don't think we're home free. In fact, I have a very bad feeling about tonight."

"It'll be fine," I said. "We'll collect the prize money, and I'll be able to pay my mortgage for a few more months." And buy a new outfit, I added to myself.

Cat's Suburban pulled up behind Eddie. She and Dante got out. Cat, ever the fashion plate, wore a vibrant purple one shoulder cocktail dress, layers of chiffon cut at a diagonal that ended halfway down her thighs. She crossed the parking lot on glitter-encrusted strappy platform sandals. Dante followed, in a gold Nehru collared shirt with a paisley ascot knotted at the neck.

He stepped close to me and slipped an arm around my waist. His hand was hot against the small of my back, even though there was a thin layer of silk between us. I tensed. He noticed. He moved his hand up and down in a small gesture of familiarity, and then pulled his arm away. The heat from his hand had spread through my entire body, leaving me in need of air conditioning.

"You two are not allowed to stand together tonight," Cat said, pointing a finger back and forth between Dante and me. "It's like it's 1968."

Once inside the store, we moved to the accessories department where a young man in a tuxedo held a tray of champagne flutes. I took one. Cat and Eddie each took a pair of sunglasses from a top-of-the-counter carousel and tried them on. A second later they exchanged pairs and checked their reflections again. I looked at the visuals and the merchandise. Heist had certainly one-upped Tradava in the merchandising department.

Until Heist had announced they were moving to our town, Tradava had been the only other local retailer. Tradava was a family-owned chain of stores based in Ribbon. They'd shown interest in changing their image and staking claim to a more fashionable client base, but from what I could see tonight, Heist had steamrollered their attempts with an aggressive ad campaign and bold assortments. If Tradava was trying to change by whispering, "come on in," to the fashion crowd, Heist was screaming through a bullhorn and the message they projected was effective.

Images from Heist's catalogs filled the store. The walls in the cosmetics department were covered with mug shots of women of all ages in flawless makeup. Models in jeans stood with hands on the back of a squad car, a pose that showed off both their curves and the back-pocket stitching of each brand of denim. Still others stood behind bars in a jail cell, in the tiniest whisper of lacy lingerie. My favorite showed a model in an orange jumpsuit scaling a pile of designer handbags to break out of prison. Their creative director had run with their theme, using gritty, Helmut Newton-like photography to create the edgy ad campaign. It was creative. Fresh. Something completely different from what Tradava would have done, and it had been executed perfectly.

I wandered away from my team, into the apparel department, taking it all in. Heist's leather jackets weren't locked up to a lockbox with indiscreet cables like other department stores but were handcuffed to a ballet bar. I continued toward the shoe department, curious how their assortment compared to what I might have bought for Bentley's. A pile of shoes, some of the most coveted styles I'd seen in the past pages of fashion magazines, sat in the middle of the department. A mannequin was at the center of the pile, staring out between stilettos as if hiding from pursuit. I touched the display. The shoes didn't move; they'd been hot glued together. Any store that was willing to install visuals like this must have an unbelievable amount of merchandise to back it up. I wandered through the department picking up samples at random intervals. The tagline on every price tag in the store said it all: *Our discounts are criminal!*

The world of fashion was one where I was comfortable, or I had been, once upon a time when I was on the industry's payroll. But being on a budget had put a serious damper on my shopping habits. I'd started wearing the clothes I found at the back of my closet. I was a walking exhibit of fashion through the ages, or at least the late seventies through last year.

Even if I didn't get depressed by the thought of waiting for last year's fashions to be discounted to 50 percent off, these days even 50 percent off designer apparel was too rich for my dwindling checking account. Wandering through Heist, ogling the merchandise, I couldn't help getting a familiar tingle. I wanted to try on these clothes. No, I wanted to buy these clothes, and go out into the world, a renovated version of myself ready for anything, the way I was when I first moved back to Ribbon six months ago.

An attractive blond man in a black tuxedo stood at the rear of the handbag department flipping through a bin of colorful clutch bags. He didn't see me. His profile spoke of male models in underwear ads: that defined handsomeness that whispers of a confidence he'd known since a very early age. He was a pretty boy, with chiseled features and a square jaw line, but with the certain hardness that comes from living your twenties to the max. My guess was that this man knew his face was his ace. He eased his way past a wall of Prada, looking to both sides. That's when I hit his line of vision.

"Who are you?" he asked.

"Just a partygoer." When he didn't move on, I held out my hand. "Samantha Kidd."

"Kyle Trent." His hand was warm and soft. He looked past me as though he was looking for someone else and then refocused his attention on my face. "What are you doing here? I thought the party was to be contained to the lounge area and the open bar."

"I couldn't help myself. I'm admiring the assortments." I fingered a teal-green, patent leather handbag that defied practicality. "It's simply amazing. Like nothing I've seen."

He scowled. "You should tell Emily."

"Who's Emily?" I asked, looking around for somebody else.

"Emily Hart. She's the handbag buyer." Again he looked past me, and then behind him, as though he'd been chased. "Better yet, don't. Her head's big enough already. She's around here somewhere. Just look for a woman in a little black dress."

"That's everyone here."

"Not quite everyone," he said, eyeing my amber silk caftan. "Anyway, I'd be willing to bet she's the only one wearing a five-carat yellow diamond ring."

He let go of my hand, which had been growing sweaty under his awkward, too-long handshake. My other hand clutched my personal handbag, knowing the Puccetti statue was inside. I fought the urge to wipe my palm against the silk of my ensemble, knowing it would leave a mark.

"Emily thrives on compliments. If you see her, tell her what you think." He continued past the shoe department and back the way I had come.

As Kyle left, I moved farther in toward the display wall of handbags. Simple white pegboard had been hung against the wall. Utilitarian metal pegs held clear Plexiglas shelves, and a soft glow from behind the pegboard illuminated the display through the small holes, backlighting the colorful assortment.

The sign above the wall read "Vongole." The Italian design house was the latest to join the ranks of it-bag designers, their designs spotted on the arms of most celebrities these days. Heist carried more of their designer handbags than I'd ever seen in one place, and that included the time I'd spent working in New York. Heck, that included the street corners in New York that sold the not-too-shabby knockoffs, too. I gazed up to the highest shelf, where a yellow matte crocodile bag called my name.

I'll just hold it for a second, I thought.

The shelf was slightly higher than my reach. Fairly certain that the stolen Puccetti statue was not at risk, I set my clutch on a glass case that held a display of wallets and small leather goods, and found a stepstool a negligent employee had forgotten to put away for the night. As I positioned the stool below the display shelf, I placed my hands on the pegboard for balance. I climbed up the three steps so I was within reach of the handbag, but I never got it off the shelf, because from my new perch about two feet off the ground, I saw something that made me forget about the yellow crocodile handbag altogether.

To the left of the display wall was a metal gate that secured the department back stock from customers. And behind the metal gate, a body lay sprawled across the floor. The case of small leather goods blocked my view of her face and her outfit, but the one thing I was able to see was the very large yellow stone gleaming from the ring on her left hand.

3

❧

EXPLAIN HOW

*E*ddie was right to have had a bad feeling. The tingling excitement brought on from the merchandise in the store turned to panic. I jumped off the ladder. My bracelets clinked against each other like a windchime as I grabbed my gold clutch and ran back to the party. I found Cat trying on a pink headband with feathers. Eddie was next to her, straightening fixtures, even though this wasn't his store.

"Have you guys seen anybody in uniform?" I asked Eddie. "Police, security, Rent-a-Cop?"

Behind them someone sprayed on too many pumps of perfume and the sweet scent of lilies and sugar filled the air. Dante leaned against the scarf case, swirling his champagne around in the flute. I tugged on the sleeve of his shirt.

"Have you seen anybody who looks official?" I asked him.

"Define official," he said.

But I didn't. I pushed past the three of them through the crowd of strangers, a difficult task in a caftan. When I reached the front of the store, two men stood checking IDs.

"Are you in charge?" I asked one of them.

"I'm in charge," said a stout bald man in a black suit, white shirt, black tie. "What's the problem?"

"A woman—in the handbag department—she's—" I stopped. I didn't know what she was. "She might need help."

"Might?" said the security officer.

"Or it might be too late," I added. I turned around and pushed back the way I had come. But before I had a chance to get the officer to the handbag department, a bloodcurdling scream pierced the store.

Everyone looked in the direction of the scream. Everyone except for Dante, who stared at me. He held his champagne flute out. I drained it in a matter of seconds and set the empty glass on the counter.

AN HOUR LATER, I would have traded a sizeable portion of my anticipated prize money for another glass of champagne. We'd been told that no one could leave the store until after speaking to the police. The crowd had been separated into groups, and Cat and Dante had been shuffled along with a different audience. I kept telling myself we hadn't done anything wrong. We'd taken on the challenge Heist advertised in the newspaper. The theft we'd committed was part of a publicity campaign. Still, I felt guilt from the theft, from carrying around the stolen statue in my handbag, and from wandering parts of the store that were off-limits. I wondered how that would translate when the police got around to talking to me. For the time being, I decided not to mention it.

A short, well-appointed man stood off to the side of our line. More than once our eyes connected. He drank a watery drink from a glass tumbler. His expertly tailored black pinstriped suit fit him well, though at a height shorter than my own I wondered where he'd found it. Custom? That costs money. Gold cufflinks punctuated with diamonds glistened from his shirt. I glanced at his shoes. Yep, money. I hadn't seen menswear like that since I worked at Bentley's. The man continued to watch me—that's exactly how it felt, like I was being watched—and I looked away, scanning the crowd, to hide my awkwardness.

The line crept slowly toward two uniformed police officers who were taking statements. There were too many of us to all be detained, so I imagined the cops were taking down names and contact information, checking that each person had a solid reason for being at this party, this night. Looking for someone who had infiltrated the fashionable happening for reason other than free champagne and a chance to shop the newest retailer one day early. Meanwhile, the advertising hanging around the store disturbed me.

This couldn't be one big publicity stunt, could it?

"Why didn't you just say you found a body?" Eddie whispered to me. "You could have told us."

"Because I don't want that to become my catch phrase," I answered, thinking of the last time I'd found a dead body and how it had complicated my life.

Six months ago, I'd moved to Ribbon looking for a fresh start. I'd found a fresh corpse instead. It was the man who'd hired me to work for him, which had raised all sorts of hard-to-answer questions from the police, the mortgage company, and the bill collectors. I managed.

Eddie bumped me with his elbow. "Look, there's your friend." He jutted his chin toward the man at the front of the line. He wore a rented tux that was too narrow in the shoulders. The sleeves were also too short, exposing the cuffs of his white shirt (no expensive cufflinks in sight). I scanned him down to his feet: round-toed oxfords with thick rubber soles.

Detective Loncar.

The detective was an older, graying man, thick around the middle, balding around the top. I've heard of women having an inexplicable attraction to police officers, something about the law and order, or the uniform, or the position of authority, but I didn't get it. Detective Loncar did his job without any hint of flirtation or sexuality. Our line advanced slowly, until we stood in front of him.

"Samantha Kidd." He turned to the young female officer to his right. "We already have her information on file." She nodded one quick nod. "What brings you to Heist tonight?"

"I'm a retailer. This is the competition. I wanted to see what they were all about."

He jotted a few notes on a tablet. "That's it? No undercover work? No extracurricular activities?"

"Pretty much."

"Still live in the same house?"

"Yes."

He jotted down a few more notes. "Okay. Sign here, please." He handed me a clipboard filled with names, addresses, and phone numbers. I set my handbag down, took the offered pen, and signed my name with a less than customary flourish.

"That's it? I can leave now?" I asked, clipping the pen to the clipboard in an efficient manner.

"Detective, look," the female officer said. She held my handbag. It had tipped on the counter, and a white bundle was exposed. Only the white bundle was no longer well wrapped, and the Puccetti statue peeked out of the top.

The detective stared into my bag for an uncomfortable duration of time.

"No, Ms. Kidd" he said slowly. "I don't think you can leave now. Follow me." He picked up my handbag and walked toward a small, dark hallway. Then he turned back to the female officer and said, "Meet us in five."

I trailed behind the detective until he reached a room, glowing with the particular blue that emanates from a Pepsi machine. "Soda?" he asked.

"Sure."

"Sit down," he said.

"Am I about to be interrogated?" I asked warily.

"Ms. Kidd, we've been through this before. We don't interrogate people in the employee lounge of department stores." He pumped some change into the machine, punched the button with a jab of his right fist, and then repeated the routine. I took the Pepsi he offered. "Have a seat," he instructed.

I pulled a plastic chair out from under the folding table. I'd been in more than enough employee lounges of more than enough department stores to know that this one, expertly decorated in black and white with punches of primary colors, would all too soon be spilled on and chipped, and the paintings would hang slightly askew. Despite the best intentions of the store to provide a nice spot for breaks, this room would show signs of employee angst in a matter of weeks, if not days.

I popped open my Pepsi and took a swig. Detective Loncar pulled a chair next to me and set his soda on the table, still unopened. He put his hands on his head, rubbing the sides where there was still a ring of hair. Footsteps sounded in the hallway, and the female officer entered, only she wasn't alone. The short businessman in the expertly-tailored pinstriped suit who had watched me earlier followed her into the room. The next person to enter was my neighbor, Nora.

From what I'd seen since she moved in, Nora fit the part of professor perfectly. On most days she even wore jackets with elbow patches. Today she was in a beige sheath dress and low-heeled pumps. She didn't look nearly as surprised to see me as I was to see her.

When everyone was seated, Loncar spoke. "Ms. Kidd, why don't you start by telling us about the statue in your handbag?"

"Heist had a contest advertised in the paper. The ad is right here." Now that the statue was out of my handbag, the only thing left were my wallet, keys, and a few pieces of paper. One of the papers was the original ad from Heist.

I handed Loncar the torn piece of newsprint I'd been carrying around since the day I first saw it. "My friends and I thought it would be fun to enter, so we decided to try to steal the statue."

"Fun," Detective Loncar repeated. The other people in the room remained silent. The Puccetti statue sat in the middle of the table like a centerpiece.

"Ms. Kidd, we know about the contest." Detective Loncar sat back in his chair. "That's not the issue here. We just want to know how you got this statue."

"I'm telling you how I got the statue."

"No, you're telling us why you have the statue. Explain how," said the businessman.

I turned to the cop. "You said I'm not being interrogated, right?" He nodded. "Then I want to know who everyone here is, and why you're all asking me these questions."

Loncar scratched his head. "Fair enough. This is Officer Rachel McCord. Next to her is Tony Simms, owner of Heist. And Nora Black—"

"I know Nora," I interjected. I looked at her. She smiled.

"Your turn," Loncar said again. "How did you steal this statue?"

"It wasn't that hard. I assembled a team. I knew there would be a limited amount of time between stealing the statue and having the college discover it was missing, and I knew we weren't the only people who saw the ad in the paper. I came up with a plan. Replace the statue with a fake. Then our competition could steal the fake and get caught, which would throw suspicion off us."

"You came up with the plan?" Loncar asked. He had stopped taking notes, and that struck me as something of an insult.

"Yes, I came up with the plan. You don't believe me?" I leaned against the back of the seat and raked my curly hair into a low ponytail off my neck. When I let go, the curls fell down my back on the outside of the caftan. I scanned the faces at the table. And then I told them about the meeting that one night last week when Cat, Eddie, Dante, and I had congregated in my living room. I told them about the fake statue, the assigned roles, and my grad student makeover, blushing when I remembered the way Dante had looked at me before he left.

"Ms. Kidd, we're waiting," said the detective.

"Waiting for what?"

"You told us you figured out what time to hit the school admissions hall and your plan to duplicate the statue and replace it with a fake before anybody else got to it. And then you got quiet, and then your face turned red."

"And?" I asked. I wrinkled up my forehead and leaned forward. "Why am I here? My friends and I can't be the only people who took the contest seriously." I searched the faces that watched me. Under different circumstances, it would have felt like a poker game.

"Let me tell her what's going on," said Nora. She looked first at Tony and then at Loncar. Officer McCord was paid no attention. The men each nodded consent.

"That contest you mentioned, yes, the college agreed to participate, but they put me in charge of the original statue, which has been in a safe place since the ad ran in the paper. A replica was put on display at I-FAD, so the real statue wasn't at risk. I was notified last night that someone had stolen the fake."

"That's it?" I asked, relieved.

"Not exactly," Detective Loncar said. "You said when you stole the statue, you left one in its place."

"That's right. Why?"

"That's why you're here. Earlier this evening, your copy was used to bludgeon a woman to death."

4

UNIQUE SKILL SET

Oh dear, I thought. Only in my head, I didn't use the word "dear."

"Samantha? Samantha?" Nora's voice sounded like it was coming through a tunnel. "Officer? I think she's going to pass out."

I held the Pepsi can up to my flushed cheeks. "Give me a second. I'll be okay," I mumbled. I chugged as much soda as I could without burning my throat with the carbonation. I suppressed a burp. "Where's Eddie?"

"I'm right here."

I twisted at the waist and saw him sitting in a chair behind me. I didn't know how long he'd been present. He leaned forward and said quietly, "They brought me in after taking my statement about the statue. They found my signature."

The room was silent. Eddie looked out at them. "You can see it right on the base if you look under a magnifying glass. It might have been a copy to everyone else, but to me it was an original."

We went over all the details of the theft more times than I could count. By the fifth time it was hard to sound like I wasn't bragging about my plan and our—well, if I couldn't call it success, I didn't know what to call it. Finally, we were let go. There would be no climactic ten thousand-dollar prize money or free champagne from Heist in my future. Only a long, hot bath, a scowling cat, and a warm, comfy bed. And a phone call from Nick that I was going to try my hardest to miss, because no matter what role he played in my fantasy life, I wasn't sure how to explain my reality, and I wasn't sure tonight was the night to test out phone sex as distraction. I got home, turned off my cell phone and my answering machine, and dove between the sheets.

The next morning, I woke, brewed a pot of coffee, and fished the paper from the front yard. Last night had made the front page: *Buyer Murdered at Retail Gala.* I sat at my kitchen table reading over details that I both knew and didn't know. The victim was Emily Hart, the handbag buyer for Heist. Like Nora had said, she was bludgeoned to death with a replica of the Puccetti statue, which had been found a few feet from the corpse.

I still hadn't heard from Cat or Dante. The police woman, Officer McCord, had gone to look for them after I'd implicated them as participants in my plan, but they'd both already given their statements and left the party.

After two cups of coffee and a shower, I dressed in a pair of pink satin cargo pants from the mid-nineties, a gray cashmere hoodie from a Barbie collector website, and a pair of high-heeled black canvas sneakers with white rubber soles. Logan trailed me around the house and jumped up on the newspaper that I'd left open on the table. I scratched his ears.

"See what happens when you let yourself get involved in hare-brained schemes?" I tried to flip the page, but he pounced on the article, attacking my hand from under the newsprint. We played this game for a couple of minutes. This should be my life. Me and my cat having fun. No homicides. No stress. No police detectives. I rested my hand for a second and Logan swiped at my arm.

"Ow!" I pulled back instinctively, but his claws had punctured the skin. I extracted them. He jumped down and started licking his paw like I'd given him cooties. Nice cat.

The doorbell rang. It could have been any number of people, but Tony Simms, the diminutive owner of Heist counted among the least expected. "Ms. Kidd. May I come in?"

"Yes, of course," I held the door open and allowed him to enter. "Would you like a cup of coffee?"

"Yes. Thank you." He followed me into the kitchen where I poured him a cup.

"Cream? Sugar?" I asked.

"Black."

I handed him the mug and accessorized my own refill with a healthy amount of milk. (Third cup that hour.)

"Ms. Kidd, I have a proposition for you," Tony Simms said.

I sank down in a chair opposite him and half-wished I wasn't wearing a Barbie sweatshirt. I glanced at the newspaper in front of him. My name hadn't been mentioned in the article. In last night's activities, I was merely an innocent bystander. Ish.

"As you know from last night, I am the owner of Heist. I have a lot of money staked in the success of that store. Millions are already invested between the construction and the inventory. Heist cannot fail."

"Some might say last night's publicity was more than you could ever have planned on your own," I said.

"Last night's publicity was not the kind we want. And now we have a murder investigation happening under our noses, but the store must still open."

"What does this have to do with me?"

"You demonstrated a unique skill set with the contest. I asked around about you. I liked what I heard. I'd like to offer you a job."

I wasn't sure where he was going, and I wasn't sure I wanted to know. And we both know that is a big, fat lie.

"You asked around about my background in retail? About my experience working for Bentley's New York?"

"About your short time at Tradava. Your involvement in the investigation of your boss's murder, specifically."

"That's not something I want to talk about."

"Samantha, I find myself needing to fill a job left vacant by a murder victim. I also find myself heavily invested in a store where a crime took place—a crime that could have been committed by any number of people, employees and customers included. Your recent experiences indicate you can work through the possible difficulties that may come with the job and, if I'm correct in my assessment of your recent history with Tradava, you'd be forthcoming with any suspicious behavior you may witness while on the job." He turned his coffee mug but didn't pick it up. "I'm prepared to offer you a generous compensation package if you say yes. Are you interested in a job?"

He wanted to hire me? No more mortgage worries. No more reading the want ads, or polishing my resume, or casing the unemployment office, or making piles of clothes to sell on eBay. All I had to do was say yes.

My dad told me once that this was the most common phrase from my childhood. "All you have to do, Dad …" followed with my childish, simplistic ideas.

Can I have a tree house? All you have to do, Dad…

Let's build a soapbox racer! All you have to do, Dad…

I have a good idea for the science fair. All you have to do, Dad…

Dad had claimed those six words were the kiss of death. But this was different. Right?

"What did you have in mind?" I asked.

"Handbag buyer. You were a buyer at Bentley's New York for nine years, right? You have the experience."

It was unnerving, him knowing my background, but I hid my unease. "Yes. I know how to be a buyer. But if I'm going to do this, there are things I'm going to need."

"Name it."

"Clothing allowance. Expense account."

He reached into the inside breast pocket of his suit, pulled out a wallet, and extracted two pieces of plastic. One was a credit card. The other was an ID for Heist.

My name and photo were on both.

The words "job" and "offer" hadn't been uttered to me in a long time. At least not by a man who was fully aware of my history since moving back to Ribbon. All I had to do was say …

"Yes."

My dad was wrong. That had been frightfully easy.

"I GOT A job yesterday," I said to Eddie. We were at Arners Diner. It was seven thirty in the morning and I was dressed in a navy eighties power suit complete with linebacker shoulder pads. It had been my interview suit upon graduating college and was perhaps an extension of the undercover college student identity I'd recently adopted. I was more than a little excited that it still fit.

I was going to show up at Heist on Monday morning, ready to be the newest handbag buyer in their corporate structure. I was pretty sure that a maniacal serial killer wasn't on the loose knocking off buyers, so the fact that I was about to assume the post of the dead woman didn't faze me much. The fact that I was about to work for a very rich man with a Napoleon complex who'd agreed to my pie-in-the-sky requests without batting an eye fazed the living daylights out of me.

Eddie's fork stopped halfway to his mouth, dangling a delicate bite of egg-white omelet. On his plate was an untouched piece of multigrain toast. I sliced through my last sausage link and raised the bite-sized piece to my mouth. Then I took a bite of my English Muffin and chewed a moment, swallowed, and finished off my orange juice. If he wasn't going to respond, I was going to eat. But when his stare continued after I'd cleared my plate, I figured it was time to go ahead and let the second shoe drop on the floor.

"At Heist. I got a job at Heist."

"What job?" he asked suspiciously.

"The handbag buyer job."

"What?" he exclaimed.

"It's a job," I said. "What happened to Emily Hart was awful, but the store needs a buyer and I'm qualified for the job."

The waitress appeared at the side of our table and asked if we wanted our coffee topped off. I said no and asked for the check. She pulled a pad out of the pocket, flipped a few pages, and tore off our ticket.

"My treat," I said, pulling the Heist credit card out of my wallet. Seemed as good a time as any to test it. I waved Eddie's wallet away. I handed the card to the waitress and sat against the back of the booth.

Eddie stood. "Dude, I can't in good faith allow you to rack up your charge card on breakfast when you haven't even started working yet." He signaled to the waitress to return.

I reached out to stop him, succeeding only in grabbing a handful of his Billy Idol T-shirt. I yanked him back enough to get his attention and then let go. "It's an expense account. I need to make sure it works," I hissed.

His eyes widened. When the waitress turned around, he flapped his hands in the air. "Never mind. We're good." He dropped into the booth. "Heist gave you an expense account?"

I had been debating whether to spill the details to Eddie. There was no way I could keep my new job a secret from him though, so I told him what I had to tell. My name came up, from my work experience, I was contacted by someone at the store. It had been too long since I had a job, and maybe Tradava and I weren't made for each other, but opportunities don't grow on trees, so I accepted the offer. I start Monday.

See? When said it like that, it sounded perfectly innocent. And it was good that I had a chance to practice, because I was going to have to tell that same story to Nick tonight.

Eddie asked enough questions to feel comfortable that I knew what I was doing, and we parted ways. But my instinct to tell someone what I was really up to led me in a very scary direction.

I headed to the police station.

5

A SITUATION

*I*s Detective Loncar here?" I asked the portly man behind the desk.

"Yeah, he's here. Is he expecting you?"

"I don't know."

On some level, Detective Loncar might have been expecting me to drop in since the first murder investigation I'd been involved with. On another level, perhaps one laced with wishful thinking on both of our parts, he might have hoped to never see me again.

"Why are you here?"

"I have to talk to him about a situation that has to do with a homicide."

The cop looked at me sideways. "A situation, huh?" He tipped his head backward. "Yo, Charlie! You got a visitor!"

The door behind the portly guy opened and Detective Loncar looked into the hallway. For three solid seconds our eyes held, until he turned, looked back into the room where he had been, and then turned to face me again. "You're here to see me?" I nodded. "That's a first."

"Can we go somewhere to talk?" I asked, ignoring his cop humor.

"Follow me."

We started down a linoleum-tiled hallway that could have benefited from a once-over with a mop. At the end of the hallway he made a right and turned the doorknob of a splintered door. The sign on the door said Questioning. I stepped backward.

"Isn't there another room we can use besides that one?" I pointed to the door.

"We're going to my office. It's through here." He held the door open until I took my first step, and then turned his back to me and walked past a small wooden table. He opened another door and went inside, this time me tripping over his heels. The door shut behind me and I stood, uncomfortably, looking around the makeshift office of a homicide detective.

"Have a seat."

I sat in a worn chair with a maple frame and brown vinyl seat. The cushion made a *pffffft* sound when I sat, like a whoopee cushion with motivational issues. Neither Loncar nor I commented on the sound.

I told him about the job offer from Tony Simms. Detective Loncar already knew about the dead body, and he already knew about my ability to insinuate myself into a murder investigation. What he didn't know was that I was capable of growing, learning from my mistakes, and partnering with the boys in blue.

After telling my story, I laid my cards on the table. Literally. I pulled the credit card and ID card out of my wallet and set them in front of the detective. He picked up the credit card and stared at it for a couple of seconds, leaned back in his chair, and then stared at the ceiling. He tapped the plastic card against his dimpled chin.

When he put the chair back on all fours, he pressed a button on his phone.

"I need a credit check," he barked into the speakerphone, and rattled off the sixteen digits on the front of my card. He scribbled a series of numbers on a tablet and pushed it toward me. "Is that your social?"

I looked at the paper. My social security number stared back at me. "Yes."

"Print it and bring it to me," he said back into the phone. He hung up and drummed his fingers on the worn wooden desk. His nails had been bitten to the quick, and the calloused tips made a hollow sound against the wood. *Badarabam. Badarabam. Badarabam.*

"You already said yes to the job, right?"

"Right."

"You were hired to do a job and you're going to do that job. But it's possible that you'll learn things that could help us with the investigation. Are you willing to cooperate?"

"I'm here, aren't I?"

"Who knows that you're here?"

"Nobody."

"You planning to keep it that way?"

"I think so."

His eyebrows shot up. "You think so? You don't know so?"

"Okay, sure. I plan to keep it that way." The fingers crossed in my lap countered the conviction in my voice.

"Good. I'll call you tonight with details."

"Do you know what time?"

"Why, you got something more important to do?"

I thought about Nick's impending call, and what I was going to tell him. I'd rather talk to him before any more conversations with the cops, less to hide. But still ...

"Whenever is fine." Turning various shades of red, I left through the back door.

NO MATTER HOW you looked at it, I was back in the fashion industry, so I had to look the part. I also had to snoop around and spy on people and somehow try to figure out why the last handbag buyer got knocked off. No matter how you looked at it, my life was about to change.

I headed home from the police station and took a very long shower. I wasn't sure if I was trying to wash off the memories of being in police headquarters or the common sense that had taken me there, but half an hour later I was scrubbed clean, hair up in a towel turban, plush terrycloth robe covering my body, fluffy pink slippers on my feet. I padded into the kitchen and searched the fridge for food.

Logan swirled around my ankles and swatted at the pompoms on the front of my slippers. I scooped him up in my arms and nuzzled my face into his fur. His front paws curled over my shoulder and he head-butted me. The light on my ancient faux-wood answering machine—a relic of my parents' life before they'd sold me the house—was red. I pushed play, peppering the space between Logan's pointy ears with kisses.

"Samantha, this is Tony Simms. I've arranged for you to go to Heist tonight. Call this number"—he rattled off nine digits— "and make arrangements with security for what time you'd like to arrive. Gabe Gaithers is expecting your call. He'll give you a tour and some shopping time." He disconnected.

Logan wriggled away and jumped to the floor. He stretched, walked over to his food bowl, and meowed. I pulled the top off a can of moist cat food and emptied it for him.

I called the number that Simms had left. A deep voice answered after three rings, and I introduced myself, unsure what else I should say.

"Samantha Kidd, yes. Tony told us you'd be calling. Come by tonight if you want. Park by the south doors. I'll let you in."

I changed from terrycloth to a navy sheath dress that was slightly more in style than the eighties power suit. My newly cut hair would have taken too long to straighten, so I pulled the curls into a low ponytail and knotted a printed scarf around it. Jackie-O glasses covered my five-minute makeup routine, and I was off.

Heist was less than two miles from my house, and don't you dare say a word about how I could have walked there. The large bald man who I'd told about Emily Hart's body the night of the party opened a door. Tonight he wore a slate-gray, button-down shirt and pleated pants that didn't quite match the shirt.

"Are you Samantha Kidd?"

"Yes."

"I'm Gabe." He tipped his head toward the inside of the store. "Follow me."

We walked through the same store I'd wandered through two nights ago, but this time it was different. Instead of being mesmerized by the gritty photography or the merchandising standards, I thought about what it would be like to be a part of this team. It had been well over six months since I'd been a buyer, and even though I'd been a good one at Bentley's, I'd chosen to leave that life behind. I didn't doubt the skills would return once I understood the store's demographics, spreadsheets, and profitability standards, but there was a certain pressure that came with that job. That pressure was why I walked away from the job in the first place.

Hindsight and unemployment had glamorized my memories of being a buyer. More recently, I'd been the unwanted jobseeker. Despite the best well-wishes from my friends, both those who knew me in Ribbon and those I'd left behind in New York, I still wondered if it had been the right decision to leave a successful career behind to rediscover myself in my old hometown. I had set out to simplify. So far I'd found one homicide and another had found me. Nothing simple about it.

"We just got in a truck of merchandise and I have to get to the dock. You okay by yourself?" Gabe asked me.

"Sure."

He handed me a set of keys. "Mr. Simms said you're to bring whatever you want to our office. We'll write it up and if there's an executive available to sign off on the forms, we'll process it tonight. These keys will unlock the fixtures and the fitting rooms." He left me in the middle of the designer sportswear department while he disappeared through the store.

The fixtures surrounding me were filled with clothes that begged to fill my closet, and I could have lost hours trying on 85 percent of their offerings. Instead, I wandered to the handbag department to see what kind of assortment decisions my predecessor had made.

"Samantha Kidd? Is that you?" asked a singsong female voice from behind me. I turned around. The woman approaching me was familiar in a vague way. She had shoulder length hair colored so blond it was almost white, blown into a fluffy style that framed her face and flipped up by her collar. On the bony side of thin, she wore a taupe jersey jacket and fluid pants with classic ivory pumps.

"Belle," she said. "Bell DuChamp." The lightbulb switched on. Belle DuChamp was the general manager for Tradava who I hadn't had a chance to work with. What was she doing here?

Belle held out a perfectly manicured hand and shook mine. A bracelet of gold links and aged antique coins clanged around her delicate wrist like chimes. "Welcome aboard our team."

"Our?"

"Heist. You'll be working with me. We never got the chance to work together at Tradava, and after what you did for them, I say it's a shame. You're a talented gal, and we're lucky to have you. Stole you out from under their noses, I'd say, even if that's not exactly the way it happened. But I believe"— she extended an arm in front of her, inviting me to join her walk through the aisle—" right place, right time. And no better time than the present." She winked at me. "Don't you agree?"

I was taken by her bravado, though I still wasn't entirely sure what we were talking about. "Ms. DuChamp?"

"Don't Ms. DuChamp me. Call me Belle. Tradava may have had those ancient political ideals and stuffy policies, but Heist is a young company. We're all on first-name basis. Even Tony Simms."

She didn't seem to have fond memories of Tradava, and considering my spotty work history with them, I was wondering if I should suggest we start some sort of club.

"Come to my office. We've got a lot to discuss."

Belle Duchamp had the figure of a twenty-year-old and the attitude of a woman in her fifties. Confidence seeped from her like she'd bathed in it. We reached a glass door, which she pushed through, much like the glass ceiling I imagined she had hit at some point of her career at Tradava. I followed her down a carpeted hallway to the last office. It overlooked the parking lot. A wooden desk sat off to the side, and a glass top conference table sat by the window.

"Have a seat." Again she gestured, this time to the red and brown plaid chair in front of her desk. The store hadn't even opened, and her desktop was in disarray. "Don't mind all this. They're still a little paperwork heavy around here, getting the store open and all." She pushed a pile of papers together, squared them off at the corners, and set them inside one of her drawers. "Tell me everything I need to know about you."

It seemed I'd misunderstood Tony Simms when he'd been at my house. "I didn't come prepared for an interview," I said.

She threw her head back and laughed the kind of full-on laugh that most women are too shy to release. I counted five fillings—three on the bottom, two on the top—before she closed her mouth.

"Samantha–Sam, can I call you Sam?"

I nodded. She reached over and patted my hand. "Relax. You got the job. I just wanted to get to know the newest superstar on the Heist team."

"In that case, I'll give you the short version." I launched into the highlights of my resumé.

She cut me off from the work stuff and interrogated me on the life stuff and dangled an awfully big carrot on trash-talking Tradava, but unlike Bugs Bunny, I didn't bite. It still felt too soon to burn that bridge, even if they didn't want me on the other side.

We talked for the better part of an hour. When she paused to look at the clock, she smacked her hands palm down on her desk. "Jesus! Look at the time. You came here to shop, and I'm holding you hostage in this stuffy office. I didn't leave you much time before they kick us out for the night. You'll be here all day tomorrow, so you'll have plenty of time. Go home, get some sleep." She stood from her desk and walked me back out to the security office. "We'll have coffee in the morning. Meet me here at quarter to nine."

She pumped my hand twice like business women in movies from the eighties did and headed back into the store. I retraced my path to the security department. Gabe pushed a clipboard my direction.

"Sign out before you leave."

I jotted my name on the first available line and pushed the clipboard back. "Do you lock up the store this time every night?"

He looked at me oddly. "What makes you think we're locking up the store?"

"That's what Ms. DuChamp—Belle—just said."

"You must have misunderstood her. We won't lock up for another three hours."

I glanced at the now-vacant hallway. If there was something in the store that I wasn't supposed to see, I'd just been railroaded away from finding it.

6

⚮

CANOODLING IN THE BOARDROOM

Instead of braving the grocery store, I joined Eddie and Cat for dinner at Briquette Burger. We sat around a large booth waiting for our entrees. Cat dredged a piece of bread through the cruet of truffle butter that rested on the center of the table and took a healthy bite. After swallowing, she tore off another piece of bread and wiped the cruet clean. Must be good, I thought; it was the first time I'd ever seen her openly gorge on carbs.

When three glasses of wine arrived at the table, Eddie raised his to me in a toast. "To Sam. For landing on her feet."

"To Sam," Cat echoed.

I smiled a nervous smile, knowing what was in store for me, and raised my glass to clink theirs. We each took a sip.

Cat excused herself to the ladies room, and I bit into the last piece of bread. I didn't need the excuse of fancy butter to accessorize a perfectly good hunk of dough.

"So you start tomorrow, right?" Eddie asked.

"Mmmhmm," I answered, chewing my way through a sourdough roll.

"The dead woman's job?"

A young couple two tables over stared in our direction.

"Keep your voice down. People are looking at us." I bit into the roll again and used both hands to tear it from my teeth. I swallowed a mouthful and washed it down with water. "I met Belle DuChamp today. Do you know her? Thin, perky boobs, chic clothes, blonde hair?" I added.

Eddie choked on his wine.

"People at Tradava call her Belle of the Balls. Because when her husband was around, she was known for squeezing them." Eddie lowered his voice. "She was the general manager of Tradava for the last eleven years. Always seemed like a pretty amazing woman, but not the most politically correct if you know what I mean."

"Actually, I don't," I said. If Eddie had dirt on someone I'd be working with, I wanted to hear it.

"I heard she had a couple of affairs during that time, with a couple members of the board."

"That's probably just the rumor mill. She was the only woman in a sea of men. Everybody says that kind of stuff."

"Well, maybe, but here's what I heard about why she got fired." He leaned in closer, dangling juicy gossip like the steak that was heading our direction. "She was caught canoodling in the boardroom."

"Who uses words like 'canoodling'?"

He ignored me. "She was on the fast track, too. Doesn't make sense, really because she's a smart cookie. Why would you throw

56

away your entire future, job security, all that, for a quick romp on a wooden table?"

"Maybe she was too dominant at home and her husband couldn't, uh, perform. Some men don't like their women to be that strong and independent."

"Speaking of which, what does Nick say about your new job?"

I glared at him. "Do not compare us with them. Nick and I are not even at the relationship stage. We aren't even in the same city."

"Maybe that's the problem."

"Who says there's a problem?"

"What does he have to say about all of this?"

"All of what?"

"The statue. The murder. The job." He made big circles with his hands. "All of this."

"He didn't really have anything to say about it. What's taking Cat so long?" I looked behind me at the restroom doors.

"That's not like Nick. Why do you think he hasn't said anything?"

"Seriously, she's been gone a long time." I stood. Eddie reached across the table and grabbed my wrist.

"Answer my question."

I shook him off. "Nick hasn't said anything because I haven't told him. Are you satisfied?

Eddie stared at me. His blond hair had been buzzed on the sides in a makeshift Mohawk, and the longer top flopped onto his forehead. "Why haven't you told Nick what you're up to?"

"I don't want him to worry."

"Why would he worry about you getting a new job?" he asked. Suspicion was written all over his face. "There's something you're not telling me."

"I have to check on Cat." I stepped away from the table and went to the bathroom. When I got there, I found her passed out on the ceramic tiled floor.

"Cat? Cat?" I untied my scarf and flapped it over her face, and then ran tap water onto a wad of tri-folded paper towels and held the stack against her forehead. "Cat?" Her eyes fluttered open and closed again. When they reopened a third time, they narrowed and looked side to side. I sat next to her on the cold tile and held her hand.

"Why are we on the floor?" she asked.

"I don't know. This is where I found you."

Her narrowed eyes widened. "I don't feel so good."

She didn't look so good, either. Green generally looks good on a redhead, but the shade Cat had gone under her normally porcelain skin wasn't her best. I helped her up and stood by her side while she propped herself on the sink. She ran her wrists under cold water and dabbed her fingertips against her hairline.

"Will you mind terribly if I don't stay? I want to go home."

"Of course I don't mind. Do you want me to drive you?"

"No, I'll be fine."

We walked back out to our table, where Eddie sat surrounded by three steak and potato dinners. Cat stopped a few steps short when the smell of food hit her. "I need fresh air," she said. she clamped her hand over her mouth and ran for the front door.

"What's wrong with her?" Eddie asked.

"She's sick." I leaned on the booth and watched Cat leave the restaurant.

He slid out of the booth. "Take the food to go. I'm going to drive her home. We'll celebrate another time, Okay?"

"Sure," I said. "Call me when she's safe at home."

He nodded and left. The waiter came to the table and asked if something was wrong. "Change of plans," I answered, and asked for a couple of to-go boxes. Logan was going to eat well tonight. And I had a second opportunity to use my new expense card too.

IT WAS AFTER nine when I unlocked the front door. The house was dark and silent. Logan was asleep on the sofa. Sweet cat. I was going to miss him tomorrow when I headed off to work.

I showered and changed into a silk nightgown and laid out my first day's outfit: a pink trench coat over a pearl gray sheath dress and gray flannel stiletto mary janes with a black patent toe and heel. I transferred my handbag essentials into a vintage black patent clutch I'd scored at a sale in New York. After I finished, I sank down on the bed and started thinking about what I was about to get myself into.

Emily Hart, handbag buyer for Heist, had been found dead. I'd been tasked to be her replacement and keep my eyes and ears open to anything suspicious. It seemed that the actual store manager didn't know my true reasons for being there. Did that mean she was under suspicion?

Come to think of it, after what Eddie had said, I wondered about Belle DuChamp. She'd been on the fast track at Tradava, worked there for eleven years. At her level, that surely put her into pension category, and she probably felt she had some job security. Had she really been found canoodling in the boardroom? Seemed a stretch. But if Tony Simms didn't tell her about me, then there might be a reason. She *had* ushered me out of the store awfully quickly that very afternoon.

The comforter on the bed started ringing. I padded my hand around until I found the cordless phone twisted up in the sheets. It was early for Nick to call, but maybe he was making up for lost time.

"Hello there, Tiger," I said in my best sex-kitten voice.

"Samantha Kidd? This is Detective Loncar."

It was going to be a long night.

7

NO DISRESPECT INTENDED

*H*ere's the plan," Detective Loncar said, ignoring the way I'd answered the phone. "You go into work like you're expected to. We're not yet sure what we want you to look for, so take note of anything you think is suspicious. I'll call you tomorrow night to touch base."

"No disrespect intended, but that's a pretty vague plan. Don't you want to tell me who the suspects are so I know who to watch?"

"Ms. Kidd, may I remind you that you have volunteered to cooperate with us, but you are not a member of the police force."

"Okay, tell me this. Is working for Heist dangerous? Will something happen to me?"

"Ms. Kidd, you were offered employment by one of Philadelphia's most influential businessmen. You legitimately have a job."

I was starting to have second thoughts about the whole thing, and not just a little because of the homicide. The cops might think Tony Simms was on the up and up, but something about him spooked me. That he'd shown up on my doorstep with identification in my name before formerly offering me a job was only a part of it.

My cell phone started buzzing around on the nightstand, and I didn't even have to look to know it was Nick.

"Detective, can you hold on a second? I have another call." I couldn't remember which button on the cordless was mute so I pushed it under the covers and answered my cell phone.

"Hello?" I said, using my sultry voice for the second time that night.

"Hey, Kidd," said Nick. His voice was low, gravelly. Sexy. I leaned back onto the pillows and hugged my knees. "What's going on in chez Kidd?"

"Not much, just getting ready for tomorrow."

"What's tomorrow?"

A muffled sound came from under the covers. I felt around with my left hand until I connected with the cordless.

"Hold that thought," I said to Nick. I set my cell on the nightstand and pulled the cordless out from under the covers. "Detective? Are you there?"

"Don't do that again, Ms. Kidd. Now, about tomorrow, just do what I said. Don't bring up the homicide, don't ask questions. Just go to work, keep your eyes open, and we'll talk at the end of the day. Same time as tonight." He disconnected before I had a chance to consent, though I guess I'd done that when I showed up at headquarters.

I picked up my cell. "Nick? Are you still there?"

"I'm here."

I pictured him in his bed, shirtless, half-covered with blankets, propped up against the pillow. Then I got a little turned on and thought it was better not to picture that. Not now, not when I had some very dreaded information to share with him. There was a very good chance that once I told him what I was up to, we were not going to be talking like one of those 976 numbers.

"You know, when you set the phone down, I thought I heard you say 'detective.' "

"I did," I said, trying to come up with a cover story. "Eddie's here. We're playing Clue."

"What's going on, Kidd?"

"Nothing! We, uh, made up new rules. Whenever someone lands in the library we have to say 'detective.'"

"You can't play Clue with two people."

I pushed my feet far under the sheet. Why hadn't I gone with Uno? "Nick, there's a new retailer in town and I'm going to work for them. You probably heard about the store before you left for Italy. Heist?"

"I read something about them expanding into Tradava's markets. From what I've heard, they're pretty high concept, right?"

"Yes. Do they carry your shoe collection?"

"No, I never got into business with them. Now that I took back distribution of my label, I have to be careful about expanding too quickly. Besides, their discount agreement is a little too deep for me. What are you going to do for them?"

"I'm going to be the handbag buyer." I climbed out of the bed and went downstairs to the kitchen. I was going to need a side of ice cream to go with all this honesty.

"Did I know about this? That you applied there?"

I chose my words carefully. "No, I didn't say anything about it because I didn't expect anything like this to happen. Turns out they were very impressed with my, uh, experience." I opened one of the takeout containers and cut off a small piece of hamburger for Logan. I tore a corner off the bread and tossed it in his bowl, too. It was free bread that came with the meal, and I was totally within my rights as a consumer to empty the basket into my carryout container.

"Why shouldn't they be?" Nick asked. "You're smart and talented. Just because things never worked out like you wanted at Tradava doesn't mean things aren't going to work out for you in Ribbon. Just think, if you'd never moved to your old hometown for a job at Tradava, we wouldn't be having this conversation. You never know what's right around the corner."

Nick was right. I didn't know what was right around the corner. But something about this particular opportunity that I was embarking on was unsettling. Maybe it was the fact that, aside from Detective Loncar, nobody knew what I was getting myself into.

I'd had more than my share of excitement since I'd moved back to Ribbon, and Nick had seen me through a lot of it. I knew he worried about me. But the two thousand miles between us created a bridge too big for him to cross if I needed help again. Maybe that's why I'd partnered with the cops. I was learning. I was growing. And maybe that's why I found myself wanting to tell Nick everything.

"I have to tell you something. Something big." Silence. "Are you still there?"

"I'm here," he said, but something in his voice had changed.

I stood with the phone pressed to my ear, watching Logan. I toyed with the best way to bring up Emily Hart's murder and how it had led to my employment at Heist. Logan swatted at the piece of meat in his bowl then licked it a couple of times. He pulled away and shook his head side to side.

"When I said Heist was impressed with my experience, I wasn't only talking about my work experience."

Logan slinked into the living room. A couple of seconds later he made a choking sound. I ran to the front room, where he hacked a few more times and then threw up. He took a few steps away from the nasty pile on the carpet and lay down on his side. His eyes went glassy and unfocused.

And I remembered Cat, passed out on the floor of the restaurant bathroom.

And the food that I'd just put in Logan's bowl.

"Nick, I'll call you back. Something's wrong with Logan."

I couldn't bear the thought of something happening to my cat. He was my little soldier, waiting for me every night when I got home. I wasn't ready for him to leave me. I'd never be ready for that, but at the hand of a piece of tainted meat from dinner? That wasn't playing fair. I didn't know how that factored into his nine lives.

The vet agreed to see him after I called in panic mode. I trundled Logan in a light blue pashmina and held him on my lap while I drove. Being captive in a car is not Logan's favorite thing, but tonight, he was quiet. That freaked me out more than anything.

The vet's assistant took him from my arms. She instructed me to fill out paperwork while she took blood and other pertinent samples that would tell if I had an overactive imagination or if my cat had been poisoned. And to kill time, since I was alone in the waiting room, I knew there was one phone call to make.

"Loncar," the detective answered.

"I'm out," I said.

"Who is this?"

"Samantha Kidd. I want out of the arrangement. They got to my friend. They got to my cat. I can't do this."

"Ms. Kidd, slow down. where are you?"

"I'm at the vet's office. My cat is sick. And my friend was sick earlier, and they ate the same food, but not at the same time. I mean, the food was for me, and I got it to go after Cat had to leave, but then I gave a piece of it to Logan, he's a cat, too, only not like my friend Cat, and now he's sick and I think maybe someone poisoned my dinner and I didn't know who else to call." I knew I sounded frantic, but frantic was about ten steps calmer than how I actually felt.

"Tell me again what happened."

I recounted finding Cat passed out on the restaurant bathroom floor, and Logan's strange behavior when batting around the meat. But the question that hung in the air that Detective Loncar was nice enough not to ask was why would someone have poisoned me at the Briquette Burger?

"You said you found your friend on the bathroom floor. Did she eat the steak?"

"No. She only ate the bread."

"Did your cat eat the bread?"

"He licked it a couple of times, probably for the butter."

"Ms. Kidd, I don't know if we're looking at our first case of poisoning through butter, but I don't think this has to do with your job at Heist. I'll send someone out to the restaurant to check it out, but you should go home and get a good night's sleep."

"But what about my cat?"

"Call me back and tell me what the vet says."

Loncar disconnected. Already this partnership with the cops left much to be desired.

I wiped away the tears that had cut tracks down my cheeks. The door opened and the vet came out cradling Logan. He made a sound, like a meow that had been recorded on a forty-five and played at thirty-three.

"He's fine. He ate something that didn't agree with him, but it's all out of his system now. Cats are funny that way. Better off than us, some might say. I gave him a sedative, but he'll sleep that off and be back to normal in the morning." He handed Logan to me, and I cradled him like a newborn.

I drove home, thinking about what was in store for me. It was after eleven when I pulled into the driveway. I set Logan on the kitchen table, next to my computer, and filled the Fred Flintstone juice glass with Merlot. One of these days I was going to update the house from early inheritance to modern woman. But before I could think about that, I had a few things I had to work out. I booted up the computer and started an e-mail to Nick.

The solitude of e-mail gave me the courage to confess my involvement in the homicide and the real reason I was working for Heist. It included phrases like *I'm working with the cops, nobody else knows about this,* and *I'm pretty sure I'll be okay, but I wanted you to know.* I signed it with a bunch of Xs and Os and prayed to the gods of internet communications that if this was the wrong thing to do, there would be a technical error and the e-mail would bounce. I turned the computer off so I couldn't see his response, turned off the cell phone so he couldn't call, and carried my now snoring cat to my bedroom. Whatever it was that I was in for, it was only hours away.

8

KNOCK 'EM DEAD

*I*D, please," said a petite woman behind the security desk at Heist. I handed her the card that Tony Simms had given me. She studied it for a moment and then handed it back.

"You're Samantha Kidd? Nice outfit. Welcome to the team."

"Thank you." I adjusted the belt on my pink satin trench coat. I followed a few other people into the store, snaking my way through the denim department to an aisle that led to the handbag displays. Tony Simms stood in by the escalators.

"Samantha." He nodded.

"Mr. Simms," I replied.

"Call me Tony."

That was better than calling him the scary small man that I wasn't sure I could trust, so I went with it. "Okay, Tony."

I hadn't expected to see Tony this morning. I got the feeling this guy would know every move I made and every breath I took. Good thing I'd brought the police into my life; they were singing my theme song.

We walked through the store, past the ballet bars of handcuffed leather jackets and the mug shots in cosmetics. In light of recent events, it was more creepy than edgy. But still, their accessories department rocked.

He led me to a small office, not much wider than the desk inside. "I'm on your speed dial, top button. Call me if you need anything. Otherwise, take today and get acclimated. Instructions on logging on to e-mail are under the keyboard, along with your passwords. Your assistant buyer will be in shortly, I imagine, and she can give you a briefing on your schedule."

After he left, I gingerly sat in the chair of a now-dead woman. I powered up the laptop and signed into e-mail. The unread ones were in red, and the first one's subject was *Welcome to the team!* It was my second "Welcome to the Team" that morning, and already the phrase felt fake and automatic, like "May I help you?" sounded to thousands of shoppers programmed to answer, "Just Looking." This welcome was from Belle DuChamp.

I read her brief note welcoming me aboard the Heist team. It had been sent on Saturday, probably after I'd left. She offered to give me a tour of the store at ten, and wanted me to sit in on two meetings in the afternoon to get a feel for the store's promotional activity and upcoming advertising. I jotted both in an unused day planner that I found in the upper right hand drawer of the desk.

The next note was from a Mallory George, whose signature line read *Assistant Buyer, Handbags. Heist—Our Prices are Criminal!* The note was brief and decidedly un-chatty, and included details on an appointment with the account representative from Vongole, apologies for having a dentist's appointment that would cause her to be a half an hour late, and no uses of the words "welcome" or "team."

I fussed around with the drawers and the notebooks and the catalogs, all of which bore a striking resemblance to my first day at Tradava so many months ago. Would I ever outlive this relatively newfound need to put myself in danger? Whatever it was I was seeking, besides the current task of identifying Emily Hart's killer, I wondered if I would find it.

The phone rang, pulling me out of my self-analysis. "Samantha Kidd," I answered, not sure if that was Heist's standard method for answering the phone.

"Who? I'm looking for Emily?" said a perky female voice.

There are some things you just don't say on the phone to a stranger, and "Emily is dead" is one of them. (Insert any name for Emily, but still, it just isn't done.)

"I'm sorry, Emily isn't here. Is there something I can help you with?"

"Who are you again?"

"Samantha Kidd, Handbag buyer for Heist." It sounded weird out loud.

"Oh. Wow. I knew Emily wanted to leave, but that was quick!"

"I'm sorry," I said again, though I'd done nothing wrong. "Who did you say you were?"

"Andi Holloway. I'm the account manager for Vongole. Actually, I run the showroom Bag Lady. Vongole is my biggest account right now."

"I think I have an appointment with you today, but I don't know what time," I said.

"Fantastic. I have some new items that you will absolutely freak out over. Four o'clock?"

I checked the day planner that, at the moment, only had three things written down, but one of them was in the four o'clock timeslot.

"I can't make four. Can you see me any earlier?"

"That could be problematic." I heard her flipping pages on the other end of the phone and pictured her juggling buyers like men on a debutante's dance card. "Can you make noon? Twelve thirty? No, make it one. Can you make one? It'll be cutting it close, but I can do it."

Sounded like I didn't have much of a choice. "One it is. Where are you located?"

She read off a Penn Street address. "It's a renovated office with space for rent. Seven stories, big Art Deco building. You can't miss it. My Bag Lady offices are on the seventh floor."

We disconnected with the pleasantries of "see you at one" and "I look forward to meeting you." It wasn't a lie. She knew Emily had wanted to leave Heist, and if that was true, then she had more than a professional relationship with Emily. You don't tell your business associates you're looking to leave your job unless you consider them a friend.

A petite woman carried a large vase of flowers into my office. So large that the only way I knew it was a woman were the skirt and stockinged legs visible from the waist down.

"Samantha Kidd?"

"That's me."

"These were waiting for you at security." She set the vase on the corner of my desk. Striking orange flowers were nestled in a square glass vase that was lined with bamboo. A card was clipped to the side of the vase. It wasn't in an envelope.

Knock 'em dead!

Though a smattering of people knew I was starting this job, only one would take the time to send me flowers. Nick's sense of humor and level of support were off the charts on this one. Maybe I should confide in him more often.

"They're the most amazing calla lilies I've ever seen," the petite woman said.

"They are pretty, aren't they? What did you say they were?"

"Bronze Callas. He must be pretty special, whoever he is. That's not a cheap arrangement."

"He is," I said, adjusting one of the waxy-textured flowers to the left.

"They last a long time, too."

"Good. I'd hate to throw it away."

We could only focus on my flowers for so long before we exchanged introductions, and considering she'd brought me flowers with my name on them, I was the only one in the dark.

"You must think I'm rude," she said. "I'm Mallory George. Emily's—I mean, your—assistant buyer." She held out a hand for me to shake.

"Hi Mallory. Samantha Kidd."

Mallory's black bobbed hair had the rigid angles of a Louise Brooks bob, and had been straightened with a precision that lent it a Japanese flavor, though her features were definitely not Asian. She wore a crisp white shirt tucked into a long straight pencil skirt. If she had any curves, her outfit kept them hidden.

"Do you mind filling me in on your background?" she asked.

"Excuse me?"

She stood in front of my desk with her handbag still draped over her arm, hands folded in front of her. "What is your work experience?"

I was taken off guard. I'd gotten this far without an actual interview, and now it seemed as though my own assistant was going to be the one to question my abilities.

"Don't you want to put your things down?"

"In a second." She stared at me, not with hostility, but with something that felt alarmingly like X-ray vision. And I was not in a position to have someone see right through me. "This is a big job," she said. "Emily had been in the handbag industry for ten years before landing here. I've been on the Heist team for fifteen. I relocated here when they opened this location. We have aggressive plans to outpace the rest of the store's sales and be the number one department. I don't think it's too much to ask what your qualifications are since you're now the buyer of the most important department in the store."

I glanced at the phone and saw the time was minutes away from ten o'clock.

"I have an appointment with Belle DuChamp at ten, so we'll talk when I return. Oh, and Andi Holloway rescheduled us for one o'clock at her Bag Lady showroom today. She said we should both come. We can talk on the way there. Does that work for you?"

Mallory looked surprised. She nodded her head and her bobbed hair bobbed. She looked at my flowers one more time, and then shuffled into her own office. I grabbed a notepad and pen, tucked my cell phone into my pocket, and traveled back to the executive offices to find the store manager.

Belle DuChamp's promise to give me a tour of the store turned out to be empty. She was tied up on the phone negotiating the price of a large purchase with a customer. She held her hand over the receiver and whispered to me, "He's so close. If I can close this, we'll blow away our opening numbers. Sorry about the tour. Tomorrow?"

I nodded. She scribbled something on a piece of paper and returned to her call.

WITH THE NEWFOUND available pocket of time, I left her office and wandered into the store. It was the perfect time to snoop. My snooping, not surprisingly, led to the handbag department.

A woman in a black nylon sheath dress accented with silver zippers was rearranging the assortment. Her dark brown hair was parted on the side and gelled back into a tight ponytail barely an inch long. Oversized silver hoop earrings weighed down her earlobes. A white can of RockStar Diet Energy drink sat just out of her reach.

"Isn't this bag fantastic?" she asked, holding up a nylon tote with the Vongole logo emblazoned on a leather piece attached to the middle.

"I like the yellow one better." I pointed to the crocodile bag I'd noticed at the gala.

"Omigod. I know. They're totally fab, right? I can't get enough of these. I have, like, ten of them in my closet, and it's not enough. Look at the blue one." She picked up a cobalt blue leather hobo bag. The color was magnificent. The logo was again stamped into the leather, in one of those very clean, linear fonts that are equally timeless and modern. "Here, try it on. It'll totally pop your outfit."

She was referring to my gray sheath dress. I'd left my pink trench hanging over the back of my chair.

I took the bag from her and slung it over my shoulder. It was big enough to carry around a laptop and just about anything else I'd want to schlep back and forth to the store.

"Omigod, it's so you. Let me find someone who can ring it up for you." She looked around the store.

"Actually, I'll take it to my office. That way I can get it on my way out."

"You work here?" She was noticeably let down.

"Yes. I'm the new handbag buyer."

"Omigod! Are you Samantha? I'm Andi Holloway, from Bag Lady!" She hopped with enthusiasm and shook my hand. My eyes darted between her and the energy drink. "This is totally funny. We're still on today at one, right?"

"Sure."

"I was just at Tradava meeting with Kyle, and we finished up early, so I came over here to merchandise. He told me about Emily." She dropped her voice and moved in closer to me. "I get why you didn't tell me on the phone. Kyle said it was awful. Just awful."

"Kyle?" It was the only thing she'd said that stuck in my head.

"Kyle Trent. Your competition."

I must have still looked confused, so she continued.

"You know, the totally hot handbag buyer at Tradava?"

9

DOESN'T ADD UP

*N*ow this was news.

Kyle Trent had been at the gala in the area of Emily's body. In fact, he'd been coming out of the shadows of the handbag department when I'd first noticed him. He had treated me like I was the one who didn't belong, and all things considered, I hadn't given him a second thought. Now I knew he worked for Tradava, Heist's biggest competitor in the city of Ribbon. That meant *he* was the one who'd been out of place. And what was it he'd said? Something about Emily, about her head being big. Had his comments been made to distract me from his presence, to make me more aware that I wasn't where I should be so I wouldn't take note that neither was he?

I was going to have to tell this to Detective Loncar. I wandered to the cosmetics department and asked a makeup artist for a tissue and a lip liner. I wrote KYLE TRENT on the tissue, handed the liner back to the suspicious employee, and balled the tissue up in my palm. It was just about noon. Mallory and I would be on our way to the handbag showroom in a short while, but I wanted to collect my thoughts, grab a bite to eat, and check on Cat, not necessarily in that order.

I stopped outside of my office when I overheard my assistant, Mallory, on the phone. "Somebody sent her a pretty expensive flower arrangement. Guess it's her boyfriend or husband. I don't think she's going to fall for Kyle's tricks. She knows Belle, too, but I don't know how. I'll find out." There was a pause of silence, and then Mallory's voice dropped. "I can't talk. Call me later." The phone clunked against the receiver while I ducked into my own small quarters. I shrugged back into my trench coat and belted it around my waist, picked up my vintage handbag, and went to Mallory's doorway.

"What time do we have to leave to get to Bag Lady by one?" I asked.

"Twelve thirty should be fine, but Andi's cool if we're a little late."

"We'll be on time. I'm going to grab something to eat. Why don't we meet by security at twenty-five after? I'll drive."

It was clear that Mallory wanted to undermine me, but I wasn't going to let her. I didn't know her deal yet, but with the tight quarters of my Honda del Sol looming in our future, I'd have approximately half an hour to find out.

I bought a Snickers bar and a packet of peanuts from the newsstand in the corner of the parking lot and sat on a public bench. I bit into the Snickers and scribbled names into my composition notebook, munching without any trace of manners, completely absorbed in my candy bar and *Harriet the Spy* routine. That's why I didn't notice the motorcycle that pulled up in front of me until the driver got off.

Dante.

He climbed off the bike and put it on its kickstand. He wore a pretty close approximation of what he'd worn the night he showed up at my house. Black leather jacket, white T-shirt, jeans, black leather boots.

I slammed my notebook shut and wiped a ring around my lipstick with my index finger to remove any traces of chocolate that may have smeared onto my face.

"What are you doing, Samantha?"

"Nice to see you too, Dante."

"You're working here now?" He jerked a thumb behind him in the direction of Heist.

"It would appear that way, yes."

"But sometimes things aren't what they appear to be."

"Okay, I'm working here now."

He straddled the paint chipped bench and faced me. "Doesn't add up."

"What?"

"If you knew you were going to be working at Heist, you would never have entered that contest. And you would never have gotten a job so fast if you hadn't applied before the contest. So somehow you got a job here, between the time that woman was murdered and today. And between that time, someone poisoned my sister. And I think it's related, and I want details."

It would have been easier to lie to Nick in Italy than to lie to Dante in front of me, but the irony was that I'd been honest with Nick despite the distance between us. I suspected what Nick would say about me being *thisclose* to a homicide investigation, but I didn't know Dante that well.

I did a little internal negotiating on whether or not I would feel better/want help/want Dante's help when something he said struck me.

"What do you mean someone poisoned your sister?"

"They found traces of poison in Cat's system. That's why she passed out."

"But we didn't have time to eat. I took the food with me when Eddie drove her home."

"She said she ate the bread."

"We all ate the bread."

"And you didn't get sick?"

"Nope." But Logan had.

"Dante, Cat's husband is on the road, right?"

He nodded.

"Are you going to stay with her, at least for now, to take care of her?"

"Yeah."

"Good."

I stood up from the bench. Dante stood too and turned me toward him. He leaned in and I could smell cinnamon on his breath. "That doesn't mean I'm not going to keep an eye on you. I don't buy this whole 'new job' thing. I don't know what you're hiding, but if you're into something, I'm going to find out." His brown eyes bore holes into my head. "If this is about you feeling some kind of rush, you're risking too much."

He stepped closer. I tried to back up but my calf hit the bench I'd been sitting on. There was no place for me to go, and parts of my body were telling my brain they didn't really want to go anywhere.

"Besides, there are better ways of getting a rush," he said, running the back of his index finger down the side of my neck and across my clavicle.

I flicked his hand away with a *Karate Kid* wax-on/wax-off maneuver. "I'm not looking for a rush."

"Good. Some things are better when you take them slow."

In the distance, I saw Mallory exit the store. "I have to be somewhere," I said, which seemed the safest of the things running through my head to say out loud. "Tell Cat I hope she feels better. I'll come by later this week to check on her." I walked past him to my car.

"Samantha," he called out behind me. "Be careful."

"Of what?" I said, turning around and walking backward for a few steps. "I'm just a buyer for a department store." I smiled and then turned away again, feeling the heat of his stare on my back the whole time.

IF MALLORY WANTED to know my qualifications, she was going to have to broach the subject again without my help. As far as I was concerned, I was fully capable of doing this job, even if "the job" involved a few things probably not spelled out in the description. I met her outside the security entrance and invited her to join me in the car.

She stopped off at a PT Cruiser, pulled a pair of tortoise-framed sunglasses from the center console, and locked the door. She matched my stride to the car, no easy feat considering I was naturally taller than she was. Her posture was bent slightly at the waist, causing her to pitch forward awkwardly. She balanced expertly upon five-inch platform wedges and came darn close to towering over my five-foot seven frame. I did a double take when I saw the size of her feet. No wonder she could balance on those boats.

We settled into the car and I immediately turned off the stereo, not wanting to blast her with the greatest hits of Tom Jones. I drove from the parking lot to the access road to the highway in silence, wondering who was going to speak first. I side-glanced at Mallory and caught her staring at the compartment between our seats. When we stopped at the next traffic light I followed her stare. Eddie had left the sketches of the Puccetti statue half-rolled up between the seats. I had to teach that boy to clean up after himself.

"Maybe I didn't ask correctly this morning, but I am curious to know what brings you to Heist," she said. Her approach was softer than earlier. I wondered what made the difference.

"I've been in the industry for more than a decade. I worked at Bentley's in New York. Just moved here recently."

"You were their handbag buyer?"

"Shoes."

"A lot of the same vendors, I suppose," she admitted. "So why did you move to Ribbon?"

"I grew up here. My parents wanted to move to the west coast, and it seemed like a good idea to buy their house. The one I grew up in." It sounded so insignificant when trying to explain it to a person who probably wasn't interested.

"Trying to go home again. Did it work?"

"The jury's still out." I changed lanes to let an aggressive driver pass.

"Why Heist?"

I wasn't sure if I should mention my brief work history with Tradava or not, but she could find out easily enough. "They recruited me after they found out I no longer worked at Tradava."

She seemed surprised. "Nobody told me you worked at Tradava."

"I was only there briefly." *Mental note: stay vague on the details.* "I'm still trying to figure out who gave them my name."

"It had to be Belle DuChamp. She's from Tradava, and she didn't leave on good terms. I heard she's very interested in crushing them."

"She was fired?"

"You didn't know? They caught her and the handbag manager getting it on in the board room. That's why it's so weird that you showed up. With Emily gone, I figured he was a shoe-in."

10

To Die For

I tried to keep our conversation to a minimum for the duration of the drive, because I couldn't exactly stop and take notes. What was becoming apparent was that Mallory George was going to be a wealth of information if I played the situation correctly.

We arrived at Bag Lady and found Andi Holloway cradling her cell phone between her tipped head and hunched shoulder while she bought a diet RockStar energy drink from a vending machine in the lobby.

"Can't talk now," she said into the phone and raised her head. The phone dropped to the floor. She scooped it up and smiled at us. "Thank God! You just saved me from a lecture from my dad. You want one?" She held up the white can as if making a toast.

"No thanks. Mallory?"

"None for me, either."

We followed Andi past a couple of smaller rooms filled with crocheted hobos and patchwork tote bags. Finally we reached a room merchandised with Vongole's collection.

Colorful handbags sat on perfectly lit shelves just like at Heist. The shelving features were a milky white Lucite, glowing from hidden lights behind them, highlighting colorful patent leather bags. Clutches with silver hardware in the colors of hard candy lined the wall, but Andi had taken advantage of the negative space on the shelves to break the assortment up into trend stories. I picked up the canary-yellow patent sample and unsnapped the clasp. Soft lilac suede lined the inside. I snapped it shut before it started whispering sweet nothings to me like a seashell from the Jersey shore. On a separate shelf sat a collection of bucket totes with chain link handles and the V logo formed out of Bakelite. Knowing I couldn't stock Heist with every bag they carried, my job got ten percent harder. And that was on top of trying to figure out who murdered my predecessor.

"I can tell you like what you see. I know. To die for, right?"

"They're gorgeous."

"They're totally freakin' hot. I mean, look at this. Look at this!" Andi's energy drink habit had turned her into a one-woman merchant machine. This was the kind of energy level not witnessed since I tried out to be a high school cheerleader. The same day I learned enthusiasm doesn't translate into a perfectly executed cartwheel.

"You don't need to worry about anything right now. This is just a review appointment, and Belle already called in an order for Heist. She'll be giving you the details later today or tomorrow or something." She waved her hand to shoo away a fly.

"Is that normal? That Belle would call in an order?"

"She totally knows what's right for Heist. You're sooo lucky to have her with you. Kyle is probably freaking out over at Tradava."

"If Belle did my job already, what did you want to cover in our appointment?" I asked, not sure I liked knowing Belle had taken control of the handbag buyer responsibilities so soon after Emily's murder.

"We're supposed to be going over your growth plans for Vongole at the store, but Belle said she'd be working on them with you later today."

I felt my forehead crease with confusion. I stopped myself from pointing out that I was the buyer, not Belle, though she was the general manager of the store, and having worked there for less time than it takes a pie crust to rise, I wasn't sure I knew enough to challenge the situation.

Andi continued. "She knows the market so well, you know? Belle ran into me in the store, and we got to talking about the inventory. S   he called me about an hour ago and told me a couple of items that you needed. She didn't want to miss out on a delivery while you got up and running in the job. I had what she wanted—don't worry, if I didn't, I'd probably steal it from somebody else's inventory to keep you in stock—we have such a good partnership with Heist!"

She turned to Mallory, who had been standing to my left for the majority of the appointment, meek as a mouse. Not the confrontational employee I'd seen this morning at the store.

"I'll send you the order in an e-mail," Andi said. "You just have to get me a purchase order and I'll ship. Okay?"

I honestly wasn't sure if it was okay, but it was too soon to know. This was not the time to pretend to be more in charge than I might be. Maybe Belle did have the ability to place orders without me. I knew of other retailers who allowed the general managers to supplement their stock with special buys. I wondered if Emily Hart had stood up to Belle and gotten in the way. Would that be cause for murder? And how much business could possibly be lost between Emily's death and my starting in the job? And had Belle been trying to hide something from me when she thwarted my efforts to see the store?

I apologized to Andi for not being ready with the Vongole growth strategy and asked if she would spend the balance of the appointment reviewing the upcoming deliveries. She agreed and walked us through the samples. Apparently everything in the showroom was already on order; Emily—or whoever had been writing the orders—didn't have much of an editorial eye. But considering how luscious these handbags were, I didn't think we'd have a problem selling them, especially at Heist's customary discounted prices. Occasionally I asked Mallory's opinion. With a little encouragement she offered up her thoughts, which were strikingly on target. She had a good knowledge of trends and of business, but I don't think she would have said a word during the entire appointment if I hadn't point blank prompted her.

Andi, on the other hand, seemed put off by my inviting Mallory to participate in the conversation. When the appointment closed in on an hour and a half, we had to leave. I had a meeting scheduled with Belle back at Tradava, and I was eager to ask her about the orders she'd placed.

Andi handed Mallory a shiny blue folder filled with line sheets and prices. "Here's everything you need on the collection. E-mail me the order tomorrow and I'll ship."

Mallory glanced my way. I tipped my head ever so slightly, allowing her to answer for herself. I was curious.

"It's a busy week. I can have it to you by Friday."

"How about Thursday by noon? I can get the orders in the system by the end of the day and we can ship on Friday. You'll have the merchandise by the following Monday."

"I don't know if Thursday is going to happen. I'll see what I can do."

"Okay, but you don't want to let this one slip. There are others out there that will snatch this up!" Andi's smile hid an undercurrent of urgency. Her casual haven't-we-been-friends-forever? attitude most likely took her a long way in selling the collections she represented, and judging from what we'd walked past, Vongole was the shining star in her showroom. The other collections mirrored what I'd seen in junior shops and flea market warehouse venues, the kind that cost pennies on the dollar to produce. I wanted to hear how she'd landed the Vongole account, but that was a conversation for another day.

"Don't forget to calculate the 40 percent discount off cost," Andi said as we were leaving the showroom. I wasn't sure I heard right.

"Forty percent from cost?" I repeated, halfway through tying the square knot on my trench coat belt. "Industry standard is five."

"I know. It's sooo much better than what everybody else offers. But like I said, we have such a great partnership with Heist that we totally want to make sure you have room to sell at those criminal prices and still make high margins. Belle negotiated the whole thing with the owner. It's insane, but good for her. And you," she added as an afterthought. "Bye!"

Mallory and I walked to the car in silence. I wanted to take notes, but there wasn't time. I needed to plan for these things better. I needed a pocket tape recorder or a solo trip to the bathroom or something. I started the drive back to Tradava.

"So, what did you think?" I asked Mallory.

"I don't know that we need everything in the showroom, but I'm sure everything will sell once we slap that discount on there."

"Is that the discount we get from everyone?"

"No. Vongole is by far the highest."

"I thought Vongole was the new It-Bag designer."

"They are. They have lots of press from the celebrities carrying them. It's the kind of word of mouth that Marc Jacobs and Chloe bags used to get."

I'd read enough magazines to know that the perfect storm of new product plus hot celebrity endorsement could launch a marketing frenzy. Witness Jennifer Lopez and the Manolo Blahnik Timberland bootie—the one from the "Jenny on the Block" video. When I was buying shoes for Bentley's, we couldn't keep it in stock, and a pair sold on eBay for eighteen hundred dollars while we were waiting on our reorder. Madness.

"I can't figure out why they would be willing to give us such a big discount when their product is in such demand. It's not the smartest strategy. You would think if they were the hottest thing going someone would have the business sense to pull back on their discount and milk us for whatever they could get. I'm not complaining, because it's good for Heist, but still, doesn't make sense. Right?"

She was right. The Heist deal was out of the ordinary and Mallory recognized it. Any number of assistant buyers would be so blown away by the low prices on Vongole's handbags and how great for anybody with an employee discount. Mallory had a way of seeing through the promotional tactics of Vongole and pointing out the imperfections, even if those imperfections were to our benefit. The discount troubled me and I wanted to find out how Belle had negotiated it, but right now, I wondered what else Mallory had picked up on, regarding Heist, Vongole, or Emily Hart.

"What did you think of the assortment?" I asked.

"They've got the best range of color I've ever seen. That showroom is like a candy store."

"That's what I thought, too."

"The bags look better in there than at Heist."

Again, she was right. Heist's assortment looked good, following the same minimalist merchandising standards as the showroom, but not as good as the samples had looked. Andi was selling the product and Heist was selling the discount.

I stole a quick glance at Mallory. She was looking at a spreadsheet in the three-ring binder on her lap. On more than one count, she'd demonstrated her value to the office. I wondered, could she do my job? Was she in line for it? I felt a pang of guilt, knowing I not only hadn't applied for the job, I wasn't even doing it for the sake of doing it well. My time at Bentley's had trained me how to be a successful buyer, but I'd also learned that the job took more than a skill set. It took passion and dedication and instincts.

I'd already acknowledged once that being a luxury-goods buyer for a large retailer wasn't my passion, but there was something about the ever-changing world of the fashion that was in my blood. I was still trying to find my place in the industry. Did Mallory have more passion for this position than I did?

We returned to the store and went into our separate offices. I had a few spare minutes before meeting with Belle and used them to scribble the questions that remained. Well, right after I buried my nose in my very attractive calla lilies and thought about what I would say to Nick later that night.

I popped my head into Mallory's office and told her I'd be in meetings with Belle for the next couple of hours. That should give her the time to work on the Vongole orders.

"Do you think you can get the orders to Andi by Thursday, or is that going to be a problem?"

"I can 'totally' get the orders to her by Thursday." She used finger quotes around totally and I laughed. "I just don't think the vendors should get into the habit of thinking we're at their beck and call. We're the customer, not them. I think Andi sometimes forgets that."

11

PR CAN SPIN ANYTHING

The executive offices of Heist's management were one floor above mine and down a carpeted hallway. Belle's secretary was busy tapping at the keyboard of her computer. Before I could introduce myself, she said, "Go on back, she's expecting you."

I thanked her and walked down the hall to the large corner office.

Several men and women in professional attire sat around a rectangular glass table by floor-to-ceiling windows. Belle sat at the end, with a notebook by her side, a calendar in front of her, two cell phones and a BlackBerry next to them. This was a woman who didn't want to miss a beat.

"Join us," she said. She waved a hand toward a chair behind two of the men. "This is the store's team of executives." She gave me a blanket introduction to those assembled at the table. "This is Samantha Kidd. She's someone to watch. I asked her to join us so we could get her up to speed on what Heist is all about. It's a crash course on our identity," she joked.

For the next hour I listened to the team that ran the store. A blonde in a too-tight suit and too-tan cleavage brainstormed with Belle about upcoming events and ways to keep people coming back to the store. Another women, in a black polo shirt and jeans, made a few comments on the store's opening expenses. And a man in a wrinkled linen shirt and faded khakis brought up the store's promotional contest, the event that had brought me to them in the first place.

"That was a great contest. It's almost a shame that there wasn't a winner," I said.

They turned my direction. "Well, there was a winner, but we decided not to announce it because of what happened. We're on the fence on how we should proceed with that."

"Who was the winner?"

"Only one group succeeded in getting away with one of the challenges."

"Which one?" I asked.

"The statue."

I sat up straighter. "That was me." I studied their expressions. "I mean, I had help. I didn't do it alone."

Wrinkled Linen Shirt looked at me with open admiration. Tan Cleavage looked skeptical, and Belle looked shocked.

"You were the one who stole the Puccetti statue?" she asked.

I nodded. "It was a great contest, only I don't think Heist got the kind of publicity you wanted."

Cleavage cocked her head to one side. "Are you kidding? That publicity was a wet dream."

Three of the men chuckled. Wrinkled Shirt leaned toward me. "PR can spin anything."

"Well, I guess that gives us our answer about what to do," said Belle, reclaiming everyone's attention before the meeting got out of hand. "The rules clearly stated that no employees of Heist were eligible to win. Since Samantha is now an employee, the contest becomes void. We can make an announcement that there was no qualified winner and move on."

Her secretary crossed the office with a pink phone message in her hand. She set it in front of Belle, who glanced at it then looked at me. She tucked the message into the spine of her desk calendar and slammed the book shut.

"When should we make the announcement?" asked Cleavage.

Belle reopened her calendar and the pink message floated out from the inside. It landed in front of Wrinkled Shirt. He slapped it down on the table and held it out for Belle. *Call Mallory.*

Belle tucked the pink paper back inside her notebook and ended the meeting. "Samantha, can you stay with me for a couple of minutes? I want to talk to you."

The rest of the staff left her office, huddled in their own conversations about visuals, publicity, merchandising, and gossip. When the office was empty, Belle closed the office door, leaving the two of us secluded.

"I want a person like you on my team. Here."

"But I am on your team."

"I don't just mean Heist, I mean here. Running the store. You pulled off that statue prank very well, and it's a shame that you weren't allowed to win, because you deserve it. I'll see what I can do about a prize."

Guess she didn't know about my new clothing allowance.

"People don't stay in jobs for long at Heist. It's a fast-moving company, with lots of opportunity. Talent gets recognized, and I think you've got talent. I want you helping to run the store."

"I'm flattered, but my experience is in buying, and I'd like to see what I can do with the handbag job first," I answered slightly mechanically. It was starting to feel like my career at Heist was a train on tracks that had no brakes, and the rails were getting shifted underneath me. "Thank you for thinking of me." I stood, thinking the meeting was over.

"I'm a determined woman, Samantha, and I'm willing to fight for what I want. I want you by my side. I think you're a risk taker. Now, I have to return a couple of calls, but meet me back here in about ten minutes and I'll give you that tour of the store I promised. And don't worry about the handbag job. I've got plans for that, too."

My hand was on the doorknob, but her last words halted my exit. I turned back.

"Belle, is there something you want to tell me about Kyle Trent?"

12

WE HAVE TO TALK

*B*elle and my eyes remained locked for at least six seconds, assuming my pounding heart was keeping a beat-per-second rhythm. She broke the stare, looked at her calendar, and then sank into her chair.

"I forgot about a late appointment. We'll do the tour another time." She picked the phone off the cradle and without looking at me dialed a number from memory. And with that, I was dismissed.

I wandered through the store. Something was up at Heist, but I didn't know what. Mallory had intimated that Kyle wanted the handbag job. And Mallory had called Belle. Maybe Belle didn't know Tony Simms had offered me the job, and this was her way of opening the position back up for the looker from Tradava. Sure, it felt good to be praised, but there was no way the attention I received had anything to do with my eight-hour performance on the job.

When I finally returned to my office, Mallory was working on the Vongole order. I considered asking her about the message on Belle's desk but didn't. I wasn't sure how to interact with Mallory just yet. I didn't know how to interact with anybody, and until I felt a little loyalty from someone, I was going to stick to myself. I went to my desk and checked my e-mail. One note, marked urgent, was from Tony Simms: *I noticed you haven't had time to shop. I'll have a few things sent by your house tonight.*

Yep, something was definitely up.

I left early, knowing I was being watched. There was no other explanation for Tony knowing whether or not I'd selected a few items to fulfill his agreement with me. And though I'd been the one to demand such a greedy perk, his insistency that I claim my due felt more like bribery than part of my compensation packet.

I needed to sort my thoughts. Logan met me at the door, still lethargic from the sedative. He grazed my ankles and purred. I carried him to the kitchen and set him on the counter. A wave of paranoia washed over me. Was I being watched right now? I carried both my laptop and Logan to my sister's old bedroom. Logan settled into a beanbag chair and I sat at Sasha's eighth grade desk, feeling only slightly less vulnerable.

The usual e-mails greeted me: coupon from the bookstore, discount offer on shoes, promotional code for the latest as-seen-on-TV item. And one from Nick: We have to talk.

Nothing good ever came from the four words he'd used as his subject line. I ignored his e-mail and went downstairs to check the answering machine.

Beep! "Ms. Kidd, this is Detective Loncar. Call me when you get in."

All things considered, the men in my life were a little too demanding. Between Nick's "we have to talk" and the detective's message, I wondered what was behind door number three. I dialed the detective's number anyway, wanting to get this part of my day over with.

"Detective? It's Samantha Kidd."

"Ms. Kidd. You done with work?"

"I left early."

"You didn't get fired already, did you?"

"No, I didn't get fired."

Rustling papers. A clunk. A curse word. "Can you come down here? I have a couple things to go over with you."

"Sure. When?"

"Now," he barked. "Unless you have other plans."

Considering my only other plans included reading Nick's note, my schedule was wide open. "I'll be there in twenty minutes." I grabbed my notebook and a few items that needed the detective's attention and headed on my way.

Detective Loncar was waiting for me by the front desk. "Ms. Kidd. Follow me."

I followed him down the linoleum-tiled hallway. A janitor pushed a dark gray mop over the tiles, barely changing the color. I hopped over the wet spots where dirty water pooled on warped tiles and moved past the questioning room to his office. I sat by the wooden table.

"Nice outfit," he said, eying my pink trench coat.

"Thank you."

"That your undercover spy look?"

I didn't answer, largely because it was. Every self-respecting fashionista knows you wear a trench coat to spy.

I filled him in on everything I could remember. I won't bore you with the details because you were there the first time, but before long he knew what I knew about Andi Holloway, Belle DuChamp, Mallory George, and Kyle Trent. I consulted my composition book a couple of times when he prompted me with questions and even remembered to share that my team had won the Heist contest, though we weren't eligible to claim the prize. I couldn't tell anyone else, and I had to tell someone. I expected him to at least say congratulations. He didn't.

"When you go into work tomorrow morning, move your flowers to your assistant's office."

"Why?" My eyes darted to the left and then the right, and then back to the detective. "How do you know about my flowers?"

"They're from us. They're bugged."

"I thought they were from—" I stopped.

"Who?"

"The card was signed with Xs and Os."

"Nice touch, dontcha think? Figured it would keep the riffraff away if they thought you were taken. You're a pretty girl, Ms. Kidd. We don't want you to have any distractions while you're at Heist."

"That is so wrong."

"It's for your own good. We think we might learn something from your assistant, so we want you to move them in there."

"On one condition." I pulled a Tupperware container out of my handbag and set it on the detective's desk. "Have someone at your lab analyze the butter on this roll."

"Are we back on your sick cat?"

"My friend was poisoned, and my cat was poisoned, and this is my only link between those two things."

"Are you trying to negotiate with the police?"

"I'm having second thoughts about helping you."

"Too late."

I put my index finger on the top of the Tupperware lid and pushed it across Loncar's desk calendar. "Find out about the butter and I'll play ball."

"Ms. Kidd, I really wish you'd start talking like a normal person."

"Is it a deal?"

"Yes, it's a deal."

"Are we done here?"

"Yes, we're done. Unless you got something else?"

I stood to leave. "Yes, one more thing. Mallory will think it's strange that I'm giving away my flowers, especially if they're from the man in my life. I'll expect another arrangement tomorrow."

IT'S A GOOD thing I had the cops sending me flowers because by the looks of Nick's subject line, the prospects of our ever being a couple were slim to none. I stared at my inbox for seven and a half minutes before I opened We have to talk.

Samantha, There's a problem at the factory and it won't be fixed for a couple more weeks. I'll call you tonight, and every night, at nine o'clock your time, to make sure you're okay. Be on the other end of the phone, or else. -N.

It wasn't the response I'd expected.

By not mentioning my e-mail, I had no context for his note. Was he mad? Concerned? Interested? Or did he simply not care?

I picked up my phone and dialed the first half of his number in Italy before I hung up. What would I say? That I wanted to know what he thought about my involvement in a homicide? I already knew what he'd say about that. No, I wasn't going to sit around worrying about what Nick thought of my life. Despite our attraction, he was there, and I was here. Fine, I thought. I can take care of myself. I turned off the computer and relaxed into the chair.

Until I heard the front door slam downstairs.

13

❧

CLOTHING ALLOWANCE

*S*am? Sam! Are you here?" Eddie called from downstairs.

Aside from the near heart-attack inducing surprise of having someone wander unexpectedly into my house, Eddie's arrival wouldn't have bothered me if I didn't have something to hide. I left the room, closing the door behind me.

"I'll be right there," I called before descending the stairs.

Eddie stood in my living room. His cargo pants carried three different colors of paint, two of which (lime green and cobalt blue) were repeated across the ironic quote on his T-shirt, one of which was smudged by his hairline (orange). A large cardboard wardrobe box with black arrows on the side indicating which end was up stood between the coffee table and the black and white chair closest to the door.

"What's that?"

"Dunno. It was sitting on your front porch. Has your name on it. Says it's from Heist."

Apparently Tony Simms had been serious.

"Aren't you going to open it?"

"No, I'll wait till later."

"You're not curious," he said.

"Not really?"

"It wasn't a question."

"Mine was."

Eddie crossed the room and disappeared into the kitchen. He returned with the kind of knife that most people kept for carving turkeys. "I want to see what you got."

"I'm sure it's nothing. Just stuff I need for the job."

"I've worked in retail for fifteen years and have never, ever heard of or seen a box this size show up on someone's doorstep on their first day on the job. And you sit here and say you're not curious." He set the knife on top of the box. "What's going on with you?"

"Nothing. I'm just trying to focus on my new job." That wasn't so far from the truth.

We both heard the muffled meow at the same time, followed by scratching. "Logan! He's probably trapped in the bedroom."

"I'll let him out. You mind if I check my email?" He jogged up the stairs without waiting for my answer. Then it hit me that Nick's e-mail might still be open. I scaled the steps two at a time, but was still too late. Eddie sat in my chair, staring at the screen. I pounced on the mouse and closed the browser.

"Sorry, that was an e-mail from Nick. Kind of personal."

"Speaking of Nick, we never got around to him the other night. What does he have to say about the job? Or the cops?"

"Nick's proud of me."

"Interesting. What did he say about the homicide?"

"Nothing."

"I'm pretty sure Nick would say something you being this close to a homicide. What gives?"

"Nothing gives. You know Nick—he'd worry."

"So you aren't confiding in him either?" His gaze hadn't faltered since I entered the room.

"It's not like he could do anything from Italy."

"Dude, if something's going on, you should confide in your friends. As in me."

"I don't know what you're talking about," I said.

He looked at my trench coat for a second, down to my shoes, and then back up to my face. I was starting to wish I wasn't dressed in cartoon spy fashion.

"I may have contacted Detective Loncar after the night of the murder."

"You're confiding in Loncar, now?" He pushed his grown-out Mohawk back, away from his forehead. When he let go it flopped to the side of his head. "The detective is a one-way street. He's going to take your information and use it to solve the homicide, but he's not going to keep you in the loop. Don't expect him to. That's not his job."

"Yeah? Well, my job is handbag buyer. For Tradava's competition, and since you work for Tradava, I'm not going to tell you what I do at Heist. It would be a conflict of interest. Even though Nick's in Italy, I can talk to him."

"Nick's two thousand miles away, so he's safe."

He sat in my chair, twisted at the waist, watching me with his intensely green eyes.

I fidgeted with the belt knotted on my trench coat, and then shoved my hands into my pockets. Eddie stood up.

"I thought you wanted to check your e-mail?"

"Nah, I can do it from my place."

I followed him down the stairs to the living room. I had met Eddie in high school but didn't really get to know him until six months ago after I'd moved back to Ribbon. He'd seen me through a murder investigation and had been the only new friend to stand by my side as my life fell apart. I wanted to tell him what was going on. I wanted to tell him we'd won the contest but weren't eligible for the prize. I wanted to tell him about Tony Simms and Belle DuChamp and Detective Loncar and Andi Holloway and Kyle Trent.

"By the way, Cat's doing much better," he said. "I thought you'd want to know. She's going back to her store tomorrow."

"Dante stopped by Heist today and told me." I thought back over what Dante had said. My face grew hot.

"She'd probably like to see you if you can manage a visit."

"Dante's staying with her, right? I'd rather avoid him."

"Why? Is there something he knows that you're trying to hide?"

We stood in my living room, Logan swirling around Eddie's purple Vans, occasionally licking the paint smears on his pants. He slinked over to the wardrobe box and ran his head against one of the corners. Then he eyed up the distance to the top of it, leaned back, and easily cleared the four feet to the top. Eddie reached over and scratched Logan's ears.

"I'll get out of here so you can open your giant package. You might be trying hard to not act like yourself, but curiosity is killing your cat."

Logan flopped onto his side and pawed at the brown packing tape that sealed the box.

"Eddie, are you busy for lunch tomorrow?"

"Why?"

"I thought I might stop in."

"Come to my office around noon."

"Deal. I'm buying."

For the first time since he'd entered my house, he laughed. "I know."

Eddie was right; I was bursting to open the giant package from Heist. I shooed Logan from the top of the giant box and sliced through the tape.

Inside, hanging from a metal rod, were four plastic garment bags. I pulled each one out and set them on my sofa. Then I pulled the blinds and locked the front door.

Each item carried the Heist price tag. The first bag contained a black skirt suit not unlike the one Tan Cleavage had worn earlier that day. The second held a black zip front dress like Andi Holloway's. The third contained a boxy menswear-styled black vest and matching trousers. Tony Simms didn't have an active imagination. He also didn't have any idea of how I wanted to dress. He was sucking the fun out of the clothing allowance one piece of dismal black apparel at a time. At least he got the sizes right.

The phone rang after I'd zipped up the pants and buttoned the vest over my bra. I flopped on to the sofa and answered.

"Are you alone?" Nick asked.

"Yes."

"What are you wearing?"

This conversation was starting off better than I'd expected. "A pair of black pants and a vest."

"Good. That means you're not dressed up like a spy in a trench coat. That means you're acting normal, at least for now." His voice softened. "Now tell me about this thing at Heist."

Truth time. I filled him on everything that had happened since my e-mail last night: the contest, the murder, the visit from Tony Simms, and the partnership with Detective Loncar. I went into detail about my first day, how busy it was and how little I'd done that was handbag related. Actually, that wasn't true. Most of what I'd done had been handbag related, and it had been related to Emily Hart's murder too. Which meant if I kept doing what I was doing, I might find a motive.

"I don't think I like this, and I definitely don't like that I'm not there," he said when I finished.

"What happened at the factory? Why won't you be coming back as soon as you want?"

"The factory somehow ran out of the leathers I bought for my collection. They can't tell me what went wrong; I placed the orders six months ago and they confirmed them, but now they're short. I'm going to have to use these designs in another fabric, find another factory, or scrap the whole thing and start over. None of the options are very appealing."

"So how long does that mean you're going to be there?"

"Easily another month. Maybe more."

I pouted and shoved my now-cold feet under the white afghan. A horn beeped out front, and I moved to the window to see who it was.

Dante was walking up my driveway, carrying a large box under one arm.

"Nick, I have to go."

"Are you okay?"

"Yes. Cat's brother just showed up."

"Does he know anything?"

"No, but like everyone else around here, he suspects something."

"Be careful. And call me tomorrow morning before you leave for work. Okay?"

"Okay."

I tossed the phone on the sofa after saying good-bye. It wasn't until after I opened the door that I remembered the vest I was wearing over my black lace bra. One of the bra straps fell from my shoulder and dangled by my upper arm.

"First a schoolgirl, now Madonna. You don't make it easy, Samantha," he said.

I hooked my thumb into my bra strap, pulled it back up, and crossed my arms over my chest to hide the plunging neckline. "What are you doing here?"

"My sister sent me over with this." He handed me the box. "She said you might need it for your new job. Something about bringing you back into this decade? I don't remember the exact quote."

"She was probably delirious at the time." I took the box and turned. "Do you want to come inside?"

"Yes, but I'm not going to."

"Why's that?"

"Because you have a man in your life who is out of town, and I have a sick sister back at the house, and I think it's better that we focus on those two things instead of how cute you look in your black lace bra."

I pulled the afghan off the sofa and wrapped it around my shoulders like a superhero cape.

"Good night, Samantha." He leaned in and kissed me on the cheek. A hint of cinnamon lingered in the air. I turned my head slightly. He didn't move away. I felt the bristle of his unshaven cheek dust my face.

I took a step backward and forced a smile. "Good night, Dante."

He closed the space between us. My back was against the sofa. He tipped my chin up and looked me straight in the eyes."I have to go out of town for a few days, but whatever you're trying to hide, I'll find out when I get back."

The afghan fell from my shoulders. He looked over my body, turned around, and left.

14

TREADING DANGEROUS WATERS

I took a long shower after Dante left, washing and conditioning my hair three times and shaving my left leg twice. To say I was distracted was an understatement. For someone who liked to plan and anticipate everything, I never saw Dante coming.

I'd certainly dated during the nine years I lived in New York. My Saturday-night suitors had come in the form of Wall Street bankers, pastry chefs, and at least three deli counter employees who satisfied my need for cured lunch meats and provolone cheese. The problem with all of those dates was simple.

Nick Taylor.

From the minute I'd met Nick on a dirty, slushy street in New York City, him in a Rocky T-shirt and me in yoga clothes, ponytails, and a knockoff Vuitton bucket hat, I'd felt an electricity I hadn't otherwise known. Where other men had either fawned on me too soon or made other intentions clear, Nick kept me on my toes. Every time I thought I knew where I stood with him, he pulled the rug out from under my sample-sized feet.

It wasn't until I gave up my job, moved to Ribbon, and left my career and connections behind that I learned he felt the attraction too. But discovering Nick's interests exposed his warmhearted, protective nature. He was an old-fashioned guy, and part of me liked that, but another part of me needed to prove I could take care of myself. Only now, with him halfway around the world, it seemed I could use a guardian angel in a Rocky T-shirt. And even though I knew that, and I recognized I was treading dangerous waters, I liked the way it felt. I liked taking chances, and I didn't know if Nick could deal with that side of me.

Dante, on the other hand, seemed to accept that side of me. From what I'd seen so far, he encouraged it.

I changed into pajamas and attended to Cat's gift. A heavy ivory envelope was tucked under the satin ribbon that held the lid on. I pulled a piece of monogrammed stationary from the envelope.

It's from last season, and that's as vintage as I'll let you go.—Cat

The box held a mint-blue knit dress and coordinating tweed topper with an oversized collar. Deeper in the box was a pair of black suede boots with three inch heels. Catnip, her store, was a designer outlet, and often last year's looks were this year's new arrivals. I'd loved this outfit from the first time I saw it in the pages of Vogue, but without a job the price had been too steep. It brought tears to my eyes to think Cat was thinking of me while I was shutting her out of my world. I punched her number into the phone to say thanks and arrange a time to visit.

"I love it. I'm going to wear it tomorrow," I said when she answered.

"Is that a promise?"

"Yes. Temporarily, thanks to you, I'll be the height of style, give or take six months. How are you feeling?"

"Better. I'm going back to the store tomorrow."

"How about dinner after?" I asked.

"Sure. Come over to the house. I can't seem to shake Dante, but you don't mind if he joins us, right? He makes a mean meatloaf."

"Sure, that's okay. But I might have to leave early," I said, thinking about my nine o'clock phone call.

"Nick can call your cell phone," she said, laughing.

"Okay, tomorrow night. I'll be there around seven thirty."

That phone call was going to prove a problem if Dante was still suspicious of my activities, but there wasn't much I could do about it now. I carried my new outfit (the one I liked, not the boring black ones from Heist) to my bedroom and curled up in bed.

When you're trying to make a long-distance relationship work, you tend to fall asleep with your cell phone. You never know when late-night texts will come through, and you want to catch every last one of them. That's why I woke at four thirty, something buzzing next to my thigh.

I fished the glowing blue screen out from under the covers and rubbed my eyes until I could see clearly. The text message was from Nick. *What is new work e-mail?*

I texted back.

Seconds later a second text appeared. *Have idea.*

***

The next morning there were two arrangements of flowers on my desk: the bronze callas from yesterday and a vase of flaming orangey-red Hawaiian stems. This time the card was inside an envelope. *Thank you for last night.—DL.* The Xs and Os were gone but it was charming how the detective had signed the card. Since he'd kept up his part of the bargain, I kept up mine and carried yesterday's arrangement to Mallory's office.

"I'm sharing the wealth," I offered, and set the square vase on the corner of her desk. "How's your workload look?"

"Okay. I came in early and finished off the Monday recaps. They're in your inbox. I'm going to work on the Vongole order next."

I glanced at the clock. "What time did you get here?"

"Don't worry. I always get in early. I like having quiet time to get stuff done. Before the phone starts ringing."

I was going to have to remember that Mallory had free reign of my office when I wasn't around. If there was snooping to be done, and I mean snooping that wasn't done by me, I'd have to cover my tracks.

I shrugged out of the tweed jacket, hung it on the back of my chair, and booted up my PC. My email was full of unread messages. Amongst the company announcements was one note from Nick.

Dear Samantha, You may remember working with my shoe collection while you were a buyer for Bentley's NY. With my recent plans to expand the Nick Taylor collection, I am adding a limited edition collection of handbags to the fall line. Attached are the line sheets of the items. You always were a great partner in the development of my shoe collection; I am eager to hear your feedback. Regards, NT.

Well, what do you know. Nick was going undercover too.

I wrote a brief reply thanking him for thinking of me first and saying I would happily consider his collection of handbags. I finished with a few details about our current assortment, vaguely disguised information for him to have while running amok in Milan handbag factories.

"Mallory?" I called out. "Do you know what factory Vongole uses?

"They use two. Luta and Lussuria."

"Why two?"

"Their basics are done at Luta, and their fashion is at Lussuria."

"Got it." I pecked at the keyboard, suggested Nick visit these two factories, and clicked send.

For the next couple of hours I looked over files in Emily Hart's—I mean my—office. Every time I'd been promoted in my past life—the successful life as a buyer for Bentley's, not the recent past that had stalled out at Tradava—I'd taken the first day to acclimate myself with my predecessor's information to get a sense of the job. To Mallory, or anyone else who might come along, what I was doing looked perfectly natural. And it's a good thing, too, because Tan Cleavage from the executive meeting showed up unexpectedly in my office.

I was highlighting numbers on one of Mallory's spreadsheets and comparing the information to a file of sell-through expectations I'd found on the computer. I wasn't so much hoping to find a clue but to get a sense of the business. It felt natural having a job again, especially one I knew I could do. Homicide notwithstanding.

Tan Cleavage entered the office, acknowledged me with little more than a nod, and disappeared into Mallory's office. I heard her and Mallory talk in low voices.

When Cleavage left, it was with Mallory behind her. She paused in the doorway. "Is it okay with you if I take my lunch now?"

"Sure, fine." I calculated the time on the clock and realized it was my turn to snoop. "I have a lunch date myself. I'll probably be gone when you get back. Are you fine on your own this afternoon?"

Mallory's eyes darted to the flowers, and Cleavage snickered in the hallway. "Of course."

I called Eddie and left him a message that I was running late and would be there by one. Then I moved into Mallory's office and jotted down her computer's IP address. I returned to my desk and used a couple of tricks to find her on Heist's network and connect to her drive. Now I could cruise her files without having to ask.

Under the guise of leaving behind additional information for her, I created a fake spreadsheet and printed it out, using Post-Its to instruct her on what I wanted. It was a dummy project, but it gave me another excuse to go through her desk.

Sitting on the corner was a red folder, labeled Orders to be Approved. I opened it and flipped through the papers. There were five outstanding orders to Vongole, totaling more than a million dollars at cost. Odder still was the note scribbled across the sheet of paper: *Mallory, our Vongole inventory is too high. Don't write any more orders until we sell through at least 30% of our current stock.*

The note was signed EH.

15

SMART AND TALENTED TOO

*E*mily Hart had put the kibosh on future orders of Heist's hottest handbag line and I wanted to know why. No, that's not true. I could respect why she'd halted orders. What I wanted to know was why Belle DuChamp was writing and approving orders if the store really was in an overstocked position. Did this have something to do with Emily's murder?

A million dollars' worth of orders would translate into a hefty little paycheck for Andi Holloway, and a surplus of inventory would provide Belle DuChamp with a lucrative opportunity for sales above and beyond her forecasted goals. I still couldn't see how Kyle Trent figured into this whole thing, but I was about to. Lunch with Eddie wasn't the only thing on the agenda at Tradava.

I found Eddie at his desk like he said, but the half-empty carton of Chinese takeout that sat on the corner told me he hadn't waited.

"I have to go to the fabric store today," he said. "Last-minutes plans. I could've had lunch with you if you'd been on time, but not now."

"What's the project?"

"What?"

"What's this last minute project?"

"I can't tell you."

"Why not?"

"Because, like you said, you're the competition. You shouldn't even be in my office right now."

"Are you kidding me?"

"Dude, you can't just waltz in here and expect me to tell you Tradava's business plans now that you work for Heist."

"I didn't ask you to tell me business plans, and you know what? We never talked about business plans before. Why would we start now?"

"I don't know. Maybe that's how you work?"

"Are you suggesting I don't have any ethics?"

He put his hands up in front of him in a defensive manner. "I don't know. When you first started at Tradava, you were knee-deep in some serious shit and you trusted me. But ever since you got this job at Heist, you're being private. Maybe you were using me when you were here at Tradava. I don't know. But a lot of people are concerned that you're on Belle's team now. She signed a non-disclosure agreement stating she wasn't going to recruit from Tradava, and then you showed up there."

"You've got to be kidding. Tradava hasn't exactly made it known they want me on the payroll. You're right, I trusted you, so you know I moved to Ribbon to work *here*. The reason I don't work here has to do with the store, not with me."

"Apparently that's the reason they're not able to legally go after her."

"Because they don't want me?"

"Not exactly. They just can't clearly qualify why you no longer work here and whether it was your decision or theirs."

It was my turn to throw my hands up in disgust. "And this is the company you want to be loyal to? You should hear them talk over at Heist. They're so passionate about what they're doing. Their executive meetings are like a think tank. They brainstorm and listen to suggestions and try new ideas. They want to stay on the cutting edge. Tradava *should* be worried about them, but not because of me."

I stood up and tugged the hem of the knit dress Cat had given me. "I thought we were friends, Eddie. But lately it sounds like my friends don't want me to succeed." I tucked my handbag under the crook of my arm and turned to leave.

He didn't say a word until I got to the doorway. "Nice outfit. Where'd it come from?"

Bastard.

Eddie was right about one thing. It would have been highly unethical for me to masquerade around Tradava as a random stranger and find my way to Kyle Trent's office. That's why, when I found him sitting by the coffee bar on the first floor, I invited myself to join him.

Kyle's male model looks weren't even slightly diminished by the lack of tuxedo or event lighting. If anything, he looked even more attractive today. He wore a crisp, textured ivory shirt, paisley tie, and grey suit. The lapels on the jacket were narrow and notched, a trend that was among the latest sartorial details to differentiate men's suits from season to season.

"Is this seat taken?" I asked.

He looked up from the catalog he was reading. I could tell he recognized me but wasn't sure why. I left my hand on the back of the tall barstool and pasted an I'm-not-threatening expression on my face. It took about eight seconds for recognition to hit. When it did, he closed the catalog and sat back on his stool. With an ever-so-slight shrug he indicated it was okay. Or possibly the shrug told me to go to hell. Sometimes shrugs are hard to read.

I gingerly perched atop the blue leather swivel stool and set my handbag on the table.

Kyle stood. "Wait here," he said.

I was not giving him this easy a getaway. I spun to the side and slid myself off the stool.

He stopped me. "You want a cup of coffee? My treat. And why don't we move to one of those tables over there?" He glanced at one surrounded by a pair of modern wooden chairs. The padded stool was certain to be more comfortable, but when I added in the privacy factor, the table and chairs won.

"Sure. Thanks." I moved to the table and watched Kyle. I'd place even money he had been fast-tracked early in his career and now held an enviable job that he'd keep for the next decade if he was smart. A few sales associates stood in line behind him, openly giggling when he smiled their direction. I bet girlish giggles followed Kyle Trent a lot. He was no stranger to attention and probably didn't spend a lot of nights sleeping alone.

He set two cups of black coffee on the table and pushed one in my direction. "Not sure how you liked it."

"This is fine," I answered.

"You're the new handbag buyer at Heist, aren't you? Samantha Kidd?"

"I am," I answered, mildly surprised he knew that much.

"What brings you to Tradava today? Are you shopping the competition?"

"I was supposed to meet a friend for lunch." I considered, not for the first time, Kyle's possible reasons for being in the handbag department at Heist the night Emily died. "Much like you were probably meeting a friend at Heist."

"I don't want to be reminded of that night, if you don't mind." The brown cardboard ring that kept his coffee from burning his hands sat at the base of his cup on the table. He spun his cup in circles. He was concentrating too hard on such a mundane task.

"You get noticed a lot, probably. You're an attractive man."

"So I've been told." He picked up his coffee and drank. I was thrown by his emotionless acknowledgement of a fact most people would take as a compliment. "I'm smart and talented too, in case you're interested."

"Interested in what?"

"In finding out what's below the surface."

I felt like a ball of yarn being swatted about by a frisky cat. I had no desire to be Kyle Trent's ball of yarn. "I'm not interested," I said, perhaps too quickly. "Besides, you could probably get any woman you want."

"Not any woman."

"Belle DuChamp? Is she the woman you want?"

"Belle's different from the others."

"Why? Because she's married?"

"Because she saw the smart and talented part."

"Did Belle get fired because she was caught—" I tried to think of an appropriate word and gave up and settled on Eddie's—"canoodling with you in the boardroom?"

"Is that rumor still alive and well?" He laughed and for the first time in our conversation, it felt like he'd let himself go. "You should check your sources. Besides, some people think Belle is still on the Tradava payroll."

"What do you mean?"

"I've heard things about you too, Samantha. You're smart. Tenacious. You'll figure it out." He slapped his palms down on the arms of the chair, elbows pointing out. He hoisted his lean body out of the chair like a swimmer heaving himself out of a pool. "Pleasure talking to you. Good luck at Heist. You've got some big shoes to fill." He picked his cup off the table and walked away, leaving me staring at the back of his very trim double-vented suit.

As long as I was at Tradava, I figured I actually would shop the competition. No reason not to, especially after two different people had made it relatively clear they didn't want to be sitting around talking to me.

I sweet-talked the creamer away from a nice old couple sitting one table away and diluted the coffee to a drinkable shade of camel. After I finished, I went to the handbag department.

There was noticeably less foot traffic here than at Heist, partially because of the hype of a new store coming to town, I'm sure, but still, it had to be hurting Tradava's business. That was how it went with new stores—big opening, big hoopla, and then how to keep up that level of interest and shift the customer loyalties from the stores they always shopped at to the new one, long term.

It was a delicate time for both competitors. Tradava had to put their best face forward: charming customer service and a familiar setting had to trump deep discounts. The history of Tradava, a family owned fixture in Ribbon, needed to cling to its loyal customer base to counter the novelty of Heist. Tradava would suffer in the short term, and no one knew what would happen in a couple of months, let alone a year.

I picked up a black and white fur handbag and turned it over in my hands. It was connected to the fixture with a thin wire that disappeared into a small locking system, much less obtrusive than the in-your-face theft deterrents at Heist. But somehow Heist owned their concept so completely that Tradava's hint at protecting their profits against shoplifters seemed more of an insult. I was able to open the clasp and pull the tissue out, inspecting the powder-blue suede lining and interior pockets trimmed in black patent leather to match the handle. It was such a pretty color combination, and the lining would be tarnished shortly after the wearer loaded in the assorted items she needed to get through the day. My own handbag carried a three-inch ballpoint pen mark, a smudge of cranberry lip liner, and a grungy corner from where a small bag of pretzels had emptied.

I snapped the bag closed and placed it in the crook of my arm so I could admire my reflection in the full-length mirror. It was lovely. An associate headed my way with a smile on his face, and I sensed I was in for a compliment and a sales pitch. I put the bag on the table and stuffed the tissue back inside. That's when I noticed the small gold metal vendor tag affixed to the interior cell-phone pocket. VONGOLE. My split-second moment of awareness gave the closest sales associate the time needed to reach my side.

"She's a beauty, isn't she?" he asked.

"She sure is," I replied.

He held the bag in the light. "One of the best bags they've done recently. We used to carry a lot of Vongole's bags, but lately not too many."

"Is that because of Heist?"

"No, they have good prices but don't carry the same quality of merchandise as us."

"They carry Vongole, though," I said.

"Yes, but Vongole's collection is big, and our buyer keeps our assortment streamlined. We don't need to carry every bag they make, just the good ones. Like this." He smiled, letting the black and white fur bag rock side to side from his index finger not unlike a hypnotist dangling a watch. "What do you think?"

"I think I'm going to have to start packing my lunch so I can treat myself soon." I smiled graciously and checked my watch. "I'm already running late. Thank you." I turned to leave before he had the chance to hit me up with a new charge application, but my path was blocked. Kyle stood in front of me, fidgeting with the knot in his tie.

"Samantha, a word of caution. I'd watch my step around Heist if I were you."

It sounded like a threat and I wanted to laugh, but didn't. "I don't think I have to point out that I know you were at Heist the night Emily was murdered."

"Of course I was with her the night she was murdered. It was a big night for her. Why wouldn't I be there?"

Something about Kyle's attitude, coupled with the knowledge of Emily's death and the memory of how he'd spoken about her did not compute. As I stood there, trying to make sense of the three incongruent pieces of information, Eddie stepped out from behind a fixture. He put his hand on my elbow and squeezed. "Dude, Kyle was at the gala as Emily's date. They were engaged."

16

SUGAR CUBE

*E*ngaged?" I said. I shifted my attention from Eddie's expression to Kyle's and felt the weight of his sorrow. He nodded. "I'm so sorry," I said. "Can we talk, like talk-talk? Away from the store?"

Kyle nodded. We left Tradava together. I was fairly sure Eddie wanted an invite, but if I was going to stay true to my word, work with the cops and not bring anyone else into this mess, I was going to have to shut Eddie out.

I had absolutely no idea what was on my schedule for the balance of the day at Heist, but I doubted it would be more important than talking to Kyle. We walked in silence to a diner in the corner of a parking lot at Tradava.

It wasn't until we were seated at a booth in the back, empty seats all around us, that I spoke. "Is that true? You and Emily were engaged?"

"Yes. I proposed two months ago. I wanted her to work at Tradava. She'd been with Heist, the store in center city Philadelphia, for a long time. I thought it would be a good step for her. She saw things differently. She wanted me to leave Tradava and work for Heist."

"How did you meet?"

"Market week, years ago. We were both handbag buyers. No matter how hard the vendors tried to keep us on opposite schedules, it was inevitable. Every couple of months we'd run into each other in New York or Milan. Last year we got stuck at the airport together. Our flight was cancelled and we sat up all night and talked. By the next morning I was calling her my girlfriend."

"Your stores didn't mind the conflict of interest?"

"We tried to keep our relationship a secret at first. When Tradava found out, they thought it was unethical. Belle DuChamp had always been a mentor of mine, but that was a turning point for us."

"She was angry?"

"She actually warned me my job was on the line if I didn't reconsider how I spent my spare time. That's one of the reasons Emily and I were keeping the engagement a secret. We knew it would complicate our work situations."

"But what about that rumor?"

"I never said I was a saint. I had a life before Emily, but that's all I'm saying. Anything I say now impacts how people will remember her, and that's not fair. I loved her. I was ready to spend the rest of my life with her." His eyes turned bloodshot, but no tears appeared.

The waitress approached our table and asked for our order. Kyle suddenly stood. "The lady is going to dine alone. It's on me." He peeled a twenty out of his wallet and tossed it on the table.

"Kyle—wait," I said.

He stood by the table and looked down at me.

"Is there a way I can get in touch with you? If . . . " My voice trailed off.

Kyle reached inside his suit jacket pocket and pulled out a small leather business-card case. He slid an ivory card out and tossed it on top of the twenty. "My cell's below my work number," he said.

I slid the card across the table and tucked it into my wallet next to my library card.

"Did you want to order something, ma'am?" the waitress asked.

"Yes," I said. I leaned sideways and looked out the door, making sure Kyle had left. "I'll have a BLT to go." I dropped my voice so the people in the next booth couldn't hear me. "Hold the bread, lettuce, mayo, and tomato."

IT WAS FIVE o'clock when I pulled back into the Heist parking lot. The only thing calming my nerves from being gone four hours was the fat from five pieces of bacon and the knowledge that my job offer from Tony Simms came with a fair amount of job security. I speed-walked through the store to my office but stopped short when faced with the assortment of flowers on my desk.

An orange bromeliad sat next to a square vase lined in bamboo shoots—similar to yesterday's floral arrangement. The card, clipped to the vase, said REPLACEMENT FLOWERS. There was no doubt in my mind. This arrangement had come from the cops.

Two arrangements of flowers was overkill, which meant the earlier arrangement wasn't from Detective Loncar. I texted Nick's phone: *Thx 4 flowers.*

A couple of seconds later I received a response: *???*

Uh-oh.

Mallory came into my office as I was sticking my phone back into my handbag. Her bag was over her shoulder. "He must be quite a guy."

I cocked my head, shaking it in a you-don't-know-the-half-of-it manner. My cell phone beeped with a text message. I ignored it. "Sorry I was gone so long. Did I miss anything here?"

"You didn't miss anything, and nobody missed you. And considering you took a four-hour lunch on your second day, I'd say you were pretty lucky."

"Let's get something straight. It's not my job to report to you."

She glared at me in a manner not unlike the kid from *The Omen*. I stood my ground even though my left boot pinched my toes and I really, really, *really* wanted to sit. My cell phone buzzed again before I had a chance to say anything else.

"I was here early this morning, and I'm going home now. You'd better check your phone. Sounds like someone's looking for you," she said.

She left without looking back once. I pulled the cell phone out and keyed up the text message: *turn your flowers around before you leave*. Honestly, Detective Loncar was turning into a high-maintenance fake boyfriend. I was ready to chuck the cell phone and cut all ties with him when I noticed who had sent the message.

Dante.

Mallory had left for the day, and I had to use the facilities. I palmed my cell phone and went to the ladies' room. Once inside, after checking under each of the stalls, I called the number.

"You got my text," he answered in lieu of hello.

"What are you doing sending me flowers?"

"What are you doing working for Heist?"

"We already covered this. They offered me a job, and I took it."

"Samantha, I know something's up with you. Just like I wrote on the card, I'm here if you need me."

"You're DL'?"

"Those are my initials. How many other DLs do you know?"

"Just one—I mean, next time you should be more clear. I mean, there shouldn't be a next time. You shouldn't be sending me flowers."

"This isn't about the flowers."

"That's what I'm afraid of."

"There's a camera inside the arrangement."

"Dante, I might not have been very easy to read the other night, but—what?"

"There's a camera inside the flower arrangement. A sugar cube."

"Which is it? A camera or a sugar cube?"

"The camera *is* the sugar cube. That's what it's called, because that's roughly the size of it."

I already knew I was going to regret the next question. "Why are you sending me flowers with a camera inside?"

"Because you're up to something and nobody knows what, but considering a woman was murdered, I think you're in danger. And you're pushing your friends away, which is not the smartest thing to do."

"Maybe there's a reason for my acting the way I'm acting," I said, wondering if I should just open up and confide in him. He didn't know me that well. Maybe he'd see my side instead of siding with Cat and Eddie.

"Sure. Maybe you're trying to figure out Emily Hart's murder?"

I stopped wondering. "What is so wrong about me trying to have my own life?"

"If that's all you were doing, sweetheart, there'd be nothing wrong with it. Only I'm having a hard time believing it."

"Well, believe it."

I would have liked to sit down for a second, but I was in the ladies room and the only place to sit was, well, not where I wanted to be sitting while having a conversation with Dante. I thought about making crackly noises and pretending we had a bad connection.

"Can we call a truce on this? I'm coming to Cat's house tonight and I don't want us getting into a thing around her. I think she's totally fine with me having a new job and wouldn't appreciate your accusations that I'm hiding something."

"Are you kidding me? Who do you think told me to send you the sugar cube?"

17

EZ MART

Cat and I may have started out on rocky terrain owing to the murder investigation six months ago, but from what I'd seen since, she was a nice, normal woman. This piece of information put her in an entirely different light. Oh, sure, I was still going by the house to check on her after work, but I was going home and changing out of the fabulous mint-blue and tweed ensemble she'd given me and into something polyester to that would offend her fashion sensibilities first.

Logan sat in the middle of the laundry basket watching me change. He was nestled on top of a pink four-hundred-thread-count sheet. He was rapidly returning to his normal self. The cat had good taste. I scooped him up, planted a kiss between his ears, and set him back down. He turned around in a circle until he ended up in pretty much the same position he'd started in.

I scribbled the notes I could remember from the day and wedged them into my handbag. Letting my hair air-dry shaved five minutes from my getting-ready routine, and the tan—even if it was fake—opened up the door to a whole palette of colors that washed out my normally fair skin.

It was a warm night. I took the top off my convertible and let the wind have its way with my curly hair. When I pulled into Cat's driveway, I was more relaxed than I'd been in about a week. Even having Dante meet me at the door only ratcheted up my pulse the amount any totally hot and slightly dangerous biker would. Good thing I was holding a chilled bottle of champagne to cool me down.

He stepped back and scanned my orange double-knit polyester scooter dress from the mod era. "I was hoping for the knit dress you had on earlier. I only got a glimpse of it through the sugar cube, but it seemed to hit you in all the right places," he said.

"I didn't want anything to happen to it."

"Shame."

The door opened behind me, and Eddie walked in carrying a pizza box. "It's about time you got here. Follow me."

We traipsed, parade-like, through the house to the den where Cat sat on the sofa, tucked in beneath an ivory chenille blanket.

"Aren't you hot?" I asked after saying hello and hugging her.

"It's chilly in here."

"It's so not chilly! It's totally warm!" I said, holding the champagne against my forehead.

"You're only hot because you're wearing a plastic dress," Eddie said.

"It's not plastic, it's polyester."

He unscrewed the cap on his bottle of water and dumped what remained on me. The water beaded up and ran down the front of my dress. Cat dabbed at the carpet with a couple of paper towels. "That is not how good clothes react to water, Sam."

"Can't a girl just come for a friendly visit without getting a fashion criticism?"

"You're the fashion person, not me," Eddie said. "At least you were." He looked at my dress and wrinkled his nose. "I'm not sure who you are anymore." He set the pizza on the card table in the middle of the room and walked out.

"I wish everybody would stop acting like me working for Heist is such a big deal," I said half to myself, half to Cat.

"I know it's not a big deal," she said.

"You don't agree with him?"

"Sam, you were a buyer in New York, right? And you've been looking for a job. And you got one that you're obviously qualified for."

"Yes. That's right." I processed her words. "That's right!"

"The only person acting like it's a big deal is you."

"Am not!"

"Are too." She leaned back against the sofa cushions and tucked the chenille blanket around her legs. "If you thought you had a chance of working for Heist, you wouldn't have entered that competition. You would have said something first."

"You and Dante have compared notes."

"Either Heist rejected your application and you wanted to get back at them by winning or you never even applied and they came to you because of your job qualifications. None of that is out of the ordinary. The only weird thing is that you kept it a secret. That's why Eddie's angry. His feelings are hurt."

"His feelings?" I asked. The idea that his reaction to my job at Heist came from something other than suspicion had never occurred to me. I looked at the doorway where Eddie had disappeared. Dante leaned against the doorframe, watching us.

"I didn't realize you were still here," I said.

"I'm leaving now. You need anything, sis?"

"Celery and peanut butter." She looked at me. "Are you going to stick around?"

"I'm all yours."

"Bring Samantha some ice cream."

FOR THE NEXT two hours we ate pizza and played Monopoly while *The Big Sleep* played on TCM. The bottle of champagne had been opened, but I barely touched it. Considering a visit with Detective Loncar was in the near future, I thought it prudent to take it easy. Cat claimed to be nauseous and sipped at a glass of club soda. After Eddie's earlier dig about my fashionista standing, I considered it a personal victory that the words "Heist" and "job" didn't come up the rest of the time I was there. I stood to leave shortly after Eddie acquired Boardwalk.

It was quarter to ten. The police station wasn't far from Cat's house, and I made a couple of turns through her neighborhood, hopped on and off the highway, and pulled into a visitor space. It still gave me chills to park between a squadron of black and whites.

Detective Loncar stood inside the front door with a black mug in his hand. "Thought you bailed on us."

"I had other things to do tonight. Important real estate transactions."

"Follow me."

We trekked along the now familiar path, over the might-be-dirty, might-be-clean gray linoleum tile, into the room that led to the room that was his office. I was starting to not notice the dinginess. I wondered if that's how it was for him. Maybe he'd long ago tuned out the monochromatic shade of bland surrounding him.

The detective poured me a mug of coffee without asking if I wanted it. I took a sip and gagged. No wonder he didn't ask first. He was just trying to finish off a bad pot so he could start fresh.

"I found something out about Kyle Trent," I started.

"Calm down for a second. Today I'm telling you something instead of the other way around. Remember those flowers?"

"Yes." I thought about the card. "You'd better start editing those cards before you send them."

"We told the florist to write whatever he wanted." He hammered a couple of keys on his computer and pulled up an audio file.

"Listen to this," he said, while his knobby, finger punched the enter key. The words were clear. "I happen to know there's going to be an opening in shoes." The background of the recording popped and fizzed like an Alka-Seltzer dropped into a cup of water, but the voice was unmistakable. Mallory George.

"That's the assistant buyer," I said.

"You know who she was talking to?'

"No, but I wasn't in the office much today."

He sat forward in his chair and narrowed his eyes at me. "Why's that?"

"I was looking into something at Tradava."

"You're supposed to be looking into things at Heist. There's more." He punched the enter key again, and Mallory's voice continued. "Either the job is mine, or there's going to be another opening in handbags."

I pointed to his computer. "Is it my imagination, or was she just threatening to take me out? She said she would make another opening in handbags. Did she mean me? I think she means me—"

"That's what we thought. You'd better watch her. She's obviously blackmailing someone. We think she knows more than she's letting on, and we need you to find out what it is."

When this whole thing started, I'd accepted the job on the basis that:

a) I needed a job, and

b) There was a pretty good chance someone wasn't going around knocking off handbag buyers.

Only now I wasn't so sure. And, because of point a, I was a handbag buyer, so if point b was in fact not true, then I was in the line of fire. That in itself was unsettling.

I started the drive home, lost in my thoughts. It wasn't until halfway to my house that I noticed a pair of headlights directly behind my car.

I pulled onto the main street and turned left, and then made a sudden right at the next intersection. The sedan followed me. It was dark, and the car had tinted windows. Maybe it was just my imagination, after what Detective Loncar had played for me. Surely this was all in my head.

I circled the neighborhood twice, unsure where to go. The car stayed on my tail. I shot through a yellow light and made an aggressive left turn, then a right, then pulled onto the highway's access ramp. The signal changed behind me. I peered down from the circular ramp to see the pursuer caught at the light. I sped up, putting distance between myself and that intersection, and pulled into a gas station half a mile up the road. The wind whipped my hair around my face. My polyester dress was cool against my skin. I got out of the car and ran inside the EZ Mart, repeatedly looking over my shoulder.

The clerk stood behind the counter talking to a pretty teenage girl. I crouched next to the Slushie machine and peered out the window. The highway was relatively quiet. This wasn't the busiest stretch of it, just beyond the mall, and it was late enough that I could track every car that passed. A red sports car sped by, easily over the speed limit. Then a minivan.

I wandered the aisles, keeping an eye on the road out front. There were no other cars in sight. I approached the counter, thinking I'd lost my tail—or that maybe Loncar was right and I needed to stop watching thrillers—when a dark sedan approached the entrance to the gas station.

Considering my Honda del Sol hadn't been produced since the eighties, my car wasn't the most undercover vehicle in the world, but it was too late to think about that now. The sedan passed the first entrance but hooked a hard right into the exit. It circled around toward my car.

I rushed to the counter. "I think I'm in trouble. Do you have a restroom?"

He glanced at my Slushie. "Most people say that after they finish one of those."

"No, I'm being followed. Can I hide somewhere?"

"Restroom's outside." He pushed a large wood block keychain toward me.

"I can't go outside. Do you have a stockroom?"

"I don't think you should help her," the girlfriend said. "Are you wanted by the cops?"

The clerk pulled the keychain back before I could grasp it.

It was too late to answer because the chimes sounded over the EZ Mart door.

18

TRAIL OF BREADCRUMBS

*Y*ou could make this a little easier, you know," Dante said, taking a couple of steps toward me. He was wearing the same uniform he'd worn when posing as a security guard the night we robbed I-FAD of the statue. I'd almost forgotten this had all started with the statue.

"What are you doing? Besides scaring me to death?" I asked. I had half a mind to throw my Slushie at him and make a clean getaway.

"Come with me." He put his hand on my arm and steered me toward the exit.

"I haven't paid yet," I said, stalling, turning back to face the clerk.

"Everything okay, officer?" the teenaged twerp asked.

"Okay, now, son. What does she owe you?"

"It's on the house," the kid said.

Dante looked at me and grinned.

"Thank you," I called behind me. I left with Dante close behind.

"Sit in my car," he instructed. He kept his hand on my elbow while we walked to the navy sedan.

"Don't you drive a motorcycle?"

"This is a rental."

"Why did you rent a car? You could have borrowed Cat's car. She's your sister. I don't think she'd mind."

"You would have recognized her car."

"I'm the reason you rented a car? You did this to follow me?"

"You went to the police station after you left my sister's house. Why?"

"That's why you left, isn't it? You waited until I left and followed me to the police? Is that why I never got any ice cream?"

"Why?" he repeated.

I ran my fingertips over my forehead a few times. This was not good. Deep breath in, deep breath out. I looked at Dante, who was waiting for my response.

"I'll talk once we're in the car."

He unlocked the doors and I slid onto the blue fabric seat. The teenagers in the Quickie Mart were watching us. "Do we have to do this here? I feel like I'm half of a peep show."

"We could go back to your place," he said.

"On second thought, this is fine."

"Samantha, what were you doing with the police?"

"I can't talk about that."

"You're working with them, aren't you?"

I repositioned myself on the front seat of the car, my back to the window. "Why do you expect me to talk to you? I barely know you."

"Compared to you, I'm an open book."

"Written in invisible ink," I muttered.

"Ask me anything."

"Okay, for starters, what do you do? Why are you here? Where did you come from? When are you leaving?"

"Those are the starter questions? I'd hate to see how you end."

"It doesn't feel good to be interrogated, does it?"

Dante relaxed, one arm around the back of the seat, the other bent, resting on the dashboard.

"I'm a photographer. Freelance. I take jobs where I get them. Sometimes that means a fashion shoot. Sometimes it means following someone around for insurance purposes. Sometimes it means catching people doing things they don't want to be caught doing."

I waited, not sure if he was going to say more.

"I live in Philadelphia. My sister lives here and I come to visit her from time to time. I'm here now because of the contest. I'm not leaving until it's all wrapped up." He stared intensely at me. I suspected he was waiting for a response. It would take longer than the time I intended to spend in the front seat of the car with him to absorb what he'd said, so I tucked it away for later.

Dante may have made a good confidante. He was close to Cat, who was close to Eddie, who rounded out the list of people I didn't want to get involved. I couldn't explain why I'd been so willing to take Tony Simms' offer, but I had. Working with Detective Loncar gave me a sense of importance. It wasn't a joke, and I wanted to keep it that way. I wanted to prove I could do this.

"Here's what I see," Dante said when I didn't speak. "You got yourself mixed up in something. I don't know who talked you into it, but you're shutting everybody out." He shrugged. "Maybe you're telling your friend in Italy, I don't know, but that's still pretty safe since he's in another country. You're not good at letting people in, are you?"

I didn't like that he'd hit the nail on the head after knowing me less than a week.

"Is this about the police or about my character flaws?"

"Samantha, I know I just met you, but I think I 'get' you. You don't want to ask for help, and you don't want to let anyone in. It's like you have something to prove." He leaned back against the seat and rubbed his hand across the bristly top of his hair, now a couple weeks past the buzz-cut stage.

Like it or not, I couldn't deny his accuracy. "What are you trying to say?"

"Something happened to you after we stole that statue, but I can't figure out what. You're following a trail of breadcrumbs that didn't start out with the loaf of bread."

"Yes it did. The breadcrumbs started at Heist," I said, before realizing I was admitting to following the trail of breadcrumbs. Instead of shouting *Gotcha!* like I expected, Dante didn't even flinch.

"What took you to Heist? The murder?"

"The statue, but that's because of the contest."

"Seems to me like there's some kind of tie-in between the statue and the murder."

I sat for a couple of minutes, my hands wrapped around the forty-eight-ounce plastic Slushie cup. Water had condensed on the outside and coated my fingers. A few drops landed on my polyester dress and beaded up like Eddie's water had earlier that night.

"The owner came to visit me. He said I had a unique skill set, and that he wanted to hire me. At first I thought he was talking about my history as a buyer, since he was in need of a buyer, but he asked me to look around, to see if I noticed anything out of the ordinary. The store was trying to shut down the bad press they got. That night at the gala, someone murdered Emily Hart with our statue. When the cops found the statue in my handbag and pulled me aside, Tony Simms was in the room. He knew everything I knew."

"You think he doesn't trust the cops?"

"No, that's not it. Detective Loncar is a good cop. He's going to do what he can to find the murderer. He's not concerned with how Heist comes off looking through this whole thing, or whether they're going to still be able to open their doors for business in Ribbon without any lasting implications. I think that's what Simms cares about. Not who killed his handbag buyer."

"Does Tony Simms know every move you're making?"

"No, at least I don't think so. I never told him I went to the cops."

"Why not?"

"I don't know. It just seemed like a good idea to keep that part to myself."

LOGAN MET ME at the front door, meowing for cat food. I filled his bowl. I hadn't wanted to confide in Dante, and truth be told I really didn't, much. But what he'd said had got me thinking, and once I get to thinking, there's really no stopping me. There was one person who knew something about the statue but was unconnected to Heist, and that was Nora. I hadn't seen her since the theft, but now seemed like a good time to visit. It was much too late to show up on her doorstep, but I could see her silhouette through the window, and that meant she was still awake, so what was the problem with a phone call?

She picked up after the fifth ring. (I probably should have hung up after four.)

"It's next-door Samantha. Did I wake you?"

"No, I'm grading papers." She stifled a yawn. "What's keeping you up?"

"I'd like to talk to you about what happened with that statue."

"I don't know that I want to end my evening by discussing a murder. Why don't you come by the college tomorrow afternoon, say, around five?"

"Is that when your classes end?"

"My last lecture ends at four forty-five. That'll give me a chance to talk with the kids who have questions before they dash back to their dorms."

Nora really was a noble professor. I agreed to meet her, because what was so wrong about cutting out of work early another day?

***

The next morning, I dressed in the black trousers and plunging vest Tony Simms had sent over to my house, only this time I wore a white cotton shirt with French cuffs under the vest and topped it with a long strand of pearls knotted like a necktie. I arrived at the store at eight o'clock. If Mallory was going to show up early, I wanted her to know she couldn't count on being alone in the office.

I spun Dante's flowers around, this time fully aware Mallory was worth watching. By the time she arrived at eight thirty, I'd already reviewed a portion of the recaps she'd put in my inbox and had caught a couple of errors, too, which always helps to level the new boss/tenured-assistant-with-attitude playing field.

"You're here early." She seemed surprised.

"I wanted to get a jumpstart on the day."

Mallory left for her adjacent office. For the next hour there were no sounds except for the clicking of keys on her keyboard.

Heist's offices may have been nice for professionalism and privacy, but at the moment I missed the old, un-renovated offices at Bentley's where all of us were crowded into one room about ten feet square. You couldn't get away with anything in that situation.

The phone rang, and Belle's name flashed on my caller ID.

"Sam, Belle DuChamp here. I'm with Tony. We want to have an impromptu meeting to discuss the Vongole strategy. Can you come to my office in about fifteen minutes? Bring whatever history you have on their business: sell-through reports, profit analyses, and pending orders. Thanks. Bring Mallory too. I'd like her to sit in on this." She hung up before I had the chance to respond. But if Tony Simms was in the building with her, it wasn't like I had much of a choice about attending.

I knocked on Mallory's doorframe to announce my presence. "Belle just called. She wants to go over the Vongole strategy. Do you have it?"

"There isn't a Vongole strategy, as far as I know."

"Then I guess we're making one up today. She asked for all the information we have on their history. I don't know where we keep that, aside from the recaps you put in my inbox."

Mallory pulled two overstuffed three-ring binders from a shelf. "Whatever you need should be in the first one, but if not, take the second one so you're prepared."

"That's all on Vongole?"

"No, this is the history of all our vendors. She'll probably want a comparison, and you don't want to not have the information in front of you."

"Okay, let me get my stuff and we'll head down."

"We?"

"Yes. She specifically asked for you to sit in." I paused for a second before adding, "Tony Simms will be there too."

The color drained from Mallory's face. She dropped the overstuffed binders. One popped open and recaps of business spread across the floor. When she reached out for them, her hands were shaking.

Something I'd said had thrown Mallory off-kilter.

19

TIME FOR A TAKE-DOWN

"Come in, sit down," Belle said.

She and Tony sat at the large, glass conference table. How much Windex did it take to keep the fingerprints off?

I sat to Belle's right and Mallory sat to my right. Tony sat across from me. If this were a game of Red Rover, Mallory, Belle, and I would have the advantage. We were down to one notebook, thanks to Mallory's shock-and-drop maneuver minutes earlier. I hoped it had the information we needed.

"Tony and I were talking about opportunities for Heist," Belle said. "Accessories are an exploding category, and we need to identify a key vendor now and negotiate accordingly."

Tony jumped in. "Handbags are like shoes. Women crave them. It's crazy what women will pay for a handbag. Doesn't matter if they need to lose ten pounds, if they're having a bad hair day, if they're getting over a breakup. Plus, the handbag business is a no-brainer. You don't have to think about sizes like with apparel. Our markup structure was at the industry standard, so we took the category and tinkered with the formula. The margin exploded."

"Tinkered with the formula how?" I asked. I was trying to keep up. Mallory was scribbling notes on a yellow legal pad.

"We get a 40 percent discount from the cost, so we dropped the retails by 30 percent. Nobody else can touch our prices. The bags sell themselves. Customers come to us first because of our pricing and stay loyal because of our assortment. Every market we've entered, we've stolen Tradava's client base overnight."

"But Tradava has a whole assortment of Vongole's bags on sale right now," I offered. "Fifty percent off."

Mallory looked up, surprised. Belle and Tony didn't say anything. I looked between their faces.

"I was shopping the competition yesterday," I finished, hoping they'd see that as an entrepreneurial spark and not a goofing-off streak.

"Those are last year's bags. We bought out Vongole's entire inventory this year so they couldn't fill any orders for Tradava," Tony said. He folded his hands behind his head and leaned back in his chair. It was the cocky body language of a college student who had just one-upped a competitor at a debate match, and with his boyish looks he kind of looked the part. I was willing to bet he'd won plenty of battles in the boardroom, even if other executives towered over him.

We spent the better part of an hour reviewing the profit analysis for Vongole. Aware that Mallory was watching me, I didn't point out the errors I'd caught that morning. Even if it was the perfect opportunity to correct the boss-employee dynamic, I took the high road.

More than once, Belle asked Mallory's opinion, calling her out of her silence, forcing her to participate in our discussion. It was a humble, almost shy Mallory who spoke when spoken to, offering up valid points about Vongole's past performances. Belle and Tony brainstormed an aggressive strategy to keep Vongole on our shelves and out of the hands of Tradava. Belle showed a devilish pleasure in plotting to shut down her former store's business. I wondered again what had happened to turn her away from Tradava, and what her relationship had been with Emily.

When the meeting was over, Mallory grabbed the unused notebook and stormed back to the office. I may not have known the answer to every question asked, but I'd more than held my own in the strategy meeting. I should have earned her respect by now.

"That went well, don't you think?" I asked when we reentered the office.

"I'd hardly say that," she spat, and disappeared into her office.

Okay, time for a take-down. I followed her to her desk and crossed my arms over my pearl necktie. "What exactly is your problem with me?"

She glared at me, slowly shaking her head. "Don't play stupid. I know all about you."

"Then why don't you tell me all about me, because clearly I don't know what's going on."

"Don't play dumb. I'm friends with the PR manager, and she told me you told a room full of strangers that you made the weapon that was used to kill Emily. Then you show up here in her job. I don't know why it doesn't look suspicious to anyone else, but it sure looks suspicious to me."

"You think I—" I didn't finish the sentence. "You're joking, right?"

"Why do they love you so much?" Her eyes widened and her voice raised.

The scent of the calla lilies, pleasantly fragrant yesterday, now caused the back of my head to throb. Mallory's verbal attack didn't help. I put my hands to my head to massage my temples.

Mallory continued. "I'm here on my merit. I've got a drawer full of performance reviews to prove it. But clearly you have some kind of relationship with Tony Simms that trumps experience and hard work. Maybe I'll be hearing about *you* in the boardroom."

"That's enough," I said. "Whether you like it or not, I'm your boss, and I don't appreciate what you're implying. You have two choices: get on board with me as your new buyer, or don't."

We stared at each other. The office felt like someone was pressing a large balloon on top of us. I didn't care what Mallory did next. I was done with her attitude.

When she didn't speak, I took my hands off my temples and put them palm side down on the Monday morning vendor recaps in her inbox.

"I didn't want to bring this up in the meeting today, but you made a couple of mistakes on the Vongole profit analysis, mistakes that significantly overstated their margin."

"What mistakes?"

I pulled out the form and circled the blank fields in freight, theft, and markdowns. "You didn't fill out all of the components of the margin calculation, so the profit is coming in overinflated."

She glanced at the paper and then pushed it back toward me. "You don't know what you're talking about."

I fanned out six other recaps on the desk. "These are all complete."

"Vongole is different. We get such a high discount from Andi that we don't take markdowns, not even coupons. It's in the disclaimer. The bags are locked up so there's no shortage."

"What about freight? Freight expense runs at 3 to 5 percent of the cost of an order. That alone will change their profitability."

"Vongole uses Simulated Trucking, and they don't charge us."

"Why not?"

"I have no idea, and that's not my job. The reports are correct. Now, if that's all you wanted to address with me, I have other work to do." She turned to her computer and pretended I wasn't there. Before I left, I remembered one more thing. "Mallory, if this is such a high margin business, why didn't Emily want you to approve any more orders?"

She stopped typing. "How do you know about that?"

I pulled the red folder marked ORDERS TO APPROVE out of her inbox and opened it up. Inside was the note that I had seen last night. She took the folder from me, the animosity gone, replaced with a furrowed brow and eyes that stared off to the corner of her desk while she appeared to think.

"I told Belle about that yesterday," she said in a normal voice. "I called her to find out why she wrote those orders when we were overstocked. If we bring in the inventory Andi has on hand, we'll risk our entire profit structure, and if we have that much inventory we'll throw off the supply and demand. We'll have to take markdowns to liquidate. And I don't understand how Vongole even has that much inventory. Four months ago we bought every bag Vongole had available so they couldn't ship to anybody else." For the moment, her animosity toward me had dissipated.

"Have you ever asked Andi about this?"

"With Andi, everything related to one of her vendors is a great opportunity. 'Omigod, like, totally!'"

She was right; Andi was not going to do anything to make Vongole look bad. But if Andi was able to play the 'Omigod, you're, like, totally my new best friend' routine, then so was I. I returned to my desk and dialed her showroom number.

"Andi? Samantha Kidd, from Heist."

I finagled a session of after-work cocktails and girl-talk. Mallory looked impressed, but before she had a chance to compliment me outright, we heard a male voice in the hallway. "Samantha Kidd?"

"That's me," I called, and stood up.

A deliveryman in a brown shirt and shorts carried a vase of pink roses into the office. "Where'd you like me to put these?" he asked, noting the two arrangements that already occupied the front of the desk. It was starting to look like Birnam Wood in here.

"I'll take them," I said and transferred the vase from his grip to the bookcase behind me.

"You must be quite a woman." He held out an electronic device that I signed with a plastic stylus.

I pulled the card out of the tiny white envelope after he left. *Don't know who sent you flowers yesterday, but here's hoping mine are better. Miss you.—NT*

I went to my desk and answered with a professional sounding e-mail:

Dear Nick, Your sketches look amazing, would love to see the real thing. Have you had a chance to meet with either Luta or Lussuria factories? Regards, Samantha.

I received a response almost immediately.

Dear S, Have not had time yet but they're on my schedule—N

I KILLED THE rest of the afternoon with buyer-related tasks. At four thirty I shut down the computer and slicked on a coat of lip-gloss. I pulled my sleeve over my hand and polished the fingerprints off my patent leather handbag.

Mallory stood in my doorway. "Before you meet up with Andi, you should know Tradava cancelled a bunch of Vongole orders, and that might be where the surplus inventory came from."

"That sounds like confidential information. How do you know that?"

"I overheard Kyle and Emily arguing the night of the gala. They didn't realize I was in here. I heard him say he'd cancelled his entire Vongole order, and he couldn't believe she'd bought all of this crap, and she yelled at him that he had no right to tell her how to do her job. They were pretty mad at each other. He said she had to pick one or the other, and she didn't answer. The last thing I heard him say was he couldn't take it anymore and was going to end it."

"What happened after that?"

"I don't know. I bolted. I didn't want to be around if they decided to make up, if you know what I mean."

"Did you tell any of this to the cops?"

"No. When I said I bolted, I mean I bolted from the store. I wasn't here when she was ... found."

"How did you hear the news?"

"Belle called me the next day to let me know."

I nodded calmly. Did I believe her? I wasn't sure. As far as workplace personalities went, Mallory seemed a little unstable.

I thanked her for the info and left. In the past eight hours Mallory had insulted me more than once, and then she made a concerted effort to confide in me. Those two actions seemed at odds with each other, but neither action changed two very important facts:

a) Last night, Detective Loncar had played a conversation for me where Mallory had threatened someone for a promotion, and

b) Today she confessed to being right here the night Emily Hart was murdered.

And whether she realized it or not, she also told me she really didn't have an alibi.

20

BOYFRIENDS

There was a limited window of time before cocktails with Andi, and I used it to meet with Nora at I-FAD. I parked in a visitor space near her lecture hall. The only other car in the lot was a highly polished silver BMW. The college was either paying more to their professors than I thought or there were some very spoiled students. When I went to school, I got around on a one-person motorized scooter that capped out at thirty-five miles per hour unless I was going downhill.

An irregular breeze wafted past me, blowing green whirlybirds from the trees. They spun in circles as they descended, landing in soft piles on the grass, to be trampled by students between classes. I picked one up, held it in front of me with two fingers, and let go, watching it spiral its way as it fell.

Students trickled out of the lecture hall, holding beat-up backpacks on one shoulder. I didn't want to waste any more time, so I pushed through the door and followed the mustard-colored carpet runner to the front. Nora stood, leaning against a marble table, talking to Tony Simms. Surprised, I stepped backward and put one hand on the door to leave, but it was too late.

"Samantha! Perfect timing. I told Mr. Simms you were coming here today, and he wanted to talk to you."

"Hello, Samantha," he said, extending his hand. I grabbed it and shook, trying to anticipate the squeeze-and-pump manner he'd used the first time we'd been through this routine.

"Hi Mr."— I caught myself— "Tony," I finished lamely.

"What brings you to the college today?"

"Nora," I answered, opting for vague over lying.

"Aren't you two neighbors?"

"Yes," I said, not sure how he knew that. "With the hours I'm putting it at Heist, I barely see her anymore." It was meant to be a joke. I hoped he saw that.

"Speaking of Heist, that's the reason I'm here." He checked his watch. "I'm late for an appointment. Nora, do you want to fill her in?"

"Be glad to, Tony."

They shook hands as a good-bye, though Nora didn't appear to care about the business squeeze-and-pump. She looked a lot more natural than I did during the whole process. The small businessman left through a side door marked only by a red neon Exit sign.

"I didn't expect to find him here," I said, this time opting for the truth over vague.

"Neither did I."

"What's this thing he was talking about?"

"Tony has been very generous to I-FAD. As a thank you, the college is dedicating a building to him. It wasn't going to happen for a month, but he wants to bump up the agenda to divert attention from the negativity that's surrounding Heist."

"Can he do that?"

"When you've given as much money to the college as he has, you can pretty much write your own ticket."

Interesting. "What do I have to do with this?"

"He wants a team from Heist here at the dedication. Turn it into a story about the store, the professionalism, the career path. Help tie it to the community. He was here to meet with the academic chair on possible internships for students and a guest professor program using Heist staff. Your name came up."

I didn't point out that I'd worked for the store for a total of three days. It was quickly becoming a moot point. "Heist is new to the area. Why isn't Tradava getting this kind of treatment? They've been in Ribbon forever."

"Tony Simms is trying to get people to connect him with the city, to give him goodwill," she said.

"If it didn't seem like such a political move, I'd say it was a good idea."

"I get the sense that Tony Simms doesn't have bad ideas, and if he decided to run for mayor, he'd probably get a lot of votes."

I turned around and looked at the door through which he'd vanished. "I'm starting to get that sense too."

"Now, what was the reason you wanted to talk to me today?"

Tony's knowledge of my whereabouts unnerved me, and I changed my mind about sticking around to talk to Nora. I told her I was running late and made plans to have dinner at her place tomorrow night. I took the next ten minutes to sit in my car to transcribe what I remembered from my encounter with Tony.

WHEN I ARRIVED at Andi's showroom, I was surprised to find Kyle there. I could tell he was on his way out, based on the dual-cheek air-kiss he and Andi exchanged. Nick used to give me those, back when he was my vendor and I was his buyer. I wondered if we'd ever get past that, if we'd transition from texted Xs to the real thing, or if the distance between us was insurmountable in terms of starting a relationship. I hated to admit that even air-kisses were better than text messages.

Andi waved to me while Kyle nodded a greeting and caught the elevator. Today she wore a black knit sleeveless dress with a cowl neck, no stockings, and flat sandals. She bounced over to me.

"Omigod, I'm sooo happy you called. It's been a long week already and it's only Wednesday. We can totally hit happy hour if we leave right now." She grabbed a purple handbag and tossed in a notebook, BlackBerry, and a laptop. "I know, most people would carry a briefcase, right? Let's get out of here," she said, and locked the showroom door behind us.

We walked across the parking lot to a restaurant overflowing with the after-five crowd. Strong tubes of neon framed the entrance. Andi shimmied her way past several of the tenants to the bar, where she perched on a stool. She thumped her hand on the top of the one next to her. "Have a seat, girlfriend!"

The bartender came over, drying a glass with a white towel. "Your usual?" he asked Andi. She nodded. "What'll you have?" he asked me.

"I'm not sure. What's your usual?" I asked Andi.

"Diet RockStar and pomegranate vodka."

"Oh. I'll have a—" I tried to think of something that sounded adult and serious. "A Manhattan."

"Oooh, fancy!" Andi said.

While the bartender disappeared to make our drinks, I wondered how I was going to keep up this newfound best friend routine. Turns out that didn't matter, because I was sitting with a pro. Andi started a nonstop stream of chatter, about the totally perfect weather, the restaurant's totally awesome calamari, the totally horrendous outfits the waitresses were forced to wear, and the totally hot hunks working behind the bar.

"Don't you just love bartenders? I married one once. Turns out the best thing about him was his name. We split up after a month, but he didn't mind that I wanted to keep it."

The bartender set our drinks in front of us and she continued. "Thanks, babe. This is Samantha. Sam, this is Cal. He's one of my boyfriends." She tipped her head back and smiled at him while running an ice cube down her throat. The bartender chuckled. "I have boyfriends all over now. They take care of me. And I take care of them. Right, Cal?" She flipped a credit card out of her wallet and handed it to him.

"Wait, I'll get these," I said, fumbling for my own credit card while searching for a way to steer the conversation to Emily Hart.

"Absolutely not! I can expense this," she said.

"At least let me get the first round."

"Don't worry! You have no idea how many receipts I have that are time stamped after midnight. Besides, you're my top client these days. I'd do just about anything to make you happy." She giggled.

It seemed she'd delivered me my opening.

"Then let's toast why I'm your top client." I raised my glass to hers. "To Vongole."

"Abso-freakin'-lutely. To Vongole."

I took a sip of my drink and recoiled at the taste, heavy with vermouth. How did Marilyn Monroe drink these? I looked at Andi. She'd finished more than half her drink on our toast. Good sign. That meant it might not be too hard to keep her talking. I sipped again, fighting the taste. I was in the middle of phrasing and rephrasing different prompts in my head when she spoke.

"It's so great to have you at Heist. I mean, it's totally sad what happened to Emily. Kyle's miserable about it. But business is business, and you're going to rock that job, I can already tell."

"I think I'm lucky to have such a strong team of supporters."

"Oh, you mean Belle? She's awesome. Such an inspirational woman. You know, when she went through her divorce, it was pretty nasty. She totally pulled herself back up and reestablished who she was and now she's even more respected than ever." She finished off her drink. "You ready for another?"

"Not yet," I said, swirling the stem of my martini glass. "What do you think of Mallory?"

She rolled her eyes. "She's a little too by-the-book, if you ask me. We all want to be successful, right? So there's got to be a little wiggle room in the numbers and orders. One time she had Heist hold a payment from us for six months because she said the collection wasn't going to be profitable and they'd have to send back the orders. She claimed it was Emily's strategy but I know it wasn't."

"What happened?"

"That's the season we started giving Heist the discount. Suddenly, everything was coming up roses and we were getting paid within a week."

"I bet it wasn't coming up roses for you," I nudged, playing the new-found BFF confidant. Fifteen percent of the discounted order is a lot less than 15 percent of the original, even if Heist bought more.

"Can you believe they totally took that into consideration? It went all the way to the top of Vongole, too. The owners agreed to pay me 15 percent on the original orders or 25 percent of the discounted orders. Either way, I win."

In all of my years in the industry, I had never heard of such a lucrative arrangement.

"Now I just have to get Tradava back into my client base," she said. She raised her hand to cover her berry-stained lips. "Oops! Shouldn't have said that in front of you, right?"

"I thought Heist negotiated an exclusive?"

She spit her drink out in a spritz of surprise, and then mopped it up with a couple of promotional Bud Light napkins before the bartender could get to us.

"No, Heist bought out my inventory so we couldn't fill anyone else's orders. But Tradava's such a big account that we put together something for them, and Kyle ended up returning it. Something about the quality not being up to standard." She drained her second drink and motioned for another round for each of us. "Poor guy, he can't get over what happened at Heist. He keeps saying it's his fault."

"Why? Because he and Emily had a fight?" I prompted, still wondering about Mallory's version of that night.

"Couples fight. That's reality." Andi waved at the bartender and pointed to our drinks. When he nodded, she turned back, suddenly very serious. "Kyle doesn't feel guilty about fighting with Emily. He feels guilty because of what they were fighting *about*."

21

RUMORS

I was surprised Andi knew they were fighting about Vongole. "I didn't think anyone knew," I said.

"Yes, Kyle does a good job hiding how much he hates her."

"Her? Her who?"

"Belle."

"Kyle hates Belle? But people say—"

"That's why he hates her. With a passion. She won't let that rumor die."

"That's what Emily and Kyle were fighting about?"

"Yes. He was always defending himself against that stupid rumor."

"That he and Belle were caught canoodling in the boardroom?"

She laughed raucously and drew the attention of several patrons near us. "'Canoodling'?! You're funny. Yeah, that's the rumor, but I can't see it being true. He was way too devoted to Emily." She sighed. "He used to send her flowers when they were at market, and room service breakfast in bed. Belle investigated him too. Accused him of expensing it to Tradava. Turns out he paid for all of that stuff himself."

"Did Belle apologize?"

"Heck no. Kyle wanted to leave Tradava and work at Heist with Emily, but then everyone was shocked when Belle was fired, and even more shocked when she was named Heist general manager a few weeks later. Kyle thought he'd have an in if he applied to the store, but then that nasty rumor started. Even if there was an open job that he was totally qualified for, he couldn't apply. Everyone would have said he got the job because he was sleeping with Belle. He kept trying to make sure Emily didn't believe the rumor, and I don't think she did, but it just kept following them around. Belle didn't exactly deny it."

I thought about that for a second. "It's not a bad rumor to have floating around about you, if you're Belle. I just can't figure out why Kyle told me some people think she's still working for Tradava. Like there are people who think she's taking everything she learns about Heist and reporting it back to someone at her former store."

"What? Girlfriend, I hear everything, and I never heard that one. She's smart enough to do it though." She reached out for her third drink. "I'm so thirsty tonight!" she said. She pulled the red plastic sword out of the glass, set it on her napkin, and took another drink. "But let me tell you, Kyle hates her. Haaaates her."

"Andi, do you have any pictures of Emily?"

"Sure." She pulled her BlackBerry out of her handbag and pushed the small buttons with blood red-painted thumbnails. "Here." She tapped a few more buttons and handed me the phone. It was a picture of Kyle Trent and a blonde with their arms around each other. Large, toothpaste-commercial-worthy smiles covered their faces.

"When was this taken?"

She took her phone back and looked at the screen. "Last year. The night he proposed to her." She stared at the screen. Her expression was less joy than jealousy.

It got me thinking that something didn't make sense. I needed to talk it through, and there was only one person I could count on for that.

"IT DOESN'T MAKE sense, right?" I asked Detective Loncar. He'd agreed to meet with me on the basis that I had information for him, info that might lead to a break in Emily's case. At least that's what I told him when I called, because it seemed the detective wanted to determine for himself how important my info really was.

I recounted Andi's gossip, though while I was repeating it, it felt more like I was in the middle of a high school love triangle and less like a murder investigation.

"I mean, it sounds like a bunch of rumors." I sat back in the folding chair and stared at Loncar, who sat behind his desk.

"How well do you trust this Andi?"

"Oh, as much as anyone else, I guess."

"She seems to know a lot of dirt on the people we're watching."

"A lot of sales reps do. It's a subtle form of blackmail. They hang out with you until you trip up and do something you'd rather not get around. It's pretty standard in the fashion industry."

"Nice industry," the detective said.

I thought about her RockStar and vodka shooters. "I thought I was going to have a hard time getting away from her, but when I said I had to leave she said she had other plans too. Until she said that, I thought she was going to stay there all night."

"You sure she wasn't playing? Sales reps have been known to close business deals over drinks."

"Did you get that from *Glengarry Glen Ross?*"

"She might have thought you were a party girl," Loncar continued as though I hadn't interrupted him.

"Do I look like a party girl?" I asked.

Loncar looked down at my pearl necktie over the white shirt and black-and-white pinstriped vest, and then back at my face. "No, Ms. Kidd, you look like an upstanding citizen," he said in a robotic voice.

"This is a very nice outfit," I said. I waited a few beats before adding, "Menswear is hot."

"Ms. Kidd, do you have anything else to tell me?"

"When Andi was talking about Kyle and Belle, her eyes turned very focused. It was like staring into the eyes of the Cheshire Cat at first, all zoned out and loopy, and then when she stood, she was completely in control."

"How many drinks did she have?"

"Three."

"She didn't get in a car, did she?"

"No. The bartender called her a cab. It was no big thing to either of them, like she does this every day. I think *she's* the party girl."

"Then maybe it is no big thing to her. People are allowed to blow off steam, Ms. Kidd."

I couldn't help thinking the detective wasn't putting the proper importance on my new information.

I PULLED AWAY from the police station, circled the block a few times to make sure Dante wasn't following me, and headed home.

Halfway there I pulled into the parking lot of an ice cream store and parked in the far corner under a light. I went inside and ordered two scoops of black raspberry ice cream in a cup, carried it to my car, and ate it slowly while I thought about what I should do next. When I was finished, I pulled Kyle's card out of my wallet and called the number.

"Kyle, this is Samantha Kidd." I hesitated, not entirely sure what I wanted to say. "I know it's late, but I was wondering if I could talk to you."

"Samantha Kidd. I didn't think you'd call. Funny thing is, I was just thinking about you."

"You were?"

There was a pause on the other end of the phone, and then Kyle continued in his languorous voice. "I have something I think you might like. Something I wanted to give Emily the night we were at Heist. I think you'll find it interesting."

I wasn't sure what he was talking about, and for a moment I wondered if he was coming on to me. "I—I'm not looking for companionship tonight."

"I don't know what it is you think I'm offering you, but the only 'companionship' I want right now comes from a bottle."

"But you said—"

"I know what I said."

"I'm confused. Do you want to give me something or do you want me to leave you alone?"

"Where are you?"

I hesitated. "The Tastee Freeze parking lot."

"Are you going to be there long? I can be there in ten minutes."

Considering he was seeking companionship from a bottle, I didn't want to be the reason he got into a car.

"I have a better idea. Why don't I come to you?"

"Fine. Here's my address."

I felt around the floor of the car for a pen and came up with a mauve lip liner. I scribbled his address on the bottom of the empty ice cream bowl and hung up.

KYLE TRENT LIVED in the Woodgate Apartments, a secluded set of buildings not far from the on-ramp to the highway. I parked by his building and glanced in the rear view mirror, wiping a smudge of black raspberry from my lower lip before getting out. The door to his apartment opened as I scaled the stairs out front.

"Come on in," he said. He wore a gray bathrobe over light blue pinstriped pajamas, and held a glass tumbler of something amber. He left the door open and I followed him inside.

His apartment was sparsely furnished. A burgundy leather sofa faced an unlit fireplace. There were no pictures on the mantle. A collection of Chinese food takeout containers covered the maple coffee table, along with two empty beer bottles and an empty bag from McDonalds. The polished, professional Kyle Trent I'd first met at Heist and conversed with at Tradava was gone, and in his place was a man who reeked of desperation and a couple of days without a shower.

"Thanks for meeting me. I wanted to ask you about Belle and Emily—"

He waved his hand in front of me. "I don't want to talk about any of this."

"But you said you had something for me?"

"I do. I have a question." He sat down on the burgundy leather sofa and pointed at me with the index finger of the hand holding the glass. "Why do you care so much about this? You didn't even know her."

I didn't know what I expected from my meeting with Kyle, but I didn't expect him to question my motives. I looked at this man, who days ago could just as easily have graced the pages of a retailer's catalog as he could be the buyer behind the merchandise. Kyle Trent, for all of his good looks, his confidence, and his ace-in-the-hole charm, was me. He was a buyer who did his job well, who was attracted to someone in his industry. Only, unlike me, who had accepted that buyers don't date vendors, that companies don't like romances that threaten the business, Kyle risked his job for his relationship with Emily and the two had fallen in love. And look where it had gotten him.

I sat on the far end of the leather sofa and leaned forward, propping my elbows on my pinstriped pants. "I didn't have to know her to see she was special," I said softly.

Kyle stared into the glass he held, swirling it around a few times. He leaned forward, set the glass on the coffee table, and held his head in his hands. His shoulders shook like he was crying.

"I'm sorry. I'm sorry I came over here, and I'm sorry for your loss. I'll let myself out." I stood and walked toward the door.

"Samantha, wait," Kyle said.

I turned around and saw him pull a white envelope out of his bathrobe pocket. It was folded in half. He held it out to me.

"I sealed it so nobody else would see it. I was planning to show it to Emily, but I never got the chance."

"What is it?"

168

"It might explain a few things."

I took the envelope. If it had to do with Emily or Vongole or Belle, then he was right, I'd probably find it interesting. If it had to do with Tradava, he was risking his job to give it to me.

"Do you want me to open it now?"

"No. Please go. I want to be alone," he said.

At home, I triple-locked the front door, undid my pearl necktie, and tore open the envelope. Inside was a printout of a spreadsheet: Vongole Gross Margin Recap, with the season and year as heading. It was Tradava's version of the profit recap I'd seen on Mallory's desk. I didn't have the Heist version at home, but I didn't need it to remember that Vongole was a very profitable vendor at Heist. That's why it struck me that on Tradava's recap, for one season, Vongole's "profits" were a hundred and seventy-five thousand dollars in the hole.

A hundred and seventy-five thousand dollar loss in one season? That's not a growth strategy. That's a business about to go belly-up.

22

OBLIGATIONS

I woke at six the next morning. I'd been up half the night, my mind abuzz with questions about the Tradava/Vongole recap. Profit and loss statements—or P&Ls, as they're called—were standard spreadsheets in the industry, recaps that indicated gross sales and backed-out expenses to let a retailer identify whether or not a business was good for the bottom line. I had questions about what I'd read, questions that could only be answered once I compared the Heist profitability against the Tradava one. My best bet was to get into the store before it was filled with employees, customers, and Mallory.

I had two cups of coffee and filled the rest of the morning with anxiety-ridden accessorizing. I stepped out of the house in a black and white polka dotted blouse and flouncy ivory and black silk skirt, a pair of pointy toed black patent leather pumps, and a black satin headband with a white camellia above my left ear. I knew I'd kissed off my attempts at undercover investigations.

Worse, Dante sat on his motorcycle in the middle of my driveway.

"You might want to go back inside and change. That's not exactly appropriate for the back of a motorcycle."

"Why are you offering me a ride?"

He held up a small metal thing with wires sticking out of it. "Cars don't run without this."

"You vandalized my car?" I asked.

I marched past him in my pointy-toed shoes and polka dots. I popped the hood of my car. Having used up most of what I knew about cars other than checking the oil, I stared at the engine, torn between touching things so I looked like I knew what I was doing and stepping away to keep the car dirt off my outfit.

Dante watched me from his motorcycle. I felt exposed. I slammed the hood back down and glared at him, trying to think of something snappy to say. Black car grunge had gotten on my fingertips, and I held them away from me like I'd just had a manicure and was waiting for my polish to dry.

"I'm not going to let this go." I turned around and went inside.

Ten minutes later, I returned wearing black skinny pants, pumps, and an ocean-blue taffeta jacket cinched at the waist. I carried a pair of futuristic silver sunglasses and accepted the helmet he handed me. Helmet hair. My morning was going from bad to worse.

"Where do you want to go?" he asked.

"Heist," I said. "I don't know where you thought I'd be going, but I'm due at work."

Dante leaned in close. "You could play hooky with me, if you want. We can drive to the Jersey Shore, make a day of it. Forget your troubles. Nobody has to know."

I flushed. "I have obligations, and now I'm going to be late."

"Hop on. I'll get you there in no time."

I climbed onto the back of his motorcycle and tried to figure out how to hold on. He gunned the engine and the bike lurched. Out of panic, I wrapped my arms around his torso and flushed. I was glad he—or anybody else—couldn't see my face.

At Heist, I went to my office and located the Vongole folder on Mallory's desk. I laid the two recaps side by side and compared the information. Both stores had achieved the same sell-through. Tradava had higher sales than Heist. So why was Heist reporting profits of two hundred thousand dollars while Tradava was almost the same amount in the hole?

I heard Mallory enter the office. She dumped her oversized handbag on the floor and sat down, cueing up her computer screen. I knew I needed the notebook that was shelved over her head, the one with the Vongole strategy, but before I could get it, she pulled it down, flipped a few pages in, and tore several sheets out of the binder without opening the rings. I leaned forward, watching her elbow propped on the outside of the notebook as she sorted through the pages. I stood up and pretended to get something from the closet so I could get a better view. She wadded the paper up and put it in her trash can. Seconds later, she stood up with her trash can and carried it into the hallway, where the trash crew would soon come to empty it.

I needed to see what she'd thrown out.

I pulled three business-sized envelopes from a drawer and scribbled addresses on the front: Cat, Eddie, and Logan (my cat is a very convenient undercover operative). Security went through our handbags every time we left the building, and I couldn't risk being caught with company information. I tossed promotional postcards into the envelopes to Cat and Eddie, and shoved the

Tradava/Vongole recaps into the envelope addressed to Logan. I stood up and walked past Mallory, waving the envelopes. "I'm heading to the mailbox. Got anything?"

"No."

"I'll be right back."

Once in the hall, I scanned the three matching trash cans lined up outside of the office, zeroing in on the crumpled piece of paper that sat on top of the can closest to our office. I palmed it and walked down the hallway and through the store. As I walked past the handbag department I smoothed out the paper, tri-folded it, and shoved it into the envelope addressed to Logan. I sealed the envelopes and carried the lot to security.

"What time does the mail get picked up?" I asked Gabe.

"Three thirty." He looked at the top of my envelopes. "They're stamped? There's a mailbox on the corner of the parking lot. They pick up in the morning too. You're early enough to make it."

I jogged to the mailbox, clutching the wad of envelopes. After dropping them into the box, I wondered if I'd done the right thing. The only actual piece of paper that proved anything until now was in the hands of the mailmen. Let's hope today wasn't the day they went postal.

Back in my office, I closed my working spreadsheet and checked my e-mail. There were four unread messages from Nick.

Samantha, I have a meeting set up with the Luta factory this afternoon. I was unaware that Lussuria was an extension of Luta's production. I will keep you posted. Regards, Nick Taylor.

Samantha, I won't be meeting with Luta after all. They are under investigation for producing merchandise that is not acceptable to export quality standards. Again, thank you for the recommendation.—Nick Taylor.

Samantha, If memory serves, you mentioned quality concerns when we last spoke. That last piece of information might prove interesting to your boss. I could be wrong but I believe his name is Loncar? —Nick

S, My initial sample collection of shoes has been flagged and is being inspected by customs. In order to focus on the shoe collection, I'm going to postpone any handbag ventures indefinitely.—N

No doubt Nick had been busy, but of all the information in my inbox, the e-mail that struck me the most was the last. He was halfway around the country pursuing his own passion, the production of his shoe collection, and yet he was researching factories for me. If his collection was indeed tied up in customs, and he had to deal with the Italian government to get it back on track, then I had no right to involve him further.

But Nick was right. I had to share this info with Detective Loncar. I called the police station.

As the phone rang, Mallory came into my office. She stood by my desk, clutching a large binder to her chest.

"I'll be just a second," I said to her.

"I'll wait." She sat in the chair across from my desk just as the detective answered. I watched Mallory open the binder and pretend to study a spreadsheet. She wasn't going anywhere.

"Hi—honey," I said. Pause. "I never got a chance to thank you for the flowers you sent to Heist."

There was silence on the other end of the call, and I couldn't tell whether Loncar knew who he was talking to. "If you keep sending me flowers, the other buyers around here are going to get jealous."

Mallory looked up at me and I smiled, pointed to the receiver, and mouthed the word "boyfriend." She looked back at her notebook.

"What's this about, Ms. Kidd?"

Okay, good. He knew who I was. "I was wondering if you could meet me for lunch? I have a surprise for you."

Mallory stood up and left. I turned away from the door and dropped my voice. "I'm sorry. The walls have ears."

"Ms. Kidd, not that I don't enjoy your company, but if you have something to tell me, then tell me."

"You know what I could do? Write notes on a brown paper bag and throw them out in the trash can at the edge of the Heist parking lot, say, around two? You could pretend you're going through the trash and take my notes—"

"Two o'clock. Heist. I'll meet you there."

"I think my plan's more covert."

"Is there a place to sit?"

"Yes, but that's not the point."

"Ms. Kidd, I'll expect you to meet me at two o'clock, Heist parking lot, with whatever information you have for me. Is that clear?"

"Crystal."

FOR THE NEXT few hours I kept myself busy with the actual functions of being Heist's buyer: familiarizing myself with the rest of the assortment, reviewing the seasonal budgets, and reading countless e-mails dictating the company's position on color, trend, accessories, and silhouettes. Where Tradava had seemed to use the throw-spaghetti-at-the-wall approach to merchandising—buy a little of everything and see what sells—Heist had a clear vision of who their customer was and how they expected her to dress for the upcoming season.

Mallory nibbled on carrots from a plastic baggie in her office, the occasional snap, and subsequent series of crunches the only sound except for the click of her mouse. I was surprised she didn't take a lunch break, until it occurred to me that maybe she didn't want to leave me alone in the office.

At five till two I picked up my handbag and left the office. Detective Loncar was in his car, drinking from a red aluminum travel mug with Kutztown University's logo on the outside. He got out of the car before I had a chance to tap on his window.

"Hi, Detective. Are you hungry? Can I buy you lunch?"

"Ms. Kidd, you said you had information for me?"

"Oh, yes, sure. There's a pizza place at the other end of the strip mall. Are you sure you don't want to talk there? It's my lunch break."

He stared at me.

"I guess you already ate." I sat next to him, hoping my stomach wouldn't growl during our meeting. "So here's the thing. Kyle Trent gave me a spreadsheet from Tradava for this handbag business, Vongole. When I got into the store, I looked at the same information for the business at Heist. It's not easy to understand someone else's spreadsheet, but once I figured it out, I realized there's a huge discrepancy in how Vongole sells to each store."

"I'm no retailer, but it seems to me it's up to each store to determine how to run their business."

"Under normal circumstances, I'd agree. Only, this isn't normal, you know? The buyer here was murdered. So I'm thinking maybe it's about business."

"Do you have these spreadsheets with you?"

"Um—no. I will, though, in five to seven business days."

Loncar's forehead wrinkled.

"Never mind that. I shouldn't even have the spreadsheet for Tradava. The important thing is that Tradava is showing a six-figure loss on the Vongole handbag line while Heist is showing a profit. For some reason, Heist doesn't factor in freight, theft, or markdowns. Doesn't that seem weird to you?"

"I'm sure this means something to somebody, but unless you tell me you found a note that says 'Kill Emily Hart because of Vongole handbags' I don't think it matters much to the case."

"No note. Not a note in sight."

"I've got means figured out, and opportunity," he said. "Now I'm looking for the motive."

"That's what I found! Listen to me," I said, slapping him on the arm for emphasis. As soon as I did, I froze, not sure if I'd overstepped my boundaries.

Loncar didn't move, didn't say a word.

I took a deep breath, and ticked points off on my fingers. "Here's how a retailer figures out their bottom line. They take their sales, and then they subtract the costs of doing business. Merchandise, markdowns, shipping and transportation costs, theft.

Like, if you had a lemonade stand. After you counted out what you made selling lemonade, you'd have to subtract out the cost of lemons, the gas you used driving to the store and back. If some kids from the neighborhood stole a pitcher when you weren't looking, that would be theft. If you started selling for $3 a cup and weren't moving it, you'd mark down to $2 a cup but that $1 would be a markdown. Are you following me?"

"I get the general concept."

"Heist doesn't use any of those expenses. For some reason, they don't pay for shipping, they don't mark down their merchandise, and nobody steals anything. But Tradava is the other way around, and they're showing a pretty big loss."

"What do you think this means, Ms. Kidd?"

"I don't know yet, but it's too big of a red flag to think it doesn't matter."

"You say Kyle Trent gave you the Tradava information?"

I nodded. "Last night. He invited me to his apartment."

"What time was this?"

I felt my eyes roll up for a second as I thought. "Let's see. I was at happy hour with Andi, then I went to the Tastee Freeze, and then I went to his house. Probably around seven."

"Did you stay there long?"

"No, only about ten, maybe fifteen minutes. He wasn't in very good shape."

"This information he gave you. Tradava would consider that confidential, wouldn't they?"

"Yes. He risked his job to give it to me."

The detective scribbled something in his small spiral-bound notebook, and tucked it back inside his wrinkled blazer. I fought the urge to suggest a local tailor who could make his suit fit better. It didn't seem like the time for fashion advice.

"Are you going to move on this?"

"Ms. Kidd, I appreciate the information." He clicked his ballpoint pen and stuck it into his breast pocket. "If you think of anything else, call."

I wasn't sure, but it sounded like he was less sincere than he'd been at the beginning of all this.

I grabbed a slice of pizza and went back to the office. Mallory had left a note taped to my phone that said she'd be back by quarter after three. I had seventeen minutes to snoop. I ate the pizza and used the remaining sixteen minutes (I was hungry!) to figure out Kyle's motivation. He'd cancelled Tradava orders based on quality issues. It seemed the new lot of available inventory wasn't up to Vongole's usual quality standards, and Belle's interest in pushing through orders quickly and stocking the shelves suggested she knew this.

It was a well-known fact in retail circles that salaries were only a portion of a vice president's income, but annual bonuses, based on statistical performances, were pretty lucrative. I pulled out a calculator and ran a few what-ifs. At the industry standard, Belle's possible bonus for the year was in the fifty-thousand dollar range.

Not too shabby.

And there was another perk in it for Belle. By bringing in the inventory—a seemingly unlimited supply of the hottest it-bag vendor—she could exceed the sales plan and secure her future at Heist. She'd be celebrated in social circles, a veritable celebrity among fashionistas. Andi had mentioned Belle's divorce. Belle was a ballsy woman, tough, and smart and driven. I wondered who'd divorced who in that scenario, if Belle's nature had been the reason for the split or the by-product of it. If she'd been left in the dust once, she wasn't going to allow that to happen again. By driving home the largest profits that Heist had seen, she would earn raises, bonuses, and stock options.

It all made sense. Kyle must have figured out Belle was manipulating the system for her own personal gain. He'd see Emily would be responsible if the strategy failed. It explained the fight Mallory had overheard, and the animosity between Kyle and Belle. Belle would have started the rumor about the two of them, causing a riff between Kyle and Emily, and giving herself the distance she needed. Regardless of business, Emily wouldn't have wanted to actively grow the Vongole business, which explained the note to Mallory. Belle must have ultimately determined Emily was a threat to her plan, and she eliminated that threat the night of the gala. Nobody would have questioned her presence on the selling floor of Heist because she was the general manager.

And the next day, Belle would have rushed to secure the last-minute orders with Andi before anybody could ask questions.

I glanced at the clock on my computer. I had about seven minutes before Mallory would return, seven minutes to call Detective Loncar. Seven minutes, as long as Mallory didn't come back early.

I made the call. "Detective, I think I figured it out."

"Make it fast," he barked. "We got some information of our own."

"Belle DuChamp—she's the one. She—" I looked up as Mallory entered my office and passed through to her own. I lowered my voice. "She had the means and the motive and the opportunity.

That's what you needed, right? I have it all here. She had to be one who killed Emily."

"Ms. Kidd, thanks for playing detective with us, but we'll take it from here."

"So you're coming here to arrest her?" I asked.

"No, we're not coming there to arrest her."

"Why not?"

"Because Belle DuChamp's body was found in the parking lot outside of Tradava this morning."

"What are you saying? That she's above suspicion?"

"No, Ms. Kidd. I'm saying that Belle DuChamp is dead."

23

DONE

While I was apparently the first to know, word about the general manager's murder spread quickly through the store. A member of the store's senior staff came around to each of our offices, telling us the store was going to close for the day.

I collected my things and popped my head into Mallory's office. Her back was to me. "Mallory, are you ready to leave? I'll walk out with you."

When she turned my way, her eyes were red and angry. "I don't trust you. I don't know why anyone else won't listen to me, but I know you're up to something," she said, spittle flying from her lips.

The part of the unduly suspected employee had already been played once by me at Tradava, and I wasn't rushing to reprise my role at Heist.

"You're upset. Anyone would be. Let's walk out together."

Mallory took a few deep breaths and powdered her face from a compact that was slightly more orange than her natural skin tone.

"Leave me alone," she said, and clicked the compact shut.

I walked through the store, past the handcuffed jeans and pile of shoes with the mannequin inside staring out. I couldn't help wondering how real events were going to affect the future of the store that proclaimed its prices were criminal.

It wasn't until I reached the parking lot that I remembered Dante had dropped me off. I called him. "I need a ride home."

"Be right there," he said.

When Dante's motorcycle blazed into the parking lot and stopped in front of me, I straddled the seat and buckled the spare helmet over my head. And when we reached my house and I saw a black and white sitting in my driveway, I thought about telling him I'd changed my mind about us heading to Jersey.

Detective Loncar sat on my front porch with two younger men in uniform. Dante let the bike idle behind the cruiser before I hopped off the back.

"You want me to stay?"

"This doesn't concern you," I said.

"It concerns you?"

"It shouldn't, but it does."

"I'm coming with you." He turned the ignition off.

"You're waiting outside."

We crossed the yard to the porch. "Detective," I said cordially, nodding once while freaking out inside.

"Ms. Kidd, we need to talk to you."

"Okay, I'll just be a second," I said, fumbling with the keys to unlock the front door.

"Ms. Kidd, there was a shootout in the Tradava parking lot last night."

"I wasn't anywhere near Tradava last night."

"Nobody said you were." He folded his hands in front of him but pointed his index finger and thumb out like a shadow-puppet of a gun. "You've been forthcoming with information regarding Heist, Tradava, and the recent murder of Emily Hart."

"I have more to tell you too."

Loncar cut me off. "We appreciate your help, but we have a suspect in custody."

"Will you tell me who you arrested?"

"No."

"So that's it? No more flowers at work?"

"No more work. You're done at Heist."

"But Tony Simms hired me to do a job."

"Mr. Simms hired you to help figure out why his handbag buyer was murdered. That question's been answered. Thank you for your help." He held a hand out to formalize the end of our working relationship.

"What about the poison?" I asked suddenly.

"What?"

"The poison? From the restaurant? I brought you samples from takeout? My cat?" My voice rose with each question.

Detective Loncar retracted his hand. "The mushrooms they used in the truffle butter were poisonous. Somehow the supplier got a few of the bad kind mixed in with the regular delivery. They're in the process of changing their supplier, and we can't pinpoint whether the bad mushrooms came from the old delivery or the new one. Unfortunate accident. Couple of people got sick—nothing serious. They tossed their supply and started fresh. No truffle butter for the restaurant for awhile."

"But my cat and my friend—"

"You shouldn't be feeding your cat human food. Your friend is a different story. No one else reported passing out. Maybe she should eat more."

This time the detective let well more than a minute of silence pass before he offered his handshake and left with the uniformed officers. I didn't know what I expected from working with him, but it was more than this—and more than this and two bouquets of surveillance flowers too. I shook his hand, but the voice inside my head screamed, *This isn't over!*

I was scared the voice was right.

Dante followed me into my kitchen. The light on my machine blinked.

"Can you wait out front?" I asked. "I don't want you to hear my messages."

I hit the playback button the second the screen door slammed.

Beep: "Sam, it's Eddie. Call me."

Beep: "Sam, where are you? It's Eddie."

Beep: "Dude, you're freaking me out."

Beep: "You didn't have something to do with this, did you?"

Beep: "Are you okay?"

Beep: "I'm calling the cops."

It's nice to be loved.

I called Eddie. He answered on the first ring. "I'm fine, and I didn't do anything," I said.

"But you know about Kyle?"

"I know about Belle. What happened to Kyle?"

"The police arrested him half an hour ago."

24

∽

STARING AT THE SHEETS

he news sucked the wind out of me. The phone clattered to the floor, and I reached for the edges of the counter to steady myself. "Dante?" I called out.

He ran inside and guided me to a chair. "Put your head down," he instructed, his hand hot on the back of my head.

I bent forward and held my head in my hands, trying to shake the sound of voices in the distance. Then I realized the phone hadn't disconnected when it landed on the floor and Eddie was still talking.

Dante noticed it too. He scooped up the phone and said, "She'll call you back."

"Dante, is Cat still going stir crazy?"

He nodded.

"You think she'd like to come over?"

For three days I did little more than sleep. There were two lessons to be learned from my short time at Heist:

a) Love doesn't conquer all, and

b) I was borderline unemployable.

Twice a day my friends checked up on me. At first I tried to make small talk, but it didn't last. I dug into the pile of discarded clothes on the floor and pulled out a black polyester tunic with green and yellow trees embroidered on it. There was a hard spot on the right thigh where someone had accidentally melted it with a cigarette back when flammable polyester clothes were in style. You didn't find cigarette holes in clothes anymore. Those were simpler times.

It was like my life. Moving to Ribbon had been about giving up the pressures of a job I knew I could do in order to retrace the steps of my life and figure out what it was I was meant to do. I hadn't sought out the handbag buyer job at Heist; the job had found me. I'd been in a vulnerable enough position that I took it. And now, I was back where I had started: unhappy and unemployed.

It wasn't the crimes that left me unsettled either, though they didn't help. It was the feeling of failing, repeatedly, that made me sick to my stomach. That's what kept me from joining my friends downstairs, even if they took turns staying at my house.

Cat brought me a tray of food on Friday. She tapped on the door. "Are you awake?" she asked softly. "I brought you grapes and cheese."

She carried the tray to the bed and sat it next to my leg. The weekend edition of *The Style Section,* the industry newspaper, was folded and tucked under a silver bud vase with a flower from the front yard. Logan stood up and walked over my knees to sniff the cheese. Cat held out her hand and set a kitty treat on the blanket. Logan lost interest in my cheese.

"You couldn't have known it was a crime of passion, Sam," Cat said. "Nobody would have believed it."

"It doesn't fit. Nobody ever mentioned Kyle being the jealous sort. I can't see him killing his fiancé. All I ever heard was how well they got along."

"Sometimes it's the ones you least expect."

"Sometimes ..." I said.

"Do you want to come downstairs and join us?"

"Not yet." I stared at the ceiling.

"Do you want me to stay?"

"No, I'd rather be alone."

EDDIE DELIVERED MY tray on Saturday, bringing his homemade macaroni and cheese. An origami monster sat on the corner by a glass of lemonade.

"Dude, time to rise and shine." He set the tray on the foot of the bed and pulled the cord on the curtains, flooding the room with unwelcome sunlight.

"I don't want to rise and shine."

"Then consider taking a shower."

I rubbed my eyes and blinked a few times to adjust to the brightness. Eddie fluffed a pillow from the chaise lounge that sat in the corner and rearranged the frames lining the top of my dresser. He picked up the pearls I'd worn to work earlier that week and tucked them into my jewelry box, along with a couple errant earrings.

"The police really arrested Kyle?" I asked.

He turned to me. "Seems that way."

"But he was your friend."

"Sometimes you think you know people, but you don't really know them at all." He picked up yesterday's pajamas and tossed them into the hamper. A pair of my panties were on the floor in front of it. He stood there looking at them before shutting the hamper, leaving them where they were.

"Dude, you can't stay in bed forever."

"I'm not ready to acknowledge what a colossal mess my life is."

He looked up. "Seems to me if you were really 'just a buyer for Heist' like you keep telling me, nothing's really changed. You get up, you go to work, you do your job. Only you're acting like you don't have a job to go to. Why is that? Why would Kyle's homicidal tendencies have anything to do with your job as buyer for Heist? As far as I know, you haven't even called in sick for the past two days. And nobody's been calling here looking for you either."

He stood in the doorway, one hand on the doorknob. Inside, I knew if I said I wanted to tell him everything that had been going on, he'd sit on the edge of the bed and listen. He'd forgive me for not confiding in him all along. He'd be what I needed. A friend.

Only I couldn't. Not yet. I didn't believe Kyle was guilty. And if I was right, that meant this wasn't over.

"I don't know what you want to hear," I said.

We looked at each other for a few more seconds before he let himself out of the room. I pulled the curtains shut, took a half-hour-long shower, and crawled back into bed. There was something I wasn't seeing, and I needed to take notes, to reason it out.

I opened the drawer to my nightstand and pulled out a wad of take-out menus I'd moved from the kitchen in an effort to cut down on my junk food delivery habit. I found a Sharpie on the floor by the closet and wrote the names of each player on top of the listings over my favorite comfort foods: Kyle Trent, Tony Simms, Andi Holloway, Mallory George, Belle DuChamp, Emily Hart. I rearranged the menus in different order, trying to see the connection between them but succeeded only in giving myself a craving for cheap Chinese food.

The house remained silent for the rest of the night. I stared at the ceiling. Eddie was right. I couldn't stay in bed forever. I pushed the covers back and opened the bedroom door. The serving tray sat on the floor. An Atomic Fireball rested in the middle of a small, white saucer, next to a note. *It's just you and me.*

I belted my silk kimono and went downstairs.

"Hello?" I called.

"The kids went to get something to eat," Dante said. He folded a newspaper on his lap.

"I got tired of staring at the sheets."

He held out the newspaper. "Want to read the details?"

"Sure," I said, taking the bundle. I felt him watching as I unrolled it and scanned the front-page headlines of the *Ribbon Eagle* and *Ribbon Times* respectively: "Respected Businessman Endangers Life in Hostage Situation," and "Fatal Showdown at Tradava Ends Murder Investigation."

I went with the Times article first. It detailed Belle DuChamp's visit to Tradava and her suspected love triangle with Kyle Trent and Emily Hart. "Ironically, the designer handbag collection that brought these three people together will most likely go bankrupt. Tradava has already distanced themselves from Vongole and, according to a statement from Simms, Heist will remain closed indefinitely to restructure their business model."

I flipped open the *Ribbon Eagle* and scanned the newsprint, a basic afternoon rehash of the information that had appeared in the *Times*. "Sources close to DuChamp and Trent confirm their business relationship but maintain the couple kept their private dalliances private. According to local entrepreneur Tony Simms, 'Belle DuChamp was a smart woman, too smart to risk her career for a one-night stand.' Other sources report when Trent proclaimed his love for DuChamp, she denied reciprocating those feelings, and threatened to turn him in. People were concerned for her safety. 'I confronted him and told him to back down, to leave her alone, but he was too upset. He pulled a gun and shot Belle. I was able to detain him until the police arrived.' "

It was hard to fit these pieces of the puzzle into the thought patterns I'd been playing with for the past few days. First Emily met Kyle. Then he killed her. He professed love for Belle and she denied him. When he tried to kill her too, Tony Simms saved the day.

I still didn't like it.

"Dante? When did you say Cat and Eddie would be back?"

"About five."

"Do you think you could give me about an hour alone?" He studied my face. "I want to take a long shower and make a couple of phone calls to tell everyone I'm okay."

"If that's what you need." He left with not much more than a good-bye, his motorcycle kicking up gravel as he peeled out of the driveway.

True to my word, I made those calls. To my parents in California. To my sister in Virginia. To Nick in Italy. Nobody answered. I left messages for all.

And then I called Tony Simms.

I needed to know what was to become of my future at Heist, though with a three-day tenure, my imagination had already served me walking papers.

I caught Tony in his office and asked him to come to my house. He agreed to come in about twenty minutes. It wasn't a random amount of time, it was the minimum I required to look at least part human. Eighteen-and-a-half minutes later, dressed in the black pantsuit Heist had delivered earlier in the week, I descended the stairs as a silver BMW pulled into my driveway. I didn't need to see the vanity plates to know it was the store owner.

My cell phone buzzed with a new text message from Dante: *10 more min.* Here's hoping Tony Simms could talk fast.

I held the door open for him before he had a chance to ring the bell.

"I heard about what happened. I'm sorry," I said.

"We're all sorry. Thank you."

I was about to invite him to sit in my living room but changed my mind and had him follow me to the dining room. We sat in opposite chairs across the table from each other. A small wooden napkin holder my sister had made in seventh grade sat between us, holding a stack of plain white paper napkins. Tony turned down my offer of iced tea, so I sipped my own while he spoke.

"Samantha, we're going to close down the store indefinitely. Regroup and restructure. If we intend to have a future in Ribbon, we need to let the bad publicity pass. The other Heist stores shouldn't be hurt by the press; in fact, it might help them. But that means we no longer need your services. In light of the recent deaths connected to Vongole, we are dropping their line. We're also moving the buying offices for all of Heist from each individual store to a central office in Philadelphia. Thank you for taking on such an important role at the store."

"It was nothing," I said.

"We're still planning on hosting the dedication at I-FAD, and I'd like you to be there. Can you do that?"

"You just said I don't work for the store anymore."

"I need you to be there as an ambassador of Heist. A liaison between the store and the college."

"What about Nora?"

"She'll be there too, but I need someone with your skill set to back me up. Someone who knows the score."

"Wouldn't it be better to have more tenured people from Heist there instead of me?"

"I'll have plenty of tenured people there. You represent the kind of new Heist blood we want. If you wanted to move to Philadelphia, I'd find a place for you in the center city store. But since you don't, consider this your last job assignment. Representing the store. You can do that, can't you?"

"Sure. Yes. I can do that." I felt backed into a corner.

He pulled an envelope out of a pocket inside his suit jacket and slid it across the table. "Consider this payment for your time at Heist."

I didn't want to look in the envelope because, after all I'd done, I didn't know if I could allow myself to accept it. I didn't want to know what I was turning down. I pushed the envelope back.

"You've more than earned it," he said. "I've written a letter of recommendation for you should you choose to pursue employment elsewhere in Ribbon. I understand you've had difficulty holding on to a job around town, and you're not to be faulted for what happened. You were no more involved in the Vongole situation than I was."

A letter of recommendation from a Tony Simms would go a long way in offsetting my career cooties. He stood and held out a hand.

"Samantha Kidd, I enjoyed having you on the payroll."

I stood too. "Tony Simms," I mimicked, "I enjoyed being there." We shook hands, me finally matching his two-pump handshake.

"If there's anything else I can do for you, don't hesitate to call." He held out his business card. I thanked him for the offer and watched him walk away.

See, now that should make me feel good. Right? A noted businessman recognized my worth to the tune of—I glanced in the envelope he'd left behind—wow.

That was a lot of cash.

I pulled the stack of bills from the envelope and counted ten thousand dollars in hundreds. There had to be some kind of mistake. I'd worked at the store for three days, and no way had I earned that kind of dough. Even if I had put myself at risk by working with a couple of greedy, homicidal sex-fiends, if the papers were to be believed.

I ran to the door with the cash in my hand to see if I could catch Tony and ask if this was a mistake. Instead, Dante stood on my doorstep. I put my hand behind my back.

"Give me a minute," I said, and shut the door in his face.

I put the money inside the front cover of the Halston biography on the coffee table, but the cover wouldn't close. I moved it to the back of the book, ignoring the fact that the book was no longer flat.

"Come on in," I said, as though slamming the door in his face was routine.

"Got your mail. Couple of days' worth." He held a business-sized envelope between his fingers but pulled it away when I reached for it. "Something addressed to your cat?"

I snatched the envelope from Dante and tore it open. Two recaps, just like I remembered. I would have done better to mail the recaps to the cops. If nothing else, it would have been evidence that I was working with them, but who was to know that this whole thing would go down before I could offer up my discoveries?

Still, I called Detective Loncar. "Hi Detective, Samantha Kidd here."

"Ms. Kidd, like I told you, we're all done here. No need for you to keep checking in with us."

"I know. I just, I have that information you needed. The spreadsheets I told you about? Remember, Kyle Trent gave them to me before he . . . you know . . . and I thought it might be important."

"You can bring them by if you want, but we already got a witness and a pretty solid case against him."

"Did he confess?"

"Do you have anything else to tell me?"

"You'd look good in blue," I said.

The detective hung up on me without saying good-bye. I stared at the recaps, wondering if Kyle had been playing me when he gave me this info. Maybe he'd been the one trailing the breadcrumbs I'd been following.

I thought it through again. Kyle had killed Emily at Heist, probably minutes before he'd run into me in the handbag department. A crime of passion. I could have easily overheard something, or seen something, and that was one thing he didn't know. So he figured out a way to keep an eye on me. Plus, he was the one who fed me information about Belle. Once he confided in me about his engagement to Emily, I wrote him off as a suspect. I never saw this one coming. And when I'd floated the rumors past Andi Holloway....

I'd forgotten about Andi. She had benefited financially from the apparent feud between Tradava and Heist's buyers, and she had a relationship with each of the buyers. In fact, even she said she didn't believe the rumor about Belle and Kyle. The romantic stories she'd told me about what Kyle had done for Emily when they were at market were the stuff of chick-lit novels, not murder mysteries. It didn't make sense.

Unless Kyle had been playing her too.

25

NOT A TOTALLY IN SIGHT

ante, I have to get out of the house. I'm going for a drive." I grabbed my keys but stopped before reaching the front door. "Is my car back to normal?" I asked.

He nodded.

I took off, only slightly surprised he didn't follow.

It was a warm spring day. The wind whipped through my curly hair, just what I needed to clear my mind. I snaked around a couple of suburban streets while deciding where I wanted to go, turning onto Perkiomen Avenue behind a delivery truck. I blasted the Go-Go's from my stereo and cruised a couple miles without a specific destination. I ended up in a parking space in front of the renovated building where Andi rented her Bag Lady offices. I entered the showroom and found Andi slumped in a chair surrounded by opened boxes of handbags.

"Andi?" I hopped to the side so I had a better view of her.

"Yes?" She spun her chair toward me. The normally peppy RockStar-fuelled woman was like a deflated balloon. "Oh, hi Samantha," she said, not standing up. "Did we have an appointment?" She stood awkwardly and used her instep to push one of the shipping boxes out of the way. Her eyes were bloodshot and puffy, and her nose was dry from too much dabbing with a tissue.

"I heard, and I thought I should ... I mean ..." Suddenly my visit seemed calculated and I didn't know what to say. "Are you okay?" It was the only sentence that felt right.

She slumped back into her chair.

I stepped around the boxes and sat across from her in silence.

"I don't get it. I just don't understand. It doesn't make sense. I've known Emily and Kyle forever. They seemed so in love. I thought they'd found it. Made me believe that I might find someone too, but not living this kind of life," she tossed a shiny red wallet on the table. "The only thing keeping me from a total breakdown is the Xanax I took this morning. I don't see it. I can't see him doing it. I know that's just denial speaking, but I completely, utterly, wholly can't see it."

She must be upset. Three adverbs and not a "totally" in sight.

My eyes strayed to the paperwork on the table. It was an invoice for the shipment she was unpacking, and the letterhead said Ace Trucking Company. I pointed to it.

"Did Vongole change their delivery service?"

She pulled the invoice toward herself but made no effort to hide it. "No, Ace delivers my samples. Simulated delivers the store's inventory." Her index finger had poked the invoice by the Ace Trucking Company logo, and she pushed it back and forth in a nervous gesture. "Only someone screwed up this time." She reached down to the box on the floor and pulled out a yellow patent leather clutch. It was the same one I'd drooled over when Mallory and I were standing in the showroom only days ago. "Here, take it."

"No, thanks," I said.

"Seriously. The factory screwed up and these clutches accidentally came in with my samples. I'm just going to end up selling them in a sample sale. I might be selling it all." She waved her hand around the showroom. "After Kyle and Emily and their association with Vongole, both stores are dropping the line to protect their reputations. I might as well cut ties too."

"How will that affect you?"

"I've been looking for a reason to cut back on my travel and try to have a real life. I can focus on my other vendors. Most of them are local." We both looked around her showroom at samples of striped cotton pajamas, sachets shaped like hearts trimmed in lace, and a collection of glass *objects d'art* shaped like hard candy. Vongole had been the shining star in her assortment.

I didn't know what else to say, so I hugged her and said good-bye. She insisted I take the yellow patent handbag, so I did. I could give it to Loncar as evidence. Then again, maybe I wouldn't.

I started the drive home and got caught behind a large delivery truck. Traffic was bad enough that I couldn't get past him. Through seventeen traffic lights I stared at his "How am I driving?" sticker until he pulled off the road into the Briquette Burger parking lot. That's when I noticed it was a Simulated truck. I called Nick with little regard for the Ribbon/Milan time conversion.

He answered on the third ring. "'Lo?"

"I just followed a Simulated truck and it's pulling into Briquette Burger. That's the trucking company that delivers the Vongole handbags. Don't you think that's weird?"

"S'mntha?"

"Hi, Nick. Sorry if I woke you, but I didn't know who else to call."

"Are you in trouble?" His words were becoming clearer as the suspicion of imminent danger to me hung somewhere over the Atlantic Ocean.

"A Simulated truck pulled into Briquette Burger. Why would he do that?"

He yawned. "Maybe he's hungry. Is that really why you called me?"

The way he phrased that question led me to believe that wasn't a very good reason for calling. "No, I just wanted to hear your voice."

"That's sweet." His breathing turned even.

"Nick?"

"Mnh."

"Go back to sleep."

I parked in the ten-minute takeout space next to the restaurant. The Simulated driver jumped down from the cab, went around back, and opened the doors. I couldn't see inside, but in a matter of minutes he'd removed three cardboard cartons and stacked them on a dolly. He pushed it to a door in the back of the restaurant. Minutes later he returned and repeated the routine.

Before he had a chance to push the second dolly load to the back door, I approached. "Can I talk to you a second?"

"Sure, little lady, whaddya want?" He uprighted the handcart and leaned against it.

"What are you delivering to this restaurant?"

He looked nervous.

"I mean, is this a regular stop for you?"

"Yeah. Restaurant supply stuff, for what it's worth."

"How long have you been delivering to Briquette Burger?"

"Couple of weeks now."

"Did you deliver some mushrooms here recently?"

"Why does everybody want to know about them mushrooms?" He pulled the mesh John Deere hat that had probably been standard issue when he got his trucker's license off his head, scratched his bald spot, and pulled the hat back over it. "We don't normally deliver produce, but when it came time to unload the delivery for this address, the crates were there."

"Doesn't Simulated deliver to Heist? The new department store?"

"Yeah, the owner's got us running all over town these days. Guess we're makin' him some money somehow."

"Who's your owner?"

"Local big shot. Tony Simms. Hey—you okay?"

The last question, I was most certain, had to do with the sudden bout of vertigo I felt at the mention of Tony's name.

"Yes, I'm fine. Thank you for your time."

I raced to the car where I'd left my cell phone in the cup holder. First call, Detective Loncar.

"Ms. Kidd, what do you want now?" He didn't seem happy to hear from me.

"Did you know Tony Simms owns Simulated Trucking?"

"Yes, Ms. Kidd. Tony Simms owns half of Ribbon."

"And that doesn't concern you?"

"That we have an entrepreneur in our midst? No, that doesn't concern me. Especially when he risked his life to come forward and pinpoint the murderer in a recent homicide investigation. Is that it?"

"Yes." I was about to hang up when I remembered the mushrooms. "Wait! Simulated was the trucking company that delivered the mushrooms too."

"Ms. Kidd." I could hear the lecture in his voice. "The Ribbon Police Department appreciates your interest in helping us. I would never want to say anything to deter you from working with us again in the future, but I think we got about all we need this time. Thank you for doing your civic duty."

The worst thing about cell phones is that there is absolutely no satisfaction in punching the hang-up button.

I called Nick again.

"Mmmmmmmh."

"Nick, it's Samantha. This is important. Are you awake?"

Silence, and then a grunt.

"Tony Simms owns Simulated Trucking. Don't you think that's weird?"

"Mmmmmh."

"Nick, I'm being serious. You're the only person who knows about what's been going on, and if we're going to do this relationship thing, then we need to be able to talk to each other. I need someone to talk to. Okay?"

He yawned audibly. "You want to know what I think? Maybe a homicide investigation isn't a good basis for a relationship. Good night, Kidd." He hung up before I had a chance to argue.

I threw my phone in my handbag and turned to my car. Dante stood next to it, arms crossed, flame tattoos in full display.

"Did I hear you're looking for someone to talk to?"

26

FAKE-BUSTING

*D*ante followed me back to my house and parked his motorcycle in the driveway behind my car. Neither of us said a word until we were inside the living room. I shared the gray flannel sofa with Logan. Dante took one of the black and white chairs.

"Here's what's really been going on," I said. "Tony Simms owns Heist, and when he offered me the job, he said, 'Heist cannot fail.' And, aside from the way he produced ID with my name and picture on it, I remember his eyes boring through me when he said that. Now, he's an intense man, I know that." I held up a palm to stop Dante from interrupting me. "And he's a successful man. But don't you think it's weird that he's connected to everything that's going south? Heist, Vongole, Simulated Trucking, the mushrooms that poisoned Cat and Logan?"

Dante leaned forward. "Keep going."

"Simms had big plans for Heist, which is why he wooed a very successful general manager away from Tradava to run it. Think about it: he owns the store, and he owns the fleet of trucks that deliver to the store. If Heist had been successful in its initial opening, they would have put a big dent in Tradava's business."

"And with their prices, they could have continued with the momentum long after opening too."

"Right. Their entire success was staked on their pricing structure." I pulled the two Vongole reports out of a folder. "Kyle Trent gave me these."

Dante leaned back and held his hands in front of him. "I'm not a spreadsheet guy."

I laid them on the table facing him just in case the red numbers made him curious. "The basic components of a product's profitability are the same from any retailer. This is Tradava's recap of the Vongole business. They're showing close to a hundred and seventy-five thousand dollar loss in one season, while Heist was projecting a two hundred thousand dollar margin surplus off discounted prices. It doesn't make sense."

"Could Tradava be mismanaging their business?"

"Vongole sold the same amount of merchandise to both Heist and Tradava, but Heist got a 40 percent discount off of the cost of the merchandise. They only passed 30 percent of that on to the customers, so they made more money on every bag that was sold than Tradava did. What I can't figure out is why Tradava can't move their inventory at 50 percent off." I leaned back against the flannel sofa. Logan climbed onto the afghan and sat behind my head. He flicked his tail, and it swatted my ear.

"When I went to Tradava the other day, there was this giant table filled with marked-down bags. Something about that pile of markdowns was off. The bags looked cheap."

"Maybe it's the merchandising?" Dante asked.

I shook my head.

"You have another theory?"

"I think the sample bags are high quality, and the bags at Tradava aren't. That's why Kyle wanted to cancel the Vongole orders. He told me the quality suffered when their business exploded."

"What about Heist?"

"The assistant buyer said something interesting. Four months ago, Vongole didn't have enough merchandise to fill their orders. Now the store is overflowing with merchandise."

I sat back, waiting to see if Dante was going to connect the dots in the same manner that I had earlier, or if I'd been reasoning a murder investigation on a sleep deprived mind and a handbag-hoarding mentality. "I think the quality suffered because the bags are being mass produced with poor-quality leathers."

"You think the bags at Heist are knockoffs."

I nodded. "I found out today that Acc Trucking Company delivers the samples to the showroom, but Simulated delivers the inventory to the store. At least to Heist."

"So there's a different trucking company that carries inventory, which could mean the stock production comes from somewhere other than the sample production." Dante followed along.

"And look at this." I pulled my yellow patent leather clutch out from inside a dingy white pillowcase where I'd kept it wrapped since coming home.

The front door opened and Eddie and Cat walked in. I had an idea. "Cat, what do you think of my new handbag?" I held the yellow patent leather clutch out to her.

She turned it over in her hands, opened up the magnetic closure, checked the lining, sniffed inside it, and snapped it shut.

"I hope you didn't pay too much for this," she said. "It's a fake. A good one, but still."

"Is that your opinion?" Dante asked.

"It's a fact." She handed the bag back to me. "I'm surprised you couldn't tell."

"I could," I said.

Dante crossed his arms over his chest and Eddie leaned forward.

"How can you be so sure?" Eddie asked.

Cat leaned on the arm of the chair Dante sat in, swinging her left foot back and forth. The heel of her bottle-green bootie bounced off the worn fabric on the side.

I looked at her, not sure which of us would answer.

"Take it away, Sam," she said.

I opened the bag. "Look, the lining is pink. Vongole makes it a point to only line their bags with the literal opposite color on the color wheel. A yellow bag would be lined in purple. A red bag would be lined in green. A blue bag would be lined in orange."

"What about a pink bag?" Dante asked.

"Any bag that isn't a primary or secondary color is lined in powder-blue suede," I said, thinking of the black and white bag I saw at Tradava.

"You're hanging your entire assessment on the color of their lining?" Eddie asked. Dante stood up and went into the kitchen. I stared at his back and considered a comment about his lack of enthusiasm for my fake-busting skills.

"I'm not done. See, the label is metal. Vongole's labels are all silver, and they're sterling silver at that. If you look closely, you can always see the '925' stamp on real silver, and it's not here. And the pull-tab along the zipper closure is too short. It's supposed to be six inches long."

"How do you know that's not six inches? Looks close."

I turned the Halston book upside down and pulled a flattened hundred-dollar bill from the back. I held it next to the pull-tab. The tab ended right around the first zero on the crisp green bill. "US Currency is six inches long."

"What's this all about, Sam?" Cat asked.

"The cops arrested the wrong guy," I said.

Eddie was still staring at the book on Halston (or more likely at the bulge where the stack of hundreds were inside the book on Halston). He folded his hands across the Union Jack on the front of his T-shirt. "It sounds good enough to us, but I think you're going to need more to make the detective take you seriously. Like proof from the factory."

"Nick checked into the two factories that claim to produce Vongole."

"Vongole doesn't have two factories. Their bags are produced at Luta," Cat said.

"That's what I was told when I started. Basics from Luta and fashion from Lussuria. But when Nick heard his factory couldn't produce his samples he checked out these two." I waited a couple of seconds for effect. "Lussuria doesn't even exist."

"So Nick's been helping you all along?" Eddie asked with surprise. "What does he think about your current theory?"

I thought about Nick's reluctance to keep talking about the homicides. "He thinks it's time I left it to the cops." I looked from face to face, trying to decipher their thoughts.

Dante returned from the kitchen with a steaming mug of coffee. "Does this guy even know you?"

Eddie and Cat left, but Dante stayed behind. I dug through the newspapers and mail piling up on my kitchen table and found Tony Simms' business card. Office, home, and cell numbers were listed below his name. I went with cell, hoping it was the easiest way to catch him.

"Tony Simms," he answered.

"Mr., um, Tony, this is Samantha Kidd."

"Samantha Kidd. I got two minutes."

"I, um ..." This was no way to sound believable to a businessman. I took a deep breath and cleared my throat and matched his cadence. "I don't think I can make the college dedication."

"Impossible! I need you there. We've already covered this. Liaison to the store, goodwill. I thought I made myself clear."

I thought about the money in the Halston book. "You did."

"Good. The dedication is at eight. Meet me there at seven."

"But—"

"Time's up. See you at the college." He disconnected, leaving me with more questions than I'd started with and fewer opportunities for escape.

"What was that about?" Dante asked.

"The college is dedicating a lecture hall to Tony Simms next week. He asked me to go to represent the store, or act as a liaison to the store, or something like that. I tried to cancel, but he won't listen."

"Tell me again what he said when he offered you a job."

"That he valued my unique skill set."

"So that's it." He leaned back against the sofa, knees apart and wrists resting on his lap. "You're the one link between all these people. He didn't hire you to investigate from the inside. He needed a shortcut. He asked you to keep an eye on everybody else, but he's the one keeping an eye on you."

27

TALK, SCHMALK

*D*ante left with the others and I suddenly felt very much alone. If I was right, and the killer was still out there, I was going to have to figure out a way to prove that and figure out a way to keep myself in one piece too. That was a tall order for someone in my size seven shoes. I didn't want to be a part of this anymore. It wasn't fun, it wasn't fulfilling, and it might get me dead.

In short, I wanted out.

I needed another person close to the situation, another ace. Nick wasn't due to come home for another two weeks and based on our most recent conversation, I probably shouldn't count on his willingness to discuss it. Then I remembered the way Andi had looked at Kyle on her cell phone picture. There was no way she believed him to be guilty, and if I wasn't mistaken, that look spoke volumes of her feelings, even if she'd chosen not to speak of those feelings out loud. I had a good sense that I knew where to find her too.

I parked in the lot outside the bar. Her shiny black Miata was parked by the front door. When I entered I scanned the interior. There she was, perched on a spinning barstool, dangling a maraschino cherry and cleavage in front of the twenty-something mixologist. Maybe I'd been wrong. She didn't look like the kind of woman pining away over another woman's man.

"What'll it be?" the bartender asked. Andi spun on her chair and recognition hit.

"Girlfriend!" she shouted, and hopped—or should I say slipped, because she didn't seem to have control of her faculties enough to hop—off the barstool. She threw her arms around me.

I hugged her back, knowing I had to play into our BFF routine again. "I'll have what she's having," I said.

"RockStar and pomegranate vodka martini?" the bartender said.

"You go, girl!" she proclaimed, struggling to right herself on the stool.

The bartender set a frothy pink drink in front of me and Andi clinked my glass. "You are so smart. Hey, Steve, this is Samantha, and she's, like, the smartest buyer in all of Ribbon. No! In all of Pennsylvania. No, wait! In the whole tri-state area!"

Not that I didn't enjoy the compliments, but I was starting to wonder if I really had it in me to pull Andi out of this moment of escapism and drag her back to reality and her unspoken love for a man suspected of killing the last two women he'd been involved with.

"Um, Andi, have you read the news today?"

"Screw the news. Have a drinkie!" She picked up her glass, shook the ice cubes around, and drained what was left. I caught

Steve's expression. He was watching her with interest too. Only our interests were obviously of different natures.

I nursed my drink while she started on another that had appeared before her without even ordering. Steve leaned in front of her. "That one's on the house."

"Ohh, honey, you know the way to my ..." She dragged her finger over her lower lip and let the tip draw a line down her neckline. This was going nowhere fast. There was no way I was going to have a real, meaningful conversation with her tonight.

"Andi, when's a good time to talk?"

"Talk, shmalk. Let's party!"

"Seriously. I mean, I need to have a serious talk with you."

"Screw serious! I just wanna have fun tonight! No worries! You with me?" she asked Steve the bartender.

He picked up an ice cube and tossed it down her cleavage.

"Oooohh! You nasty boy. Now who's going to help me fish that out of there?"

I couldn't take any more of this. I unfolded a Bud Light napkin and pulled a pen from my handbag. I jotted my cell phone number down after my name and folded it carefully. When she wasn't looking I tucked it into her handbag. She was too preoccupied to notice.

I opened my fake Vongole clutch and pulled out my keys. When I looked up, I spotted a woman with a jet black bob sitting in the corner booth. It was my assistant buyer, Mallory George. She buried her head in a large menu, but I wasn't fooled. She'd been watching me from the second I'd walked in.

The sun was halfway visible above the horizon as I drove home. Was it possible that I was making too much of situation that was already resolved? No. Definitely not. Two people were dead, and something was still not right. And just when I thought I was out on my own, I was pulled back in for the dedication at I-FAD. Heist was like the retail mafia. And even the envelope of money I'd moved from the Halston biography to between my mattress and box spring did nothing to comfort me.

The lights were on at Nora's house. I parked in my driveway and crossed the lawn, pushing a couple of crabapples out of my path. "I've been expecting you," she said, holding the door open.

She wore a Mercersburg sweatshirt pulled over a turtleneck and jeans. Blucher moccasins, standard issue at most prep schools, adorned her feet, and a stained white cotton apron dangled loosely over her clothes. She was the best candidate I'd ever seen for a makeover, but if given the chance, I wouldn't change a thing. Some people just know who they are.

"I saw you through the window. I was hoping you were heading my way. Care to test out a new recipe?"

"Sure." I followed her to the kitchen. Her house was laid out much like my own if you held the floor plan up to a mirror. She used an ice cream scoop to measure out a perfectly round dollop of rice into a bowl and scooped something vaguely orange over it. "Thai curry. It might be a little spicy. Want some bean sprouts?"

She handed me a fork and set a bowl of sprouts on the counter. I scooted up onto one of her bar stools and dug a forkful into my mouth. Exotic flavors of basil and coconut hit me a split second before the heat.

"Water?" I choked out.

"Milk will be better. Is it hot? I wasn't sure. I may have added too much liquid pepper. You're okay with mushrooms, right?" She filled a glass with milk from the refrigerator and handed it to me. I drained it and toyed my fork around in the rice for a while, not sure if I wanted any more.

"Nora, with everything that's been happening around town, do you think it's good timing for the dedication at I-FAD? Don't you think it should be postponed?"

"Tony was on the fence, but I convinced him to go for it."

"He was going to cancel?"

"He was concerned for everybody's safety. I think it's wise that he arranged extra security."

"Detective Loncar?"

"The detective on the Hart case? No. Well, I didn't ask for him specifically. The college is hiring extra security officers to work for the night, Heist security guards will be there, and we'll have a large presence of campus police. Between that contest and the matters at Heist, there's bound to be some kind of activism. I admire that the students want something to protest, because it's good to stand up for things, but in the event their activities get out of hand, someone's got to be there to keep things under control."

"You think the students are going to riot against Tony Simms?"

She laughed. "I've gotten beyond the age when I can predict what the students are going to do. What I do know is that several of the students participated in the promotional activities of the Heist contest and were not happy when there was no winner announced. You know, Simms owned each of the landmarks mentioned in the contest, and in each case there was really no chance for anyone to actually win."

"My team won. We swapped the Puccetti statue for a fake."

A knowing smile crept onto Nora's face. "Wait here," she said. I sampled another scoop of curry after she scaled the stairs, and refilled my glass with water to wash it down. The water ignited the heat in my mouth, and I ran to her fridge for milk.

When I turned back around she was coming down the stairs holding a locked metal strongbox. She set it on the counter and pulled on a pair of white gloves, the kind a magician wears while waving his hands as distraction before the voila! moment. She spun the dial on the padlock until it opened, and pulled out a bundle wrapped in white sheets. She unwound the fabric and exposed a wooden statue that bore striking resemblance to the one I'd swiped from the college only a week before. I swallowed a mouthful of milk in one gulp and pounded on my chest until the pain went away. She pulled the statue away from me to avoid me from tainting it with DNA evidence.

"This is the real Puccetti." She kept one hand on the base of the man while the other gently patted him on the head.

"You've had this one the whole time?"

"Yes." She kept a finger on the head of the statue and spun him around to face her. "It's been killing me not to tell you."

"But Tony Simms told me we'd won the contest. In fact, the team at Heist said one team succeeded in pulling off the stunt, and Simms said he would see to it that my team was paid the prize money. Why would he say that if we didn't actually steal the original like the contest wanted?"

Nora's eyes flicked from my face to my bowl of curry, now virtually untouched. "Come into the living room with me. I can finally tell you the backstory."

28

THE REAL MCCOY

*H*eist wanted a massive publicity event," Nora said. "One that would have a viral word-of-mouth feel that would energize shoppers. The idea was to be so different from what this town has seen that it would instantly feel cool."

"How do you know all this?"

"Once Simms heard the concept from the PR manager, he wanted to go full force with the idea. Originally it was a much smaller scale, like a scavenger hunt, but Simms knew he had the unique option of using his own holdings around Ribbon as the bait, and that would accomplish two things. He'd instantly connect Heist with landmarks from Ribbon, and he'd get the kind of publicity he wanted."

"So Tony owned all of the prizes," I said mostly to myself.

"The Puccetti has been in his family for generations. His father donated it to the Philadelphia Museum of Art decades ago. It's been at I-FAD for about five years now. There was a nice amount of publicity that went into the exhibit, and he wanted to leverage that publicity by naming the statue as one of the objects for the contest."

"I get it. He fooled the public by using a fake at the museum, so the real one was never at risk."

"That's when I came in. The college appointed me keeper of the real statue. No one was ever going to know."

"Nora, that statue has to be worth millions. You kept it in your house?"

"Of course not! It's been in my safety deposit box. Just yesterday Tony asked me to make sure it was back in place for the dedication. I picked it up today and am delivering it to the school tomorrow morning."

"Who else knew the statue had been replaced with a fake?"

"Simms, the PR manager of Heist, the dean of the college, and me. We didn't tell campus police because we wanted them to take the protection of the statue seriously. When you stole it, they came to my house to deliver the news."

"We saw them that night. We were celebrating, at least we were until we heard the sirens. We thought they were coming for us."

"They weren't happy when they heard they'd been duped."

I peered closely at the little wooden man on her counter. "So that's the real McQueen."

"Don't you mean McCoy?"

"We called him—never mind."

"For what it's worth, yours spooked a lot of people. You must know some talented people to have come up with a knockoff that good on such short notice."

I did. I thought back to Dante, showing up at my meeting with a folder of surveillance photos of the statue, and Eddie, who'd taken those photos and made the fake. I remembered our assignments:

Cat as executive professor, Dante as security guard, me as undercover student. Undercover grad student.

"You can't repeat any of this, you know," she said. "I shouldn't have told you at all, but I've wanted to tell you the truth since you showed up at the Pilferer's Ball with our fake."

My mind was abuzz. In addition to the people I'd been watching at Heist, Nora's information now made me think I-FAD could be involved. She'd been at the party, so who else? The killer, who had bashed Emily Hart's head with Eddie's copy of the Puccetti statue, would most likely be at the dedication. And while the press had reported about the murders, news of the statue as weapon had been kept quiet. The only people who knew were those in the inner circle: my friends, colleagues, and the killer. Whether or not the killer knew the statue would be at the dedication was one thing, but if he—or she—knew what I now knew, he—or she—would expect the real statue to be in place.

I was short on both time and ideas, but in the brief moments, when I ignored the fear of trying to trap a killer who had escaped the police, one fact remained consistent. The killer had used the fake statue to murder Emily Hart, and I could trick him—or her—into thinking I had evidence to prove that. I excused myself from Nora's house and all but ran home and called Eddie.

"Can you make another fake Puccetti statue?" I asked.

"Consider it done."

"How long will it take?"

"Seriously, consider it done."

"I know it's no big thing, but I need to know the timetable."

"I made an extra when I made the first one."

"I know you—what?"

"I needed a prototype, and I thought it might be a cool little item to remember our adventure. Meet me at Arners tomorrow morning. Seven thirty."

"Okay ..."

THE NEXT MORNING, I dressed in a sequined tank top, a pair of navy chiffon harem pants, and a cropped white denim jacket with frayed edges. I buckled on blue T-strap sandals on a two inch heel, grabbed the yellow handbag, and headed for the local family owned diner. Eddie was already in a booth when I arrived, even though I was seven minutes early.

"You're up to something," Eddie said while munching on a piece of dry wheat toast.

"What makes you think that?"

"There's no way you'd agree to a seven thirty meeting if you didn't really need this. And by the way, MC Hammer called. He wants his pants back."

"One more crack about my clothes and I'm taking scissors to your Frankie T-shirts when you're not looking." I poured a cup of coffee from the pot on the table and waved at the waitress, pantomiming my order of bacon and scrambled eggs. "Speaking of weird accessories, what's with the bowling bag?"

"I couldn't exactly walk in here with a wooden statue that looks a lot like a piece of art that was recently used in a homicide, could I?"

"Yeah, but a bowling bag? At seven thirty in the morning?"

"I've seen the handbags at Tradava. Bowling bag, doctor's bag, knitting bag. That's what they all are. Someone else's bag. Pretend it's Chanel and call it a day."

"Chanel never made a bowling bag. Vuitton did. Chloe, too. But not Chanel."

"Whatevs." He washed the dry toast down with coffee. "What's with all the questions? According to you, you just wanted a keepsake."

I'd slept on Nora's information, and on my theories, and kept returning to the statue. I shrugged. "It was nice knowing we pulled it off."

"I had my doubts, but your plan worked. Is that what you did at Bentley's before you moved here?"

"I told you what I did. I was a buyer. There's a lot more to it than picking out pretty shoes. There's plans, projections, strategies for three months, six months, one year, three years. Then there's the constant what-to-do-when-things-don't-sell pressure. You don't get to make one strategy and call it a day. Sometimes trends don't hit and you're stuck with merchandise. That's when you have to figure out a new way to drive your business and liquidate your inventory."

"Trends. That's what you were supposed to be doing at Tradava. Trend specialist."

"Yes."

I could almost feel the heat from the light bulb over Eddie's head. He had now seen my natural planning and problem-solving abilities firsthand. "What's next for you?" he asked.

I felt the conversation shift. I knew he was taking about my work history and lack of job leads, so regardless of my suspicions that I wasn't ready for what was next because I was still dealing with what was now, I answered the question on the table.

"I don't know. Temporarily I'm at a standstill."

I thought again about the money Tony had given me. It made me uncomfortable. In the past twenty-four hours I'd moved it from the Halston book to my mattress to the never-used salad crisper. If I deposited it in the bank, I could pay my bills for a few months and figure out my next step. Only, depositing it indicated I was keeping it, and as much as Tony Simms claimed I'd earned it, I still wasn't sure what he was paying me for. A few days on the job or my silence?

"I'll do the thing at the college for Heist, and then I'm officially unemployed again," I finally said. "Maybe I'll call Andi, see if she has any contacts." I checked my watch. "Better give her a couple of hours to sleep off that hangover, though."

Eddie looked suspicious. "You really think a party girl is going to have a job lead for you?"

"It seemed pretty clear to me she was looking for an escape last night. So maybe she knows how I feel."

"I hope for your sake she does."

"For what it's worth, she told everyone in the bar that I was the smartest buyer in the entire tri-state area. Too bad I didn't have a tape recorder with me."

"You are smart, dude. That's why we listen to you."

"Since when do you listen to me?"

"The gala? Swiping the statue? Your genius plan?" I stared at him, stunned by his frank compliment. "Seriously, you're way too hard on yourself. Just because you can't keep a job around here doesn't mean people aren't in awe of what you've accomplished. Even yesterday I overheard a couple of the Tradava executives talking about," he made air quotations with his fingers, " 'that trend specialist we used to have. The one with the great personal style'.

And you know as well as I do that fashion people can be a little judgmental."

I perked up. "People from Tradava said that? What else did they say?"

"Let's just leave it at that, shall we?"

"What else did they say, Eddie?"

He averted his eyes, cleared his throat, and mumbled. "They said too bad corpses followed you wherever you went."

"They didn't."

"Those weren't the words they used, but they kinda did."

"What about Belle DuChamp? She was killed at Tradava, and I was nowhere near the store. I was out having drinks with Andi."

"No one really understands that one."

"What do you mean, no one?"

"Just saying, you've made yourself quite a reputation around these parts."

"Sometimes I wonder why I hang around you."

"Because I don't buy into the gossip? Because I like you for who you are? Because I'm willing to stare death in the face and hang out with you, knowing that just being in the same room with you might increase my chances of impending doom?"

I reached out and whapped his arm.

He rubbed his bicep with the other hand and smiled. "The same goes for Cat, you know. When this whole thing started she was in it for the shopping spree. Now that she's seen what you're capable of, she's impressed. She put her life at risk by associating with you. Probably Nick too. He must be proud on some level."

"Nick would rather not talk about Heist anymore." I thought about that last conversation we'd had.

"It's probably not going to get any easier," Eddie said.

"What?"

"The long distance thing."

"Nick's coming back in a couple of weeks."

"Dude, he's a shoe designer. He's going to spend half the year in Italy. I know you know that. I just don't know if you *know* that." Eddie tipped his head and scratched the short blond hair that had grown in on the side of his Mohawk. "There is one person you could talk to."

"You mean Dante?" I leaned back into the red vinyl booth and stared up at the ceiling, trying to figure out what to say. "He's different from Nick, that's for sure. It's almost like he encourages me to get involved."

Eddie leaned forward and propped his elbows on the table. "Can I ask you a personal question?"

"Shoot."

"You moved here to start over, to leave your old life behind, right?"

"Yes, but that didn't exactly work out—"

Eddie cut me off with a raised hand. "Nick's somebody from that life. That former life."

"You're from my former life."

"That's different. We know each other from high school. That's like the you you were before you became the you you are."

"Sure, that's clear."

"What I mean is, we got to know each other when we were still figuring out who we were. You took a side street after that—the one that landed you in New York. That's where you met Nick. He doesn't know the person I knew at Ribbon High School, the person

223

who risked her own reputation to save me from a cheating scandal that would have impacted my future."

I pushed the fruit around on my plate for a couple of seconds while the memory came back to me. Eddie as the new kid in high school. The football player who copied off his test. The accusation that Eddie had been the one to cheat. And me, in the principal's office the next day, admitting in confidence that I'd seen the whole thing. Eddie's scholarship to art school was safe after that, and until I read what he wrote in my yearbook, I didn't know he knew what I'd done for him.

"I think Nick sees that part of me too."

"Sure, but he met the professional out to prove something to the world. Who you are today, the Samantha who moved back to Ribbon to start over, came second to him, not first. Dante's like a breath of fresh air—"

"—that smells like cinnamon—" I interjected.

"You know what I mean. You're here in Ribbon, and in your first six months you did something nobody believed you could do. Maybe you should run with that."

"But Nick—I can't explain how I feel about Nick. Since the first time I met him, there was something there. A spark. And for all that time I worked at Bentley's, we never acted on it. Now we can." I speared a slice of pineapple from Eddie's plate and took a bite.

"What I don't get is Nick's behavior." He popped the last piece of crust into his mouth and washed it down with coffee. "He knew you were involved. He wouldn't tell you to leave things to the cops unless he knew the cops were already involved something. Why back away now? And why not want to talk about it? I think you're just trying to bait me again. Unless Dante's right about Nick not knowing you at all."

He got a second slap for that.

"SAMANTHA? THIS IS Andi Holloway. "I just found your note in my handbag. I'm concerned. Call me."

I ran to the phone on my counter. "Hello, I'm here," I answered breathlessly. "You got my note?"

"Yes. I'm not sure what it means."

"I wanted to talk to you last night, but you had a couple of distractions." I trailed off, not sure the best approach was to tell her that I'd watched her get sloshed, or ask how it felt to wake up next to a different bartender seven nights a week. Actually, I kinda did want to know about that last one.

"Oh, those boys, we just like to have fun. It was nothing. So, what did you want to talk about?"

"Kyle Trent." There was silence on the other end of the phone. "Andi? Are you still there?"

"What do you know about Kyle?"

"I don't think he killed Belle DuChamp."

"Who do you think killed her?" she asked.

I took a deep breath, and then exhaled. "Tony Simms."

"Give me your address. I want to hear your plan to get that bastard." This time there was no mistaking the click on the other end of the phone.

29

CONFLICT OF INTEREST

By the time Andi arrived, I'd fleshed out my thoughts on the take-out menus. I held them in my hand like a fan, ready to make my case for her. My denim jacket hung from the back of a dining room chair. Three sequins had fallen from my tank top and landed on the table next to a dusting of pretzel salt.

"Are you ordering food? I already ate," she said, glancing at the menus.

"These are my notes." Andi pulled a chair away from the table and sat. I'd been sitting for too long and instead paced back and forth on the other side of the table. "You told me Simulated Trucking delivers Vongole handbags to Heist. Right?"

"Right."

"That's the key." I looked down at what I'd written on the menu from B&S Sandwich Shop. "Tony Simms owns Simulated Trucking."

"Tony Simms owns a lot of things," she said.

"Why is everyone so willing to accept that? It's a conflict of interest. Tony owns Simulated, and Tony owns Heist. Simulated delivers the handbags to Heist."

"I never thought much about it."

"There's more." I flipped the menu over. "Heist has a growth strategy in place for Vongole, but didn't Tradava cancel orders because they felt the bags weren't up to the appropriate quality standards?"

Andi sat up straighter. "How do you know that?"

"Kyle told me. He thought it was suspicious."

"He was right to be suspicious." She sat back in her chair, plucked a small pretzel out of the bowl I'd set in the middle of the table, and tapped the pretzel on the placemat. "Last season, Kyle brought it to my attention. I contacted the factory in Italy. They said the leathers came from a new source, and they weren't using them anymore."

"Did they offer to take the bags back from Tradava?"

"Better. They offered to pay all markdowns if Tradava liquidated them."

I thought about the pile of Vongole handbags on the Tradava selling floor. The pile-it-high, let-it-fly merchandising certainly didn't improve the appearance of the bags, but if Vongole was paying markdowns, Tradava probably encouraged the bargain-basement mentality.

Andi leaned forward. "What else do you have?"

I tossed the sandwich menu onto the table and flipped open the Chinese menu. "Emily was trying to exit the Vongole business. She must have known something was up."

"But that doesn't make sense. Belle bought out my inventory."

"I know, right? I thought that was weird too. That's when I realized Belle had some additional interest in the Vongole business." I held the menus in my right hand and flapped them against the fingertips on my left. "But before we get to how Belle ties in, let's follow this." I squinted to read my writing over the fried rice options. "Kyle and Emily were engaged. No doubt, their loyalties were to each other and not to their respective stores."

"Which would have pissed off their respective stores," Andi interjected.

"I think that's when Belle started the rumor about Kyle, to get between them—"

"—So Emily would stop listening to him—"

"—and get back onboard the Vongole gravy train."

Andi's eyes lit up. We were finishing each other's sentences. She wasn't pointing out any flaws with my logic. She saw what I saw.

"Tony ultimately pockets the profits from Heist," I added.

She crushed the pretzel in her fist. "Between Tradava's cancellations and Heist dropping the line, Vongole wouldn't be able to recover. We have a lot tied up in those two accounts."

"How would it affect your showroom?" I asked.

"I'd be fine, if that's what you're wondering. Vongole is my biggest account, but I rep other lines. I could pick up another handbag line and use my contacts to fill the void. I never did because I'd have a conflict of interest between two different vendors." She brushed her palms together, sprinkling pretzel crumbs like pixie dust over her placemat. "How did you put all of this together?" she asked.

"It started with the contest."

Her brows pulled together, and three small wrinkles appeared between them. "What contest?"

"Heist had a contest." I told Andi about the ad in the paper, the Puccetti statue, and how it had tied us to the murder of Emily Hart. "If Eddie hadn't knocked off the statue, I wouldn't be sitting here talking to you right now. The publicity contest is the key."

"How so?"

"Tony Simms owns the statue. He's the only one who would have had access to the knockoff we left the night we stole it. That statue was what he used to kill Emily. Tony probably knew the statue was a fake and our fingerprints would be all over it."

The three wrinkles between her eyebrows marked her thought processes, and her eyes stared into mine in a manner at odds with the vacant party girl from the night before. She was thinking about what I had said. She was gauging if she should confide in me. My plan needed her, and she needed a push.

"Andi, I saw how you looked at Kyle in that picture on your phone. I think he means a lot to you, more than just a buyer/designer relationship. And I know how that feels. The guy I'm—Nick Taylor—he was one of my vendors when I was a buyer at Bentley's. We had to be professional because of our jobs. But that didn't last forever, and now there's no conflict of interest, and even though he's in Italy and I'm here, we're trying. Just like you and Kyle could try if he was clear of this mess and had a chance to move on. You can help him get that chance, if you want, but he's never going to move on if he's suspected of something he didn't do."

She sat back against the wooden chair. I surprised myself with the personal information I'd shared, and part of me wanted to take it all back. But it was true. And if it helped convince her to clear an innocent man and trap a guilty one, it was worth it.

"Here's what I think has been going on with the handbags." I sank into the chair opposite her. "The showroom has the real samples, produced in Italy by quality factories. After the orders are written, a different factory produces the bags with imitation skins and cheap hardware. Somebody in that equation is pocketing the difference."

"You think Kyle knew. Tony killed him to keep him from talking."

I nodded. "I think Belle knew too."

She lobbed questions at me, questions I answered deftly, having recently spent a week reasoning out these very same conundrums from a cocoon of down comforting and stuffed animals. By the time the sun went down and the air grew chilly, we were on the same page.

Unfortunately, that page indicated one very scary thing. I was about to meet the killer at the dedication at I-FAD, and with the exception of a handbag rep with a happy-hour habit, nobody believed me.

"The thing is, Tony Simms didn't get to be Tony Simms by accident," I said. "He's a smart guy. We have to make him think we know everything. We have to get him so worried that he's about to be caught that he trips up. We probably aren't going to have any backup from the cops either, considering they have Kyle in custody."

"Let's hear your plan," she said.

I studied her face and took a deep, steadying breath. "He murdered Emily with the statue, right? So we make him think the cops have the wrong statue, meaning that we pulled another switch and the one we have his fingerprints and her, um, blood."

"That's going to take some doing."

"True, but it can be done."

"And you? How are you going to protect yourself?"

"I'm going to call in a favor from a friend." I made my apologies—some prior commitment I pretended I'd missed—then triple-locked the front door and found my cell phone in the bottom of my handbag. I stared at the keypad for a solid twenty seconds before I called the only person who had the skills to help.

30

UP AT NIGHT

I need you," I said when Dante answered.

There was a long pause on the other end of the phone. I stood very still, not sure if I was on the verge of a bad decision. Finally, he spoke.

"What time does your man call?"

I blushed even though he couldn't see me. "Nine. Ish"

"Ish?"

"Nine. Exactly at nine."

"I'll be there at nine twenty."

"See you then." I exhaled a long breath I didn't know I had been holding.

If I were a different kind of person, I should have been able to walk away from it all myself, but I'd gotten involved too far, and the only way I knew to make sure I came out of it alive was to get the person that I believed to be a killer behind bars. I had learned that, somewhere in me, under the fashionable exterior and the business savvy that had launched my career, that there was also a need to see justice done.

I couldn't explain it. I wished I could. Truth be told, since Kyle Trent had been arrested, I couldn't sleep at night, I couldn't eat during the day, and I'd lost my desire to accessorize.

I couldn't live like this.

When the phone hadn't rung by nine thirteen, I called Nick.

"Hey," I said. "It's me."

"What's going on?" he asked. His voice was cool.

I knew he didn't want to talk about the homicide. But with the meeting at I-FAD in my immediate future, there wasn't much else I could think about. The best way to maintain a truthful conversation with Nick was to tell him everything. That, I knew, to be right. Only I wasn't ready to hear what he had to say, even though he'd been remarkably supportive until recently. I was on the verge of doing something really, really dumb—or genius, depending on how you looked at it—and I didn't want his reaction to sway me from my plan. I adopted what I knew to be a successful manner of communicating the truth, without sacrificing my privacy. I finished all of my sentences in my head.

"Just hanging out." I glanced at the wall clock and climbed on a dining room chair to mark the time Dante was going to arrive with a yellow Post-It note.

"Are you glad that whole mess is over?"

"I'm not exactly sure it's over," I said without thinking, distracted by the Post-It that had only partially stuck to my clock and now dangled by a corner.

"Kidd, why do you do this? Why can't you just let it go?"

"You sound like you're judging me."

"I just want to understand how your brain works."

"My brain works like it's always worked. I like to solve puzzles. I like to figure things out. I like resolution."

"Is it the fact that the cops figured it out without you that's keeping you up at night?"

"How do you know I'm up at night?"

"It's just an expression. You're up at night?"

"No, not really,"

"You just said you were."

"Okay, so I am."

"Kidd, what's going on?"

The doorbell rang. "Nick, I gotta go." I hung up without saying good-bye.

I opened the door for Dante. He pushed past me and strode into the kitchen. I followed Dante. He opened a few cabinets, pulled out the canister of coffee, and made a pot before facing me. "That Simms guy was right about one thing."

"What's that?"

"You possess a unique skill set."

"He was talking about my background as a buyer at Bentley's."

"Sit down, Samantha," he ordered. I noticed the brown nylon duffle bag that sat on one of my chairs. "I agree with him. You do possess a unique skill set." The pot of coffee was only half full, but Dante pulled it out and filled two mugs. He pushed the pot back into the machine and carried the mugs to the table.

He set one of the mugs in front of me, and moved the duffle bag from the chair and sat down. The bag landed by his feet.

"You're not planning on staying over, are you?" I asked.

"We'll get to the bag in a second." He drank from his mug. "I'm going to tell you a couple of things tonight, and I don't want to hear that you repeated them. Got me?"

"I, um, I don't want to agree to anything until I know what I'm agreeing to," I stated in a sentence that started rather tentatively but ended with conviction.

"You still don't trust me, do you?"

"You're Cat's brother, so yes, technically, I trust you. Only I don't completely trust you for other reasons."

He raised an eyebrow.

"But we're not getting into those reasons tonight. In fact," I stated, gaining spitfire momentum, "I don't think we should be getting into anything tonight. In fact," I repeated, because it seemed as though my little speech was as much for me as it was for him, "I think after this cup of coffee you should be going. Because I have a very nice man in Italy, and just because he's not here is no reason I should entertain you in his absence."

"You called me."

"Maybe that was a mistake."

"Samantha, I'd be lying if I said I wasn't jealous of your very nice man in Italy, but that's not why I'm here."

"It's not?"

He reached down to the duffle bag and unzipped it. I tried to look inside but didn't recognize anything. He pulled out a square metal object with wires sticking out of the top.

"Did you take that thing from my car again?"

He set the contraption on the table. "This didn't come from your car."

"Whose car did it come from?"

"One at the junk yard."

"What are you saying?"

"There was nothing wrong with your car the morning I showed up here."

"You tricked me?"

"I knew you were up to something. So yes, technically I tricked you, so I could see where you were going and what you were up to. Once I followed you to Heist, I figured you'd either come out with files or paperwork that I could read, or the sugar cube would pick up something you did. And it did. You got very excited about a couple of papers."

"The spreadsheets I mailed to my cat."

"Why did you do that?"

"I knew they were important. Kyle was going to give the recap to Emily but she was murdered. He gave it to me because he thought it was suspicious."

"Why'd you mail them?"

"Heist might not have liked it if they saw me taking recaps on their profit margin out of the building, especially considering what happened to Emily, but I was pretty sure Vongole was at the middle of the whole thing. I thought about putting the recaps in my shoe or my bra, but I was too scared they would fall out or somehow someone would find them."

"Who did you think was going to look in your bra?"

Considering Nick was in Italy, it was a good question. Considering I was talking to the only other person I found myself inappropriately flirting with, I chose not to answer.

"So your instincts told you to mail them to yourself—your cat."

236

"Yes, and I mailed two other envelopes at the same time so security wouldn't be suspicious when I waved a stack of hand-addressed envelopes in front of them. And I ran them out to the mailbox on the corner of the parking lot so they wouldn't be sitting around in the store. They were delivered a couple of days ago."

"Addressed to your cat."

"That's because I was afraid of addressing them to myself."

"I know a lot of women, and I know how a lot of women think. And I don't know a single other woman who would do what you did in that situation."

"What can I say? I'm special," I said, not entirely sure he'd intended what he said as a compliment.

"Remember I told you I sometimes get hired to take photos for investigations?"

"Yes."

"I learned stuff. How to get information, how to trip people up, how to hide things. I have a knack for it."

"I'm sure you do."

"You have a knack for it too, only the opposite. People thing you're going to zig, you zag. You're unexpected." He studied me for a moment. "The problem is you have no idea what you're doing."

I set my coffee cup back on the table with a bang, letting the brown liquid splash out of the mug and onto the placemat. "I got this far, didn't I?" I asked.

"And some people might say it's a wonder, but I won't, because, like I said, I agree with Tony Simms. You possess a unique skill set."

"Dante, if there's something you're trying to say, just come out and say it already. It's getting late."

"For all I know, Kyle did kill those people."

"That's a load of crap and you know it."

"Let me stay tonight and teach you a couple of things to help you."

"I—I'm kind of in a relationship," I said with less conviction than I should have.

"Assuming this Nick guy cares about you, I'm sure he'd appreciate knowing I'm going to arm you with knowledge that will protect you when you go off tilting at windmills."

He might have had a point. Whether or not it held water was a different issue.

"You think someone else is the killer. That's a big accusation." Dante sat forward and propped his elbows on his thighs. "Not that I don't follow you, but you're going to need a solid set of connectors to get anyone to buy it. Why don't you spell it out for me one more time?"

I let out a big sigh. I didn't want to be mocked or shot down anymore. "It's going to take a lot of time for me to go through what I know and try to convince you."

Logan entered the kitchen and nuzzled his head in the duffle bag. We watched him pull his head out, and then step his front feet in and circle a few times. Less than a minute later he was curled up inside, purring.

"I hope your entire lesson plan isn't under my cat," I said.

"Drink your coffee. I'm going to check out a couple of things."

He left his mug on the table and walked upstairs. Logan raised his head and watched, stretched, stepped out of the bag, and followed him. I reached down to the bag and dug through it. But before I could determine what Dante brought, his tattooed arms reached down and grabbed the nylon webbed handles and hoisted the duffle away from me.

"Bring the coffee." He turned back toward the stairs and disappeared.

"Where are you going?" I asked with a little more than mild alarm. My bedroom was up there.

"My sister's not the only one around here who knows how to accessorize."

"Accessorize?" I called behind him.

"Yeah." He stood at the top of the stairs, staring down at me. "You're getting another makeover. This time on my terms."

31

MAKEOVER

I climbed the stairs and went to my bedroom. Dante wasn't there. Not sure if this was his idea of a prank, I whipped the closet doors open, expecting to find him staring back at me. He wasn't. I dropped onto all fours and bent my head down, peering under the bed, butt in the air.

"Do you want to tell me what you're doing?" he asked from behind me. I pulled my head out and looked up at him propped against the doorframe, holding Logan and scratching his ears.

"This isn't a bedroom kind of thing. I'd prefer to do this in the room over here." He jerked his head back and to the right.

"What exactly do you prefer to do?" I asked, scooting to my feet and dusting a few cobwebs off my harem pants.

"Luck has brought you further than anyone expected."

"It's not luck. Everything I've done has been completely reasoned out."

"Like I said, not a single woman I know would jeopardize her job and send her cat confidential paperwork from her place of business."

"But it was—"

"Not a one."

"But–"

"You have some kind of talent for this stuff, but you also have a knack for finding trouble. I can't in good faith send you out there to the world at large thinking luck is going to protect you."

"What do you plan to do? Outfit me in Kevlar and wire me with a camera that looks like a tube of lipstick?"

Dante looked at my tank top for a second, and then back at my face. "No, I kind of like the way you dress." He pulled a couple of things out of the duffle bag and placed them on the old wooden desk in the room. A Bay City Rollers poster hung on the wall, one of the few things left from when it was my older sister's room. My parents had never tossed the last of her high school belongings, and I had yet to figure out what I was going to do with the room, so I'd left it empty.

"What do you call this room?"

"My sister's old bedroom."

"You might want to start calling it your crime lab." He pulled a few items from the duffel. "I've been doing some digging. I'm not 100 percent sure you're making this whole thing up."

"Really? You believe me?"

"Not entirely, but I'm not going to discount your suspicions, either."

This was it. This was the time to flat-out tell Dante what I thought. I was bolstered by the fact that I'd shared this very knowledge with Andi and she hadn't balked.

"I think Tony Simms is the killer."

Once again, our eyes held for several seconds. Even Logan, who had followed us into the room, sat as still as a Puccetti, waiting for the inevitable reaction.

"So that's the real reason he wants you there. If he can keep tabs on you, you can't get to him."

I stared at Dante while he made his point. There was more, and I knew it, and I wanted to know if he would go far enough to say it out loud.

"But if he's keeping tabs on me, then I can keep tabs on him too."

"Simms' plan isn't just to watch you, sweetheart. If he's the killer and thinks you know something, he'll kill you too."

"What am I thinking?" I jumped up from my chair and spun around, not wanting to face the tough guy who was listening to me and leveling with me, because my inner tough girl had run screaming for the hills. "Why am I doing this? What is wrong with me?"

I started to leave the room, feeling hot tears on my cheeks, feeling desperation obliterate my confidence. I wanted to get out of there before Dante saw me break down. I tripped over his duffle bag and fell toward the door.

He caught me with both arms and spun me around. I buried my head into his T-shirt and took deep breaths. "Shhh. Breathe. Calm down," he said, one strong arm holding me and the other stroking the back of my head. I was shaking.

"All I wanted was a job where I could wear nice clothes. And instead I'm a failure."

"Look at me." He gently pushed me away from him and took my face in his hands. His thumbs swept the tears from under my eyes like wiper blades. "You are not a failure. Get that? You are ... not a failure."

"You're not the person whose cotton I should be using," I muttered. Clearly this was not a time to be worried about grammar.

"Does your guy in Italy wear cotton?"

"Sometimes."

"Then pretend I'm him."

It was such an innocent statement said with no ulterior motive. If ever Dante had an opportunity, he had one now. He didn't go there. Aside from the heat from his arms, there was nothing hot about the way he held me. In that one second, Dante got more personal than he had in my fantasies.

I excused myself and went to the bathroom. I splashed cool water on my face, put drops in my eyes to offset the redness, and delivered a pep talk to my reflection.

"Why are you doing this? Why can't you just let it all go? You're going to be all alone if you can't stop doing this. Alone or dead." Nice options.

There was a tap on the door. "Samantha? You're not going to be alone. I'll be there too."

I dried off my face and opened the door. "You're going to help me?"

***

BY THE TIME Dante left it was well past one o'clock in the morning. The pot of coffee had kept us going for hours, but the emotional rollercoaster I'd ridden had left me drained.

True to his word, Dante taught me a couple of tricks of the PI trade, and true to my word I promised not to repeat anything he'd said. He was right. It was crazy to think I'd gotten this far on instincts alone. After triple-locking the door, I changed into pajamas and crawled into bed. I had a daunting task ahead of me. Tomorrow morning, stage one of our plan, I was going back to Heist.

32

EVERYTHING GOES

I wanted to get in and get out. If I timed everything well, no one would know I had been there—well, besides the security team I'd have to walk past. But I was ready for them. I flashed my ID to the glass window that separated us.

"Sign the sign-in sheet," Gabe, the portly security guard, was working. He waved toward the clipboard and the pen connected by a dirty white string. His swivel chair squeaked under his weight as he spun away from me.

"Here's my ID," I waved again.

"Store's closed, and no one goes in or out without signing in."

"Fine." I scrawled my name on the first available line and scanned the names above mine. Only about half a dozen were on the sheet, and none looked familiar.

I rested the pen on the top of the clipboard and went to my office. The store was glowing with light, and if it wasn't for the lack of employees, you'd think it was open for business. As I rounded the corner from the contemporary department to handbags, I found the stock team throwing merchandise in giant plastic garbage bags.

"What are you doing?" I asked.

"Everything goes," said the shortest guy of the bunch.

"Where?"

"To the Heist in Philly. We're transferring as much of this inventory as we can." He hoisted a full bag onto his shoulder like Santa Claus and bent at the waist to counter the weight. Many of the handbag shelves were empty, though scads of the inventory had been dumped on the selling floor. Other members of the stock team were scooping up the inventory and dumping it into the plastic bags too.

"Wait! Those bags aren't cheap!"

They looked at me like I was nuts. "There's a cloth bag inside each one. Put the bag in the cloth and *then* throw it in the plastic." I opened a purple clutch and pulled a Vongole-stamped felt bag out from against the yellow suede lining, placed the bag in the felt, and pulled the drawstring shut. "See?"

"We don't have that kind of time, lady," said another member of the operations team. "We have an hour to pack up this department before we move on to shoes."

"Fine. Just don't let anybody else see how you're treating the merchandise." I stepped over a pile on the floor, hopped to a narrow pathway through the mess, and continued through the store.

Honestly, what did I care at this point? I already knew the bags were fakes. And I knew if there was a loss to be had from the mistreatment of these bags, it would fall on Tony Simms' shoulders. I wasn't the buyer anymore. I wasn't connected to the store in the least. I wasn't going to drive to Philly to buy one of the patent leather creations at 80 off, or whatever ridiculous discount they were going to pass off to get rid of them.

To get rid of them.

Those bags weren't going to make it to Philly.

No wonder no one cared how the bags were packed. These bags, these fakes, were part of the bigger picture, part of what would make sense of the killings. Once this evidence was destroyed, no one would be the wiser about Simms and his activities.

I had to get Detective Loncar to the store, to get him to see the merchandise, and to see the inventory was being moved. If he could follow the truck, he would know the truth. I dumped my bag on my desk, picked up the receiver, and called him.

But before he answered, I heard a noise in the office next door.

33

STEALING FILES

I set the receiver back on the cradle. If the stock team was packing up inventory, there was no reason for anyone to be in the buyer's offices. As quietly as I could, I crossed the carpet between my desk and the doorway.

Mallory was filling a large canvas tote bag with files. She didn't notice me at first, but when she did, the files fell to the floor. Manila folders spilled out recaps and past orders and photo sheets with selling information.

"What are you doing here?" she asked. I had been one second short of asking the same question.

"I came for my personal things."

"You haven't been here long enough to have personal things. You came here to steal files."

"I'm not the one rifling through the file cabinet."

"You don't know this business like I do. I've taken too many chances, and you're not going to ruin this opportunity for me."

"What opportunity? The dedication tomorrow night?"

She turned pale. "Tomorrow night? But I won't be ready."

"You shouldn't go. I wouldn't if I hadn't been asked by Tony. I'd be as far away from there as I possibly could get."

"Tony asked you to go? I thought you didn't even work here anymore!"

"How do you know that?"

"It's not about what I know, it's about what you think you know. I've worked too long and too hard to get noticed around here and some nobody isn't going to get all of the credit that I deserve. I don't care what you have on your resume. With everything I've been through, *I* deserve the recognition, not you!"

"I don't know what you're getting at, but I think you've got the wrong idea about me, Mallory," I said. "I just came here to get my flowers."

I went back into my office and picked up the arrangement Dante had sent. I didn't know if the sugar cube was still working or picking up anything she had said, but I didn't want to take any chances. The arrangement from the cops was sitting on her desk and I wanted that one too, if only for the wireless mic.

"Stay home tomorrow night, Mallory. Please. Listen to me. Nobody's going to notice whether or not you're there. It's not going to be a big deal."

"Are you kidding? None of this would have started if it wasn't for me and I'm darn sure going to see that it's finished." In her anger she took a few steps toward me, closing the gap. She shook a balled-up fist in the air as though she was claiming to never go hungry again.

I stepped backward, but the toe of my shoe caught on a piece of paper that had fallen from the files, and I slipped. I let go of the flowers and grabbed for the desk to right myself. The vase landed on the floor, the flowers still secured in the green sponge at the base. The miniature camera fell loose, lying inches from Mallory's foot. We both stared at it for a tense couple of seconds.

Mallory looked up, her face red in splotches that continued down her neck. "I don't care how you got this job or what you plan to do after this, but I am going to finish you. I intend to be at that dedication, and I'm going to make sure Tony Simms knows you're up to something."

She picked up the camera and stormed out of the office.

I WASN'T LOOKING forward to telling Dante I'd lost his camera, or that in doing so I may have tipped off a murderer to the fact that I was on to her, even if she wasn't the suspect I'd been figuring out how to trap. I was mixed up. The only thing clear about my thoughts was that I was barely making sense.

Mallory. Was it possible? Had I misjudged her so much during my short time at Heist? She'd done a good job of pulling the wool over my eyes, but I mentally ticked off my checklist. She had admitted to being around Kyle and Emily the night of the murder. I'd overheard her threaten Belle DuChamp. She had done little to hide her open displeasure when I'd started working at Heist and I didn't know why. This couldn't all be about a promotion or a career path. Unless ...

Could it be?

There was one simple answer I hadn't wanted to see, and that answer was yes.

Yes, Mallory knew I was doing more at Heist than replacing the murdered handbag buyer.

Yes, if Mallory had murdered Emily over the Vongole knockoff scheme, she'd be threatened when I showed up unexpected.

Yes, Mallory was going to be at the dedication. She had said it like a threat, not a fact.

And yes, it was entirely possible Mallory was the killer.

I sped home. I parked in the garage and pulled the door down to hide my car. Logan stood guard over his empty food bowl yowling for dinner. I snapped open a can of gourmet cat food and spooned it into the bowl. He buried his head, and I sank down on the linoleum tile floor, legs splayed in front of me.

"How can you eat at a time like this?" The sounds of wet cat morsels being gulped down answered me. He pulled his head up and stared at me for two long seconds. Then he walked over and head-butted my forehead. I scooped him into my arms and held him close for comfort. The phone rang. I held Logan to my chest and stood. I answered on the third ring.

"Ms. Kidd, this is Detective Loncar." Long pause. "I know Tony Simms asked you to be at the event at the college, but I am strongly suggesting you don't go. Do you understand?"

"But you said everything was over. If everything is over, then I'm free to do what I want, right? Your case is closed. Unless you want to admit you have the wrong person in custody and you have some questions for me. Do you have any valid questions for me?"

"Just one. Do you want to explain to me why Mallory George wants to file a restraining order against you?"

34

_G_ ood thing cats always land on their feet, because when I processed the detective's question I knocked Logan off the counter.

"She what?" I asked.

"I don't know what you did to her, but she was clear that she doesn't want you to be anywhere near her or the dedication."

"Because she's the killer."

"Ms. Kidd, a week ago you said Belle DuChamp was the killer. Yesterday it was Tony Simms and today it's Mallory George. Who's it going to be tomorrow? These accusations are borderline defamation of character."

"The only person I haven't said was the killer is Kyle Trent."

"I'm sending a car over. If you leave your house, we'll know. It is my very strong recommendation that you stay away from I-FAD for the next forty-eight hours."

"Why? The dedication is tomorrow, right?"

"And the dress rehearsal is tonight." He hung up.

I looked out my window. A gold PT Cruiser drove slowly down the street. That was Mallory's car. I remembered it from the day I drove her to the Bag Lady showroom. Considering she claimed she wanted to keep a distance spelled out in a restraining order between us, her presence in my neighborhood was suspicious. I called Dante.

"Are you close? How close? Can you come get me now? Right now? I have to be gone from my house like really, really, really fast."

"Samantha, slow down."

"I don't have time to slow down. Please. I'll tell you everything when you get here."

A motorcycle pulled into my driveway. We weren't going to talk about how fast that actually was. I scooped Logan up and kissed him. "I'll be back soon, I promise." I took the stairs two at a time, grabbed Dante's duffle bag and ran back downstairs and out the front door. I straddled the bike while buckling the helmet on. Dante peeled out of the lot just as I wrapped both arms around him. He circled the block, and a police cruiser passed us. I gripped tighter.

He turned his head around to me. "Are they headed for you?"

I nodded. He revved his engine and shot through the intersection. I closed my eyes and leaned my head against the orange and red flames on the back of his jacket.

He sped past most cars and pulled onto a narrow drive that took us up the side of Mt. Penn. We passed basketball courts and kids playing hopscotch. The road was narrow and windy like the Autobahn. We slowed by a white iron gate.

"We're here."

I didn't know where "here" was, but I was vaguely certain no one else who might be looking for me would know where "here" was either. Safe enough for me.

I took off the helmet, and he locked it to the back of his bike. "Follow me."

He pulled the handles to the duffle bag out of my grip and started up the concrete stairs that wrapped around a porch that led to a wood and glass paneled door. He unlocked it and entered a room no bigger than a small hotel room.

A wooden, fold-out futon sat under a window facing a flat screen TV mounted on the opposite wall. Tall, metal bookcases that held books on their side flanked the TV, and an oblong piece of marble sat on two concrete blocks below them, holding magazines on cars and photography. Next to the futon was a desk with a computer and chair. Silver cups filled with colorful markers lined the back of the desk. Blues, greens, and purples in one cup, oranges, yellows, and reds in the other.

Dante dropped the bag next to a turntable and opened a small fridge. When he stood, he held a beer out. I took it and drank a fair amount even though I'm more of a wine girl.

"Sit."

I collapsed on the sofa.

"Talk."

"I, um, may have been wrong about Tony Simms being the killer."

Dante demonstrated great patience after I made that statement, allowing me to gulp my beer, supplying me with a second one when the first ran low. In fact, it wasn't until my cell phone started going crazy from inside the pocket of my pants that he prompted me with questions. I muted the phone and started talking.

I recounted what had happened at Heist that morning, barely believing that less than a day had passed since Mallory had caught me—or vice versa. I ended with her reaction to seeing the camera on the floor.

"I'm sorry. I'll pay you back whatever it cost when I get a chance."

He waved my apology away with his hand. "That's not important. You said the cops told you she filed a restraining order against you?"

"Yes. And that can only be to keep me away from the dedication. But there's no way I can stay away now. She's going to murder someone else. Maybe Tony Simms. Maybe Nora. Maybe she'll take out a bunch of students. Who knows how far she'll go?"

"Calm down. None of this makes any sense."

"I know."

"No, you most likely don't know." He set his beer on the table and leaned back against the futon.

"What most likely don't I know? I mean, what don't I know most likely? I mean, what do you mean?"

"Do you need some kind of sedative?"

Mental note: chill out. "Tell me what you mean."

"There's no way this Mallory person can get a restraining order in a couple of hours. The cops would know that. They would also know you've been working with them. And they would know you've been saying the real killer is still out there. So if this Detective Loncar wants to talk to you so badly that he sent a car to your house, it might be because he finally has reason to listen to what you have to say."

"Detective Loncar has already shown up on my doorstep once before." I didn't add that he'd read me my rights, hand cuffed me while I was in my bathrobe, and taken me to the police station. It wasn't a happy memory. "When he said he was sending a car to get me, I wasn't going to hang around for a repeat fashion intervention a la Copper."

"The handcuffs were copper?"

"Copper, like James Cagney. You know, 'Come and get me, Copper!'"

"You seriously learned everything you know about the police from old movies, didn't you?"

"I resent that." I said. I fidgeted with my hands, crossing and uncrossing my arms, sitting on my palms, trying to find a position that didn't look or feel completely vulnerable.

I looked around the interior of the room. "What is this place? A safe house?"

"This is where I live." A smile crept along Dante's face, and then blossomed into a full-blown grin. "At least when I'm not at my apartment in Philly."

I immediately looked around for insights into Dante's personality. While I watched, he reached out to a small metal box that sat on the table next to the futon. Inside was a stash of Atomic Fireballs. He pulled one out, bit into the plastic, and popped it into his mouth.

"Do your parents have any idea how badly they screwed you up by naming you Dante?"

"You might offer me an apology."

"For what?"

"That 'safe house' crack. Just about confirmed what I thought about your knowledge."

He was right, and I knew he was right, but I was full of pride and indignation. I stood up and marched across the room to the one interior door that had been shut.

"What's in here?"

"Bathroom."

I went inside and shut the door behind me. This was as good a place as any to let the steam cool down from behind my ears. I sank to the white tiled floor and started thinking.

Within five minutes, I knew I had to talk to Loncar. Someone's life was at risk. I still didn't know whose. It could be mine. Or Kyle's, or Tony's, or Andi's, or Nora's or any unrelated person who came into contact with Mallory.

I won't let you ruin this for me, she'd said. *After all I've done, I'm taking what I deserve.*

I stood up and opened the door. Dante stood directly on the other side, one hand up, ready to knock.

"Can I use your phone?" I asked.

He handed me my cell phone. The number was already on the screen. I punched the connect button and waited.

"Ms. Kidd, where are you?" Loncar demanded.

"I'm at the grocery store," I lied.

"I want you to listen to me carefully. Mallory George wanted to file a restraining order against you. I explained that unless the two of you were lovers living in the same house, what she was seeking didn't pertain to your 'relationship.' Now I want to know what you did that makes her think you're a danger to her, and I'd feel a lot better about this conversation if we had it in my office."

"No disrespect, Detective, but that's not going to happen. And I'm going to hang up every twenty-nine seconds so you can't trace this call."

He sighed heavily. "Ms. Kidd, that's not necessary."

"I'll call you right back." I hung up.

Dante reappeared in front of me. "Done so soon?"

"I don't want him to trace the call."

"You have to stop giving me ammunition."

I held my hand up to silence him and hit redial. "Detective Loncar? It's Samantha Kidd."

"Why does Mallory George want a protective order issued against you?"

I stared at the blond hardwood floorboards and traced a line between the seams with the toe of my shoe. "I've been thinking about that."

"Give me the abridged version. Try to keep Hollywood out of it."

Dante and Detective Loncar probably would have a great time hanging out over drinks.

"She told me she was at Heist the night Emily was murdered."

"What's she stand to gain?"

"I don't know for sure. She's the assistant buyer. You're the one who played back the recording of her threatening me. I also heard her threaten Belle DuChamp. At first I thought she just wanted a promotion, but this is too crazy. Nobody wants a job this badly. At least, not this job. Not at this level. You don't kill to be a buyer. CEO maybe, or something like that, but not buyer. The perks just aren't that great."

"You don't hear about people killing to be CEOs either. I've heard of a lot of motives. They pretty much boil down to love, family, money. You don't see the connection to any of them?"

I shook my head.

"Ms. Kidd? You still with me?" the detective asked over the phone, since I hadn't answered him out loud.

"The answer is no. I don't see the connection to any of those motives. But she's trying to keep me from the dedication."

"You feel pretty positive something's going down at that dedication?"

"I do." I waited for him to order me to stay home, or to tell me my active imagination had run away from me into a fourth dimension.

"This Mallory George said you've been secretly filming her in the office. That's a violation of privacy."

"You were secretly recording her! How is that any different?"

"Where'd you get the camera?"

"A friend who is looking out for me."

"I thought that friend was in Italy."

"Different friend."

"What's his motivation?"

My eyes flickered to Dante, who stood in the kitchen watching a pot of water. "Same as yours."

"Put him on the phone."

"No can do. I'll have him call you."

Dante locked eyes with me, and I snapped the phone shut.

"Detective Loncar wants to talk to you. Here's the number." I scribbled it on a paper towel and tossed it into the sink. "Call him, don't call him. It's up to you."

Dante snatched the phone and dialed the number with his thumb.

"Detective?" he said into the phone. I couldn't hear the other side of the conversation. Then Dante dropped the hand that held the phone to his side and told me to go back into the bathroom while he finished the conversation without me.

And just in case you're wondering, I knew Dante was purposely keeping the tone light, and Detective Loncar wouldn't be listening to me if he didn't believe maybe I was right. And having two men converse secretly over how to best protect me while a potential killer orchestrated one last hit did nothing to calm my nerves.

So I called the other man who would have something to say about my current situation.

35

TIME'S UP

*A*fter I left a message with Nick that included phrases like, "I need to talk to you," "Things have gotten out of hand," and "Please don't think I am a drama queen needing attention, but even the cops are starting to listen to me now," I hung up and waited.

And stared around Dante's bathroom.

And at his shower.

A shower would feel good. A shower would go a long way toward cleaning my aura, or at least the smell of fear that had begun to travel in small circles with me.

I opened the door to the bathroom. Dante was still on the phone, making notes on a lined steno pad. Fine. Let them figure out I was right. For the next half hour, it was going to be their problem and not mine. Yes, I said half an hour. For once it wasn't my hot water bill.

I locked the door and peeled off my clothes, tossing them into a pile next to the sink. The water sprayed the walls of the shower, producing a cloud of steam. I climbed in, dunked my face under the spray and doused my hair. It felt good. It felt better than good. I rested my forehead against the walls of the standup shower, and the insistent pulse beat down on my shoulders and back. Tensions calmed. Muscles relaxed. I lathered the bar of Ivory soap into a foam of suds and washed my face and body like I was exorcizing a demon.

I repeated the routine with Dante's shampoo and conditioner and then sat on the floor and let the water wash over me like a tropical rainforest. I could sit here for hours. I could sit here all night. I didn't have to ever come out of here again, except maybe for the occasional serving of pretzels. For the first time in days, I was totally relaxed.

Then a shadow appeared on the other side of the shower curtain and a deep voice broke my trance. "Time's up."

The water suddenly shut off, and I was left sitting in the middle of a shower. Naked. With Dante on the other side of the flimsy plastic curtain. I jumped up, and in an attempt at modesty, turned my back toward the curtain. A fluffy white towel hit me on the head.

I wrapped the towel around my torso. Dante pulled the plastic curtain aside as I secured the corner by my bust line. "Detective Loncar thinks there might be some truth to what you're saying, but he's not ready to admit Kyle is the wrong guy. It appears as though your new 'evidence' started a ticking clock on the amount of time they have to tie everything together with a big bow."

"So we're going to the college tonight? I don't have anything to wear."

"This isn't a date."

"That's not what I mean. I bolted from the house and all I grabbed was your duffle bag. I don't have anything to wear to shake down a killer."

"Your term papers must have been fun to read."

"I majored in the history of fashion. I didn't need to use phrases like 'shake down a killer' when writing about Emilio Pucci."

He shoveled his hand under a neatly folded pile of clothes. "Put these on. They should work."

I flipped through the pile. White shirt and work pants. "Are these your clothes?"

"Let's not get into where they came from. Hurry up and change."

I turned back into the bathroom and dressed. The button-down, collared, short sleeved shirt was part of a uniform. The name Doris was embroidered onto a red patch sewn over the right breast. The pants were a men's flat front boxy cut, narrow fit through my hips and ridiculously full at the waist.

"Hand me the duffle bag," I said through the cracked door.

He handed it to me. I unclamped the black nylon shoulder strap, adjusted the length of it, and clamped it over the waistband of the pants like a cinch belt, creating the kind of paper-bag waist that made Isaac Mizrahi famous. I rolled the cuffs of the pants up until they were slightly above my ankles and then buckled my feet into my blue patent leather T-strap sandals.

"I'm ready," I said and left the bathroom.

He walked toward me and reached his hands on either side of my head, flipping the collar up.

"Good idea. The flipped-up collar works," I said, catching my reflection in the glass of a framed pin-up girl on the wall.

"Put this on." He lowered a skinny blue necktie, already tied, over my head like a noose.

"That might be a little much."

"These people are going to expect you to have on some kind of weird getup."

"Why? It's not a costume party."

He stood back, eyed me up and down, and tightened the necktie. "Because they know you, and you always have on some kind of weird getup."

"I resent that."

"The tie is wired with a transmitter. If you speak clearly I'll be able to hear everything you say or anyone close to you says."

I fingered the blue fabric. "This tie is bugged?"

"Yes, and it cost more than two hundred dollars, so don't spill anything on it."

WE ARRIVED AT the college about twenty minutes later. Dante spun the bike around the mostly empty parking lot and then pulled under a couple of maple trees that kept us out of sight.

"Get off."

"You could be a little more polite, you know," I said, stepping down on my right foot and hopping backward so my left leg could swing over the back of the motorcycle. I unbuckled the helmet and hooked it onto the clip.

"This isn't the time to joke around, Samantha. Are you scared?"

"Yes I'm scared."

"Good. You'll be more careful if you're scared."

"Where are you going to be?"

"I don't know yet."

"Then why did you tell me to get off?"

"I'm not coming in with you." He handed me the duffle bag. "McQueen's in here. You need to put him on the platform where the real statue was."

"I don't think this is going to work."

"Listen to me. You need to have a reason for being here. McQueen is your reason. If anybody says anything, you say you're there to replace the statue. If things get hairy, you put him on the pedestal and you leave."

"Okay, sure. I can do that."

"I'm going to be able to hear whatever you hear, but if you stand too close to something with background noise, I'll have a harder time. So try to stay away from general noise."

"But I'm the bait."

"McQueen's the bait."

"So I'm what dangles the bait. I'm the fishing wire?"

"Try not to get tangled up." His eyes held mine for too long. I couldn't read his thoughts, and I wasn't sure I wanted to.

"Can I pretend you're Nick again?"

He looked at me for a couple of seconds and then touched my cheek. "You can do this." He revved the motor and pulled away, scattering pebbles over the toes of my shoes.

I hoisted the duffle from the ground and scaled the steps to the business school. Nobody else was around. I pulled McQueen from the duffle and stuck him on the pedestal, and then left out the front door. After descending the stairs, a shiny red sports car sped into the lot and shot directly toward where I stood.

36

NOTHING IS GOING TO BRING HER BACK

*K*yle got out of the car and slammed the door. His eyes were glassy and unfocused, shifting his male model looks into fallen pop star territory. "Where is he?" he yelled as he ascended the stairs. He stumbled halfway up.

Andi followed more slowly. She grabbed my arm, her eyes wide with fright. "The police couldn't charge him with the crime so he was released. I was watering his plants at his apartment when he walked in. I told him what you figured out and he freaked. You have to stop him. I'm afraid he's going to do something bad."

I pulled away from Andi and ran after Kyle. "He's not here, Kyle. Nobody's here."

"How did that get here?" he asked, staring at McQueen.

"Tony wanted it here for the dedication." I moved closer to the glass case of trophies and then took a step backward, into the hallway that led to the lecture hall.

He stood, rooted to the marble floor, staring at the statue as if he'd seen a ghost. "That bastard. He must have the police in his pocket if he got them to release evidence for his event."

"That's not the one that he used—" I cut myself off. Kyle had been in love with Emily; she'd been his future. Whether or not the statue in front of us was the one that had been used to bludgeon his fiancé, it hardly was a point worth mentioning.

"You put this here, didn't you?" he asked. "He asked you to put it here and you did."

"Yes."

"What are you trying to prove? She's dead. The love of my life is dead and nothing is going to bring her back. Not taking on Tony Simms, not shutting down Vongole, not a single thing you, or Andi, or anybody else can do. I have to try to move on, to learn to get up and go every single day without her. Can you imagine that? Learning to live without the love of your life?"

Kyle was not in a good place. His eyes were bloodshot, more so than they'd been when he arrived. A vein pulsed alongside his eyebrow. He spoke carefully, like he needed to make extra effort to get the words out clearly.

Andi remained in the parking lot. She looked scared. I made a face at her and waved her closer when I thought Kyle wasn't looking.

"Kyle, why don't you let Andi drive you home?"

I walked Kyle to the door and guided him to the steps out front. It seemed like yesterday that Eddie and I ran down those steps with the Puccetti statue hidden in my handbag. I held Kyle's arm as he descended the stairs. He walked to his car in a trance. I didn't know if he had tuned it all out up to this point, if seeing the statue had triggered something that he'd been able to keep buried behind emotional walls, and I was afraid to ask.

Andi looked at the keys, at me, and then at Kyle. "I can't drive stick."

Kyle aimed his remote at the car and sat in the driver's seat. He didn't start the engine. He draped his arms over the steering wheel and bent his head, his shoulders shaking with sorrow.

As I stepped away from the car, I realized the one thing I'd wanted by bringing the fake Puccetti here was to elicit a response from someone. There were too many suspects. I knew the person who had used the statue to murder Emily would have a hard time with the sight of it on its pedestal. From the looks of Kyle Trent, he was the definition of "hard time."

Had Detective Loncar been right all along? Had something I'd said or done released a killer from custody?

I had to talk to Dante. I backed away, up the stairs, and into the admissions hall. After the door closed behind me I looked at the pedestal.

The Puccetti was gone.

I glanced back at the parking lot. Exhaust puffed from the tailpipe of the red car. As I turned to my right, something wooden and solid swung at me and connected with left cheekbone.

The momentum knocked me down. A foot connected with my midsection. I curled onto my side and wrapped my torso with my arms—the same way I'd curled up in the back seat of Cat's Suburban the night we stole the statue. Pain yielded tears that blurred my vision. Something fell to the floor next to me.

Twenty-four inches of wooden man.

I forced myself onto my hands and knees, fighting each movement like a battered Rocky Balboa. I slowly crawled down the hallway to the bathroom where I'd hidden after stealing McQueen a week ago. I pulled myself into a standing position. After I opened the door, I moved across the black and white checkerboard floor and bent over the closest sink, splashing cold water on my face. Pink water, tinged with blood from the strike on my cheek, trickled down my face into the basin.

A rock smashed through the small glass pane of the crank window in the tiny lavatory, landing in the sink next to me. "What just happened?" Dante asked through the now-shattered window.

"Somebody hit me."

"What? Speak more clearly. Your voice is muffled."

I glanced down at the tie, now wet in patches thanks to the water I'd splashed on my face.

"Samantha, I can't hear you anymore. Get out of there. I don't have a good feeling about this."

"Kyle's here. He's drunk. He freaked out when he saw McQueen."

"I can't hear you. Move closer to the window."

I stepped around the broken glass on the floor and looked for Dante through the metal frame. "Kyle. Red sports car. He shouldn't be driving."

"I'll try to catch him. Meet me out front."

A toilet flushed behind me. The stall opened and Nora stepped out.

She caught my eyes in the reflection of the mirror above the row of sinks. "Samantha! What happened?" She grabbed a handful of paper towels, ran them under cool water, and turned around and held them gently against my face.

"I-I'm fine." I pushed her away. "I'm not sure what happened."

"Let's get you out of here. I'll take you home."

"Not yet." I backed away from her into the rose pink metal door to the stall.

"What's wrong?"

My face throbbed, and I couldn't think straight. When I looked at Nora, I felt like someone was hurling neon Frisbees at me. I was having a hard time standing up.

"Can you give me a couple of minutes? I'll meet you out front."

"Sure, if that's what you need." She tucked her sandy blond hair behind her ear and left.

I smacked the tie a few times and moved closer to the window. "Dante? Are you out there?" There was no answer.

I splashed more water on my face and dried off as best as I could. When I pulled the door to the bathroom open, I looked up and down the hall. There was no sign of Nora, no sign of anybody.

I couldn't risk going out the front door. Not when I didn't know where Dante was, or if someone was waiting out there to ambush me. I crept the other direction to the lecture hall and ducked inside the heavy doors.

"Samantha, I was starting to think you weren't going to make it," Tony Simms said. He was the picture of calm, or, he would have been, if he hadn't been tied to a folding metal chair.

The door closed behind me. "Watch out!" Tony called.

Someone pushed me into the back row of seats, but I threw my arms out in front of me and broke my fall by landing in the velvet-covered theater seats. I heard the sounds of metal clanking against each other. I sat up and saw Andi feeding a padlock through a heavy chain that secured the lecture hall doors.

"What are you doing?" I asked.

Andi turned quickly and dropped the padlock key. Her normally slicked back hair had come loose and pieces hung in spikes around her face. Dark circles colored her under-eye area and she was missing an earring. I mentioned none of this, and she didn't mention the trail of blood that dripped onto the collar of my borrowed shirt once owned by a woman named Doris.

"Tony is going to pay for what he did."

"This is crazy. Call the police. Let them arrest him. This isn't our job."

She stared at me as though she didn't understand me.

"He has to pay," she repeated. "I'll never have a life until he pays."

"I'll help you," he said. "Let Samantha go."

"You've done enough!" she spat at him. She stormed down the aisle and screamed at him. "You can't control me. You can't touch me!"

"Andi, calm down," I said.

She pulled a gun out of her pocket. Something wasn't right. It was as if the plastic game pieces had popped from the game of Concentration and everything I thought fit didn't. But as the pieces fell into new and different arrangements, the scattered information pointed me in an entirely different direction.

"Andi?" I said, approaching her.

"Shut up!" she screamed. I didn't know which of us she was yelling at.

Could Dante hear us? Or anybody? Where were Nora and Kyle and the cops?

"Why couldn't you let me live my life?" she asked. Touches of white saliva spotted the corners of her mouth. "I killed her. I should have let it go, but you tried to protect me. Now two people are dead."

"Nobody has to know what you did. It'll be our secret," Tony said.

Detective Loncar's words resonated in my head. Love-family-money. The Concentration game pieces snapped back into their slots, and suddenly I knew why Andi Holloway drank so much, why her father would never let her leave the family business, and why she was so desperate to take down Tony Simms.

"You never let me try to achieve anything for myself. If you had believed in me, just once. If you had let me fail, let me learn about hard work, about what it feels like to succeed on my own, everything would have been different." Andi kept the gun aimed at Tony. "But you didn't and now there's no way out."

"I worked hard to succeed so your life would be easy. I can get you help."

I fell to the floor and crawled the last few feet to the door. The key had landed somewhere around here. I padded my hands across the carpet in search of it. My fingernail snapped in half. I stifled the instinctive cry of pain, not wanting to draw attention to myself.

"I know all about your 'hard work.' You were never there for Mom, and you were never there for me."

I flipped my cell phone open and powered it back on. The screen glowed neon blue. I cued up the text screen and typed "Simms daughter Andi Holloway need help" and then hit send. Who could think about verbs and apostrophes at a time like this?

I had to keep Andi from doing something rash until help arrived. There was a chance Dante had heard the argument and called the cops, which meant there was a glimmer of hope, a chance the good guys would burst through the door. If I could just stay alive until then.

"Andi, I made mistakes with you. I see that now. I should have been there for you, but it will all end tonight. I can help you. Put the gun down."

"I'll never get away from you. If I'd have been caught, it would be over. But now I'll never have a normal life. You did this to me. You made me this way." Snot bubbled out of her nostrils as she sobbed and screamed.

"You won't have to live with the memory of killing Emily Hart if you let me help you."

"You're right. I don't have to live with the reminders, but you do."

A gun fired.

Tony Simms shouted.

I screamed.

Sirens blared.

And Andi Holloway collapsed on the cold marble floor. Her body toppled like the Puccetti statue had from its pedestal and a puddle of blood seeped out of the self-inflicted gunshot wound that ended her life.

37

OUT OF MY SYSTEM?

The day Nick was scheduled to arrive in Ribbon was spent cleaning, showering, and changing into outfits from at least five different decades. I may have worn my best underwear and changed the sheets on my bed. I'd rather keep that to myself.

I didn't know how I would feel when I saw him. The last time we spoke, things had been strained. I braced myself for what I would get when I opened the front door, whether it be lecture or hug.

I opened the front door. Nick stood on my porch, dressed in a cream knit turtleneck and plaid pants. He held a dozen pink roses wrapped in butcher paper tied with twine in one hand and a shoe box in the other. His curly brown hair moved with a breeze that passed over us. His eyes, deeper brown than I remembered, sparkled with the reflection of the waning sun, highlighting golden flecks in the middle of their normal root-beer-barrel shade.

We stood there for a second, not talking. I was close enough that I saw his eyes go from mine to the fading bruise on my cheek, to my lips, and then back to my eyes. All of the flirtation, the innuendo, the chemistry from life before he'd gone to Italy flooded back.

"Kidd," he said.

"Taylor," I said back.

"These are for you." He held out the roses. "This too," and extended the shoe box.

I took both. "Do you want to come in?" I asked.

Nick stepped forward. I stepped back. He stepped forward again and I tried to step back but the door to the hall closet behind me made that impossible. Nick put his fingers under my chin and tipped my face up to his. His lips brushed against mine once, twice, and then pressed down in our first kiss. I dropped the flowers and the shoe box and buried my fingers in his hair and his hands moved down my neck, shoulders, and body.

When the kiss ended, he pulled away and touched his fingertips to my bruise.

"Does it hurt?" he asked.

"Not anymore."

"Do you want to talk about it?"

"Not anymore."

I took his hand and led him to the sofa. We sat next to each other. I tucked one bare foot under me and faced him. He reached out and twirled a lock of my hair through his fingertips.

"I didn't expect the curls and the tan."

"I didn't expect the ..." I looked at the front door where we'd kissed. "Roses."

The lid had come off the shoe box when it fell, and one pale pink strappy sandal had fallen from tissue paper, resting on its side. The twine had come undone, and stems of roses scattered across the hardwood floor.

"I should put them in water." I stood up. Nick caught my hand and pulled me back to the sofa.

"Leave them," he said. We kissed again, like two teenagers with five minutes left before curfew. "I hated that you were in the middle of a dangerous situation again and I couldn't help you. It helped knowing you were working with the cops."

I thought about my frustrating partnership with Detective Loncar. I'd expected something from him after the dust had settled on his investigation, maybe a thank-you note, maybe the key to the city. At minimum, I thought I deserved a third bouquet of flowers.

I was still waiting.

Nick had helped me. From across the world while he was working on his own agenda, he'd taken time out to do what he could. He deserved to know the details the rest of us knew. "Andi Holloway was Tony Simms' daughter. She resented him, resented that he wasn't a part of her life other than handing her job opportunities and money. He wasn't a father to her. Andi was desperate to find someone who cared about her, to treat her like a full, visible, valuable human being. She saw how Kyle treated Emily and thought if Emily was out of the picture, that could be her."

"She killed Emily at the gala?"

"Yes. That's how I got involved. Andi took the statue from I-FAD. She knew it was part of Tony's art collection. She didn't know we'd replaced the one that was there with the fake Eddie had made. I think she thought she was killing Emily and framing Tony. The cops found it, and I got called in to explain it all to Detective Loncar."

"And Belle?"

"The working theory is that Tony killed Belle to protect Andi. Tony's not saying anything, but he's definitely not innocent. He's the one who started the rumor about Belle DuChamp and Kyle Trent. He wanted Andi to think Kyle was a rat. He'd also been the one to funnel knock-offs into the two stores that carried Vongole, knowing that eventually the business would go belly-up and he could offer his daughter another job."

Tony Simms had kept his daughter in his pocket, the way I'd put the Puccetti statue in my handbag, and Andi had carried that anger and resentment around with her like a purse filled with baggage. She'd been in and out of psychiatrists' offices dealing with abandonment issues. Just like she'd told me, she'd married a bartender early, divorcing him quickly but keeping his name.

Her hatred for her father ran much deeper than I ever could have imagined. If he'd been more of a real dad, not a mere figurehead, maybe this would have worked out differently. Instead of knock-off handbags and false success, Andi Holloway might have had a real life with ups and downs, failures and successes, highs and lows. But desperation to have her own identity forced her into a declaration of her own independence. Some might say she punctuated the declaration with a bullet.

"What about Kyle?" Nick asked.

I picked up a postcard I'd received a few days ago. It pictured a forest in black and white, with one small tree in the middle. The leaves on the tree were green. The message on the back was short and sweet: *Thank you for believing in me. Life goes on.—Kyle* After his signature there was a PS: *There's an opening at Tradava if you're interested.* I handed the postcard to Nick, who read it and then set it down on the table.

"So that's it," I said.

"Is that it?"

I leaned against the sofa cushion and thought about what I hadn't told Nick.

Mallory George did not apologize to me face to face but sent me an arrangement of bronze callas to rival the bouquet Detective Loncar had sent me at Heist. Her note was simple: *I learned a lot from you.* I taped it to my bathroom mirror and read it every morning before restarting my job search.

I finished cleaning my closets and donated half of my wardrobe to charity.

I didn't apply for Kyle's job.

A week after the showdown at the college, I went to Cat's house for dinner. Eddie was there, but Dante was not. After dinner I drove to Dante's apartment with the freshly laundered clothes he'd loaned me to wear to the college. The necktie lay folded on top of the pile.

I hadn't seen Dante since the night at the college when everything went down. And with Nick back in town, I didn't know if I was ready to analyze the way Dante made me feel. I carried the clothes to his front door. The lights were out, so I left them with a note. *Thanks for the education.*

When I got back to my car, I looked up the stairs. Dante leaned against the wooden banister in front of his door. I waved, and he tilted a bottle of beer in my direction. The next morning there was a note under my windshield. *I don't meet many women like you, Samantha Kidd.*

I tucked that card in my underwear drawer.

Nick pulled me close and kissed the tip of my nose. "I'm glad you worked this out of your system," he said. "It is out of your system, right?"

I looked behind him to the small crystal bowl that sat on the end table, now filled with Atomic Fireballs. Things were different now. Different-good or different-bad, I didn't yet know.

"Kidd, you didn't answer the question. Is it out of your system?"

I smiled and kissed him again.

From Diane:

Samantha Kidd is a favorite character of mine. She left her fashion buying career in New York in order to simplify her life and discover what makes her happy, but she hasn't figured it out yet. What she has figured out is that even though she approaches problems differently than others, she's often first with the solution. In The Brim Reaper, her next adventure, she's in it up to her eyeballs as a hat exhibit at the local museum turns deadly and Eddie is suspected of murder.

If you love Samantha, I'd like to introduce you to another one of my characters: Madison Night. Madison is a business woman. She owns her own decorating business, Mad for Mod, that specializes in midcentury modern décor. She dresses like an extra from a Doris Day movie, which is perfect for promoting her business, but a little confusing to strangers who expect her to act helpless and demure. She's quite happy with her independent life (her faithful Shih Tzu, Rocky, provides all the company she needs) until a series of crimes make her see that maybe life shouldn't be spent in emotional isolation. If you'd like to get to know Madison and company, you can check out Pillow Stalk, her first adventure!

Sincerely,
Diane

P.S. Please consider leaving a review for this book. No matter how brief or how long, reader reviews make a difference. Thank you!

About The Author

After two decades working for a top luxury retailer, Diane Vallere traded fashion accessories for accessories to murder. She is a national bestselling author and a past president of Sisters in Crime. She started her own detective agency at age ten and has maintained a passion for shoes, clues, and clothes ever since.

Sign up for The Weekly DiVa to receive news about girl talk, book talk, and life talk. Get notice of new books, advance notice of contests and giveaways, inside stories, and chances to contribute to books in progress: https://dianevallere.com/weekly-diva

Acknowledgments

Writing a novel is like swimming a race in a river: the water is cloudy, the conditions unpredictable, and while you're not alone, you feel pretty isolated. It's only after you've finished the race and come out of the water that you can focus on the people who cheered you on from the riverbank:

Thank you to my parents for your constant support. You raised me to think I could achieve anything if I worked hard enough, and now, for better or for worse, I believe it.

Thank you to Angela, Amy, and Cynthia, the best retail mentors I could have asked for. Little did any of us know my experience as a buyer would serve as research for a murder mystery!

Thank you to Ramona DeFelice Long for your editing and content insights. You're a gem! And to Monica O'Rourke, who proves you can find professionals on LinkedIn, thank you for your thorough work on this manuscript.

As far as cheering goes, a shout-out to the Sisters in Crime Guppies, the most supportive pond a writer could find. Thank you Krista Davis and Sheila Connolly for your quotes, and to Josh for your suggestions of the Ace Trucking Company and Vongole sort.

And of course to lifelong friends like Jen, Gino, and Kendel, for your ongoing friendship. You're in here somewhere, and not as a corpse.